This book is dedicated to my friend
Kathleen Bailey
18th May 1968 – 15th February 2010

S. L. Powell was born in Shetland and by the age of seven she had lived in Somerset, Norfolk, Dorset, Australia and Dumfries and finally the Isle of Wight, where she stayed until she was grown up. She lived on boats for many years, but currently lives in a house in Oxford with her husband and daughter, and combines writing with working for a charity. *Fifty Fifty* is her first published book.

Find out more at www.slpowell.co.uk

FIFTY FIFTY

S. L. POWELL

PICCADILLY PRESS • LONDON

First published in Great Britain in 2011
by Piccadilly Press Ltd,
5 Castle Road, London NW1 8PR
www.piccadillypress.co.uk

A catalogue record for this book is available from the British Library

ISBN: 978 1 84812 123 2 (paperback)

1 3 5 7 9 10 8 6 4 2

Printed in the UK by CPI Bookmarque Ltd, Croydon, CR1 4PD
Cover design by Simon Davis
Cover illustration © tanakawho

CHAPTER 1

Gil poked a finger deep into his breakfast porridge and immediately whipped it out again. The porridge was even hotter than usual, which meant there was almost no chance of beating the record he'd set yesterday. Still, he ought to give it a go. He watched the kitchen clock, waiting for the second hand to flick round to twelve.

Ten. Nine. Eight . . .

'You've got money for lunch, have you?' said Mum from behind him.

'Yeah,' said Gil, hunched over his porridge bowl with the spoon in his hand, concentrating. *Six. Five.* Crap. 'Yeah' was the wrong answer. He'd have to find a way to get round Mum later. *Three. Two. One . . .*

Lift off. Gil started to shovel porridge into his mouth as fast as he could. It burnt his lips and skinned the roof of his mouth, and the gloopy stuff in the bowl glistened and

1

oozed like pale lava.

Come on, come on, thought Gil, jiggling the hot porridge between his teeth, trying to cool it down.

He watched the seconds steadily flicking away. The quicker he finished his porridge, the more time there was for . . . well, for what, exactly? That was the problem. It just left more time for the argument that was always sitting quietly in the spaces between him and Mum and Dad these days, waiting for them to come too close to each other. Then it would suddenly blaze up from nowhere, like the crackle of static electricity.

'Slow down,' said Mum. 'What's the hurry? You'll burn yourself.'

She hadn't even looked round, as far as Gil could tell. How did she know he was eating too fast? He swallowed the last lump of porridge and noted the time. Two minutes twenty-four. Disappointing. Nowhere near his personal best. And it would drag his average down, too.

Dad swept into the kitchen and grabbed his phone from the top of the fridge.

'I'm off,' he said. 'Gil, your job when you come home from school is to tidy your room, please. It's a complete tip.'

'You went in my room?' said Gil.

'The door was open,' said Dad.

'So? It's my room. I decide who's allowed in.'

'Oh, really,' said Dad. 'Is that so? Well, it doesn't alter the fact that your room is a mess and needs tidying.'

Gil looked up properly and saw Dad – Dad in his smart-but-casual work gear, always black trousers and a blue jumper, with his phone in one hand and his laptop in the other, and that look of invincible rightness on his face – and felt the zap of electricity jolt him into a reply.

'Is that so?' he said, slowly. 'Well, sorry Dad, but I've got plans for after school.'

'Your plans for after school,' said Dad, 'are to come straight home and sort out your room.'

'But I'm going into town,' said Gil.

'Are you?' said Mum. 'Who with? Louis?'

Gil ran his tongue around the inside of his mouth, feeling the shiny raw patches where he'd blistered it with the hot porridge.

'Actually,' he said casually, 'I thought I might go on my own, for once.'

There was a moment of silence while Mum and Dad looked at each other and Gil felt the feeling hit him again. It was a new feeling, and he hadn't got used to it yet. It was like the moment in a dream where you are running, and suddenly you can't feel your feet on the pavement any longer and you realise you are running in the air. It made Gil feel dizzy, as if he couldn't breathe, as if he wanted to stop but couldn't stop, and it scared him. But it was exciting too.

'That is completely out of the question,' said Dad, and at the same time Mum said, 'Oh but Gil, you know we don't really want you to go into town on your own.'

'So you keep telling me,' said Gil. 'I still don't get it, though.'

'I could meet you when school finishes and we could go together,' said Mum.

3

'Mum. I'm nearly fourteen. You can't pick me up from school any more, you really can't.'

'In any case, Rachel,' said Dad, 'you're forgetting that I've just told Gil he's to come home and tidy his room. End of story.'

'Oh, yes, of course,' said Mum. 'Well, maybe you could go on Monday instead, with Louis.'

'I don't want to go with Louis.'

'Oh dear, have you fallen out?'

'Mum, for God's sake! I just want to do something by myself for once. What's the big deal?'

'You are not going into town on your own,' said Dad. He had put down the laptop, and now he shoved his phone in his pocket so he could fold his arms.

'Perhaps I could meet you in town one afternoon,' said Mum. 'So you wouldn't have to be seen with me at school.'

Gil looked down into his empty bowl. He'd reached the point where he had to be careful not to meet Mum's eyes, because if he did he would start to feel sorry for her, and then it would make him angry. He knew there would be a look in her eyes like a puppy that has no idea if it's going to be punished or rewarded.

'You do know that all the boys in my year are allowed into town on their own now?' he said, staring at the scraps of porridge that were slowly beginning to harden into glue.

'You're not just any old boy, though, are you?' said Mum.

'Look, I'm not four, all right? I'm not a baby.'

'You're only thirteen,' said Dad.

4

'So, basically, you don't think I'm old enough,' said Gil. 'You don't trust me.'

'Don't put words in my mouth, please,' said Dad. He hadn't moved.

'If you trusted me you'd let me have a front door key.'

'You don't need a key,' said Dad. 'There's always someone here to let you in.'

'So, according to you, I'm not even old enough to be home alone,' said Gil. When Dad didn't respond, he went on. 'So when *will* I be old enough?

'We're not prepared to discuss it right now,' said Dad.

'No, Dad, I want to know. How old do I have to be? Fourteen? Fifteen? Eighteen? Forty-eight, for God's sake?'

'I said we are not prepared to discuss it,' said Dad. 'This is not the time.'

'What the hell do you think is going to happen to me?'

Gil saw Mum's eyes widen slightly. It was a stupid question. He knew exactly what she thought would happen to him. The bus might crash, or he might be abducted, or he could choke on a piece of chewing gum as he walked down the High Street, or he might be mugged at knifepoint in that little alley behind HMV. He could see it all running through her mind in a big fast jumble, like a violent film trailer.

Gil felt himself begin to buzz quietly. He should stop now, he knew that, before he slammed into the wall ahead of him. But the wave carried him, his legs carried him, running over thin air.

'Mum, listen,' he said. 'You know I'd be careful.'

'Drop it,' said Dad.

'We'll think about it another time,' Mum said, getting up. 'I promise.'

'Yeah, right. Like I really believe that,' said Gil. He saw Mum's shoulders twitch and half-regretted the comment. It was becoming too easy to hurt Mum. 'Look, if you'd let me have a phone I could text you every five minutes to say I was OK,' he went on.

'You are not having a mobile phone,' said Dad.

'Why not? Everyone else has had one since they started secondary school. Even the really sad people at school have got a phone.'

'You know perfectly well why we don't want you to have a phone yet,' said Dad. 'We've been through this before. There are no scientific studies on mobile phone use which have fully explored the long-term effects, and the government advice is still that children should be discouraged from using mobile phones. And quite apart from that, the evidence shows they increase your chances of being mugged and bullied.'

'Oh yeah! Scientific studies. Government advice. I completely forgot,' Gil said, with as much sarcasm as he could manage.

Mum had moved into the farthest corner of the kitchen, as if trying to move out of range of the argument. Gil wondered why she didn't just leave the room.

'Science is the best tool we have for understanding the world, Gil,' Dad said. 'We have to take it seriously.'

'I hate your stupid science.'

'That's a bit short-sighted of you,' said Dad. 'Without

science there would be no mobile phones, for example.'

'If science proved your brain was in your bum you'd believe it.'

'I'd certainly consider it,' said Dad. 'If the evidence was convincing.'

He was always right. Always, always, always. Evidence, logic, facts. There was never any way through it or round it or under it or over it. It was beginning to drive Gil crazy. He stared at Dad and Dad stared back, with the kind of smile that made Gil start to rock his chair backwards and forwards, smashing the chair legs on the hard kitchen floor.

'So if phones might give you brain cancer, how come you and Mum have both got them?'

'We use them carefully,' said Dad.

'And you don't think I would?'

'Gil, when you are older you will understand what a responsibility it is being a parent,' said Dad. 'We have a duty to look after you, even if you don't yet see that it's for your own good.'

'Blah blah blah blah blah,' Gil said. 'You talk such a lot of *crap*. I hate you.' He shoved his chair back quickly and stood up.

'Gil,' said Mum. 'Please.'

'Please what? It's not me that's the problem. It's *him*.'

'Get in the car,' said Dad. 'Now.' He took a step forwards and Gil automatically stepped away. He wondered if Dad was going to try to pin him against the wall. He'd never done it before, but it would really freak Mum out.

'I can't go to school like this,' said Gil, bouncing on his

toes in case he needed to run. 'I haven't even cleaned my teeth.'

'I don't give a damn,' said Dad. 'You're coming with me.'

His hand shot out to grab Gil's arm. Gil dodged him and ran round the table.

'You shouldn't be driving to work anyway,' Gil said. 'You're destroying the planet.'

Dad made a noise that was probably meant to be a laugh. 'Oh yes, I'm destroying it single-handedly, I know. Global warming is all my fault.'

It was a mistake, Gil realised, running round the table. He'd got himself trapped in a corner and the kitchen had turned into a cage. His hands ached, and looking down he saw that his fingers had made themselves into fists, even though he didn't remember telling them to. It was an effort to find something he could spit back at Dad.

'Well, Dad, it's your generation who've well and truly screwed it up. You've just behaved like a bunch of selfish gits and left the mess for us kids to clear up.'

'That is *enough*. You are coming with me *now*.'

'If you come any closer,' said Gil, 'you'll get this over your head.' He grabbed his porridge bowl off the kitchen table and waved it wildly in Dad's direction.

'Oh, for *God's sake!*' screamed Mum suddenly, dropping something with a crash into the sink. 'Just stop it! *Stop it!*'

Dad froze in mid-step, his eyes full of astonishment, and for a moment even Gil was thrown. Mum never lost it. She never got more than mildly irritated, never screamed at anyone.

'Rachel?' said Dad. 'I'm sorry – is it all getting too —'

With his last shred of energy Gil hurled the porridge bowl at Dad. He heard Mum cry out at exactly the moment that he saw Dad catch the bowl neatly, just like a frisbee, and then he ran from the kitchen.

He took the stairs two at a time, slamming the bedroom door behind him, and immediately started to build the barricade the way he had before. He dragged his homework desk across the door and put the chair on top of the desk, weighing it down with as many heavy objects as he could put his hands on. And then he lay on the bed and waited. Next time I'll throw the kettle, he thought. Or one of Mum's teapots with the tea still in it. He won't be able to catch that. He tried to laugh but it made his lungs hurt.

Dad took a while to come. In the end, though, Gil heard Dad's footsteps plod up the stairs and stop outside his door. The handle rattled.

'Come out of there, Gil.'

'You can't make me. You can't force me to do anything.'

'Oh? Really?'

There was a thump on the door and Gil saw it move. He could almost feel Dad's whole weight pressed against it. The desk tilted slightly, and the chair slipped a centimetre.

'So you're going to break the door down, are you, Dad?' Gil said. 'That's very mature of you.'

The door relaxed again. There was silence for a while, and Gil gazed through the bedroom window, thinking about the fire drill that Dad made him practise from time to time. *Unlock the middle window. The key's above the curtain rail. Step*

9

out on to the conservatory roof – the joists, Gil, the wooden beams, not the glass, or you'll go straight through. Edge across to the wall, crawl down backwards, hang at full stretch off the end of the wall, drop into the back garden. Safe. The fire drill had seemed like a huge adventure when he was little, and now it felt like just another of Dad's pointless rules. But it might come in useful as an escape route if Dad decided to lay siege to his bedroom.

'Gil, listen. You're not an adult yet. We have to do what we think is right.'

'I don't care,' shouted Gil. 'I'm not listening.'

'Look, I'm sorry if I made you angry. But you must believe that the things we do are in your best interests.'

'I *don't* believe it. I don't believe anything you say.'

'Gil, I've got to go to work now.'

'Why don't you just sod off to work, then? Your precious, wonderful work. It's so *important*, Dad, isn't it?'

'Is this how you speak to your teachers? Honestly, Gil, I don't understand what's got into you recently.'

YOU have, you loser, thought Gil, but he didn't say it aloud.

'You can't go on like this,' Dad said through the door. 'For your mother's sake, please try to sort yourself out.'

That meant Mum was upset, but Gil made himself not think about it, in the same way that he was making himself not think about the way she'd screamed at him and Dad.

'Have a good day at school, Gil.'

'Yeah, yeah,' said Gil. 'Whatever.'

There was silence, and then Dad's footsteps went away

10

down the stairs, and Gil heard him talking quietly to Mum below. After a while the front door clicked shut and the car engine started.

All at once Gil felt exhausted. The wave that had carried him this far had smashed itself to pieces and he looked at the day that lay ahead of him with something like desperation. *Have a good day at school?* What kind of crap was that? Every day was a clone of the day before. Each day was exactly the same, from the moment he got up until the moment he went to bed. Identical clothes, identical meals, identical arguments.

Nothing ever changed, nothing moved on, nothing was sorted out. You could fiddle around with a few of the details – swap the porridge for cornflakes, or wear a new pair of trainers – but it made no real difference. Everywhere he turned Dad was there, blocking his way, breathing down his neck. He was stuck in an endless loop.

He had to find a way out, before he completely lost his mind.

CHAPTER 2

Twenty minutes later, mainly because he couldn't think of anything else to do, Gil dragged the desk away from his door and started to go downstairs. Halfway down he decided to go back to his room and fill his wallet with the remains of his pocket money. After all, it might be worth being prepared.

Mum was sitting at the kitchen table with a half-finished cup of tea. She looked up when Gil came in, and Gil wondered if she might have been crying, but she managed to make her voice sound almost normal.

'That was all a bit unnecessary, wasn't it? It's a good job that bowl didn't smash.'

'Yeah. Sorry,' Gil said. He couldn't think of a way to make his apology any bigger. Mum seemed to have recovered. Maybe she hadn't screamed quite as badly as he'd imagined. And anyway, it was all Dad's fault.

'You're going to be terribly late, you know,' she went on.

'Yeah, I know. Can I have three pounds for lunch?' Gil held the wallet behind his back.

'I thought you said you had money? I gave you ten pounds yesterday, didn't I?'

'I had to give some of that to Louis,' said Gil. 'I owed him. From last week.'

It wasn't a very convincing bluff, but Mum got up obediently and Gil almost felt guilty. It was getting easier and easier to blag money off Mum. She hardly bothered to put up a fight these days.

'Actually, make it five,' he said. 'I need some for tuck shop too.'

'Honestly, you cost me a fortune,' said Mum, but she handed it over anyway.

'Bye, then,' Gil said, picking up his bag and slipping the wallet into it.

'Don't you need a coat?'

'No. See you later.'

'Bye, darling,' said Mum.

Gil walked away out of the front gate, knowing that Mum would watch him from the half-open door until he was out of sight. He resisted the temptation to turn at the last moment to wave to her. Instead he watched his feet as they walked him along the pavement in the direction of school, the direction they took him every single morning. But today didn't feel quite like one of his identical days, and Gil wondered why. Then he realised it was because he was really late. He couldn't remember being this late for school

13

before, and it felt weird. The streets were nearly empty, and when Gil stepped into the playground there was an echo he'd never heard before. The noise of a thousand kids was shut up inside the school walls. He walked towards reception, feeling nervous.

Don't be stupid, he told himself. And then, with his hand on the door, he thought, Crap. What am I doing here?

Suddenly it was blindingly obvious. He needn't have come to school at all today. He could have skived off, gone somewhere else, done something exciting and dangerous. That would really have been like sticking two fingers up at Dad. But Gil had never deliberately skipped school before, and the idea hadn't occurred to him until now, when it was too late and he could see the secretary frowning at him through the glass door. Oh, well, another time, thought Gil, pushing the door open.

'Name?' said the secretary.

'Gilbert Walker. 9Q2.'

'Why are you late?'

Gil made his face droop sadly. 'I had a really, really bad row with my dad. Sorry.'

The secretary's face softened a bit. 'Oh. OK. You're not one of our regulars, anyway. Don't make a habit of it. You should catch the end of registration.' She pressed a button below the desk and the entrance door buzzed to let him through.

As Gil opened the door of his classroom, the noise burst around him like a small bomb. Mr Montague wasn't there. At the front was a woman Gil had never seen before, obviously a supply teacher. She was trying to keep order and failing badly. As Gil slipped quietly into the room the whole class turned towards him, pointed and howled with laughter. Gil stopped and stared, more irritated than embarrassed. What the hell was going on?

'There she is, Miss,' shouted Ben from a desk at the back of the class. Gil's lip curled. Ben, the moron who made all the other morons in the year look relatively normal. And Louis was sitting next to him. Fantastic.

The teacher was looking at Gil with a puzzled face.

'You are . . .' she said.

'Gil Walker.'

'Gil?'

'Yep, Gil, as in the things fish use to breathe with. It's short for Gilbert.'

'Oh dear, I'm terribly sorry. I thought it was *Jill*. I was expecting a girl.'

The class exploded with laughter again. Gil rolled his eyes and waited for them all to get over it. Even Louis seemed to be in hysterics, although if he was under Ben's spell that wasn't surprising.

'Simmer down, simmer down,' called the teacher just as the bell rang and everyone stood up and made for the door in a thunderous, giggling mass.

'That was sick, man,' said Ben loudly as he and Louis came towards Gil. 'Hey, Jill! Shake what your mamma gave you, girl!' He poked Gil savagely as he went past and began to cackle again like a demented chicken. Louis was still laughing, but when he saw Gil's face he made a brief effort to compose himself.

'It *was* funny,' Louis said, defensively. 'Really. You should have been here.' He started to imitate the teacher, putting on a silly high voice that sounded just like her. '*Jill Walker? Jill Walker? Is she here, children? Has anyone seen Jill this morning? Now, simmer down, simmer down, please!* That teacher is so dead if she does registration again this afternoon!'

'Yeah, right!' laughed Ben.

Gil felt Louis and Ben both looking at him.

'Why aren't you laughing?' Louis said.

'Yeah, why aren't you laughing, *Jill*?' said Ben immediately.

'Because it's not funny,' said Gil. He had never felt less like laughing in his life, and he vaguely wondered why. Louis *always* made him laugh. He was brilliant at imitating people, and the teacher *had* made a complete idiot of herself, and really Gil should be laughing about it, even though the joke was partly on him. But today, somehow, it wasn't funny any more.

'Yes it is,' said Louis.

'Yes it is, *Jillian*,' echoed Ben, mocking.

'Oh, sure, it's hilarious.'

'What's your problem?' Louis' eyebrows wriggled in surprise. 'God, you've really had a sense of humour failure, haven't you?'

'I'm just sick of you laughing at me,' said Gil. 'You're always doing it.'

The second he'd said it Gil knew it wasn't fair, and Louis' mouth dropped open in outrage.

'I am not! I do not! I wasn't laughing at you!'

'Ooo-oooh! Are you two gonna have a fight?' said Ben, his eyes shining.

'Get lost,' said Gil coldly.

'That's not a nice way to talk to your friends, is it, Jillian?'

'You,' said Gil, 'are not my *friend*.'

Ben just grinned, wider and wider, until Gil felt he wanted to fill Ben's mouth with his fist.

'*Louis* is my friend,' Ben said loudly. 'Aren't you?' He grabbed Louis in a friendly head-lock.

'Sure!' croaked Louis. 'Why wouldn't I be?'

But Louis was laughing again, as if he really didn't mind Ben strangling him, and Gil bristled with irritation. He turned and walked away up the corridor. After a minute or so he heard Louis calling him.

'Gil! Hey! Wait up! Gil!'

Gil didn't wait. He was halfway up the stairs on the way to maths before Louis caught him up.

'Why didn't you wait?' puffed Louis.

Gil shrugged. 'Didn't want to spoil things between you and your new best mate,' he said.

'Ben? But he's a laugh,' said Louis. 'He has some really cool ideas.'

'What, better than me, you mean?'

'Well . . . um . . . not *better*, but . . .'

Gil looked sideways at Louis. He looked exasperatingly cheerful, and Gil felt another surge of irritation. Ever since they'd known each other there'd been an unspoken agreement that it was Gil who had the best ideas, and that Louis would always go along with them, and that they would laugh about

17

it together afterwards, even if they got told off. Like that time when he and Louis were being Arctic explorers and they'd climbed into the big chest freezer in Louis' garage so they could pretend it was a snow cave with polar bears digging through the roof, and then they'd forgotten to shut the lid of the freezer and all the food got ruined. That was Gil's idea, and even though Louis' mum was pretty laid back about most things and the freezer was nearly empty, it got them into terrible trouble. But they'd still laughed about it afterwards and said it was one of the best games ever.

'Ben's a loser and a moron,' said Gil. 'And a jerk. Oh, and a retard.'

'What's the problem with you today?' said Louis. 'Why were you so late, anyway?'

Gil was silent. He wasn't sure he wanted to talk about it.

'OK, don't tell me, then,' said Louis, sounding hurt, and Gil began to relent.

'Oh, I just had another mega-row with my dad. *When you're older you'll understand . . . blah blah blah . . .* You know, all that crap. It's so boring. He won't let me have a phone, he won't let me go into town on my own – it's really starting to get to me.'

'That's because you're an only child,' said Louis.

'Is it?'

'Yeah, you're the only one. That's why they're so protective. If you had brothers and sisters it would probably be a lot easier. I mean, look at me. I can pretty much get away with anything. I watched an 18 last weekend with my big brothers, and mum and dad didn't say a word. It was cool. Well – a bit scary. But mainly cool.'

'There's not much I can do about that, is there? I can't exactly magic up a few older brothers.'

'No,' said Louis. 'God, I'd hate to be an only child. It'd be like having nowhere to hide.'

'Yeah,' Gil said slowly. 'That's exactly what it feels like.'

Nowhere to hide. Sometimes Louis said things better than Gil could say them himself.

But by the end of the day Louis had begun to feel like a parrot on his shoulder – prattling away into his ear, laughing his arse off at things that weren't funny, asking for help every thirty seconds with stuff that was so easy Gil could do it in his sleep – so that Gil was desperate to shake him off. And when the bell went for home time Gil suddenly found himself wondering what he was going to do. Was he really going to go straight home and tidy his room, like a good boy?

'So, do you want to come over to my house?' said Louis, following Gil out of the school gates.

For a second Gil was tempted. Louis' house was warm, noisy, messy, full of people. Gil's house was cool, quiet, tidy, mostly empty. He liked Louis' house, even when Louis got on his nerves, and there were no time limits on watching the television or using the computer, as long as Louis' big brother didn't come and boot them off. And maybe he could call Mum and say, *Look, I know Dad said I had to sort my room out, but I'm only round at Louis'. I'll be home soon.* Maybe Mum would feel sorry for him, and tidy the room herself. It wouldn't be the first time.

'Ben's coming too,' added Louis eagerly, spoiling everything.

'Ben,' said Gil. Ben had called him Jillian roughly thirty times over the course of the day. Gil felt certain that if this continued on Monday he would have to punch Ben somewhere he wouldn't forget.

'Yeah! Did I tell you what he did yesterday after school?'

'No,' said Gil, in a way that was meant to signal the end of the discussion, but Louis was already laughing.

'He nicked a PE kit off this geeky little Year Seven and he tried to *set fire to it*! He carries this cigarette lighter round with him and . . . and . . .'

Louis paused to get his breath back, while Gil stared at him in complete astonishment. What the hell was happening to Louis? Two years ago *he'd* been the geeky little Year Seven and Gil had spent half his time protecting him from people like Ben.

'I bet you weren't even there, were you?' said Gil.

'It was so funny,' giggled Louis, not answering Gil's question.

'Fine,' said Gil with sudden decision. 'You go off with Ben. I'm going into town.' This was it, then, he thought in surprise. He'd actually said it out loud.

'We'll come with you,' said Louis immediately.

'No,' said Gil. 'You don't get it. I'm going on my own.'

'But I thought you said you weren't allowed.' A look of confusion crossed Louis' face and Gil felt quietly pleased with himself.

'I'm not. I'm still going, though.'

'But Gil . . .'

Louis' expression was so serious that Gil nearly burst with laughter. Louis was so short and skinny, such a *kid*. But he'd been going into town on his own for ages. And he had a mobile phone, of course. It really didn't seem fair. And now here he was, looking up at Gil as if Gil was the one who needed protection.

'What about when your mum and dad find out? Your dad'll go crazy, won't he?'

'I couldn't care less,' Gil said. 'Bring it on.'

'I really think you should let me come with you,' said Louis. 'Then maybe you won't get into so much trouble.'

'*Get into so much trouble!*' mimicked Gil. 'Oooh, I'm so scared!'

'Shut up,' said Louis. 'I'm just trying to help.'

'Yeah, well, don't. You're being a pain in the butt.'

'I am *not!*'

'Yes you are.'

'Fine. Go on your own.'

'Yeah, I will. Have fun with that retard Ben.'

'So what am I supposed to say if your mum calls our house to see if you're there?'

'You can tell her what you like. I don't care.'

'OK.' Louis shrugged. 'But when it all goes wrong, remember I told you it was a bad idea.'

'Stop telling me what to do,' Gil said. 'You're as bad as my parents.'

He walked away to the bus stop, and Louis didn't follow.

CHAPTER 3

When Gil got round to counting the money in his wallet he was disappointed to find there was hardly anything in it. He'd already managed to spend most of the five pounds that Mum had given him, and once he'd paid the bus fare and put aside enough to get home later he had less than ten pounds left. And without money, town wasn't nearly as much fun as he'd expected.

He wandered past the shops, feeling the blast of warm air and music that poured out of each doorway. He browsed computer games for a while, but there wasn't enough cash to buy even the second-hand ones. His plans for buying a secret mobile phone evaporated. He had money for a McDonald's – Dad really disapproved of McDonald's – but after standing outside for ten minutes trying to decide what to have he realised he just didn't fancy a burger or fries or even a McFlurry.

Suddenly, when he could do anything he wanted, there wasn't anything he really wanted to do. It was all a bit of a let-down. Now it looked as if he would get into big trouble for something that didn't even feel like a proper rebellion.

Well before it began to get dark, Gil found himself back at the bus stop. It stood near a small scrubby park with two fairly big trees, some patchy grass and a bench or two. It was a place where alcoholics and drug addicts crept into corners in the hope the police wouldn't spot them.

This was as exciting as it was going to get, Gil thought, looking around him. He was on his own, standing next to a park occupied by drinkers and druggies. Dad would go mad if he knew. There were even a couple of policemen hovering in a side street.

It was then that Gil spotted a man in one of the two big trees.

Gil stared up at him. The man didn't seem to be climbing the tree, or lopping off branches with a chainsaw, or anything sensible like that. He just looked as if he was relaxing. Lounging, even. He was lying on a big sloping branch about three metres above the ground, with a hand tucked under his head, gazing up at the sky.

What on earth was he doing?

There was a hammock slung above his head, and Gil could see other objects hanging from the bare branches – a saucepan, a bucket, a rucksack, clothes that swung in the breeze as if they were hung out to dry. He wandered closer to get a better look. There were some placards propped up at the base of the tree. *Trees are the lungs of the world,* said one.

Save our green spaces, said another. *Free the trees.* Gil lifted a leg to step over the low wall that surrounded the park.

'You can't go in there,' said a voice suddenly. One of the policemen had crept up on him.

'Why not?'

The policeman jabbed a finger towards the tree. 'Illegal protest,' he said. 'These trees have got to come down sooner or later. We've got instructions to stop anyone else trying to join him up there. So don't even think about it.'

'For God's sake,' said a voice directly above Gil, 'he's just a kid. Leave him alone.'

The man in the tree had rolled over so that now he was draped along the branch like a lazy leopard. He didn't look all that old, thought Gil, maybe only twenty or so, and although it was March his face was still really tanned, as if he spent most of his time outdoors. His fair hair fell over his face as he grinned down at Gil, one arm dangling casually just out of reach of the policeman.

'He can talk to me, can't he?' the man went on. 'Or are you trying to ban that too?'

The policeman growled and muttered. 'Stay this side of the wall,' he said to Gil eventually, and retreated a few metres.

Gil watched a bus pull up at his bus stop, and decided he could afford to miss it.

'So . . . uh . . . what are you doing up there?' he said.

'Well, they can't cut the tree down if I'm living in it, can they?' said the man.

'You're *living* up there?'

'Yup. Been here four days now.'

'Why do they want to cut the trees down?'

'Usual stuff,' said the man. 'More shops. Greed. Money. Capitalism. All that.'

Gil considered the possibility of living in a tree. He imagined the phone call he'd make – if he had a phone, of course. *Oh, hi, Dad. No, I'm not coming home for dinner. I'm staying in a tree. I'm going to be here for a while, actually. You see, I'm a green activist now, trying to make up for the total mess you've made of the world.* He thought about how furious Dad would be and it gave him a shiver of enjoyment.

'What's your name?' asked the man.

'Gil. Gil Walker.'

'Gil, eh? Cool name.'

'Oh. Thanks. Who are you?'

'Jude,' said Jude.

'Jude who?'

'Just Jude. It's simpler that way.'

'How do you . . . *manage*? I mean, do you come down from there at all?'

Jude laughed. 'You're wondering how I go to the toilet, aren't you?' he said. 'All the kids ask me that.'

Gil opened his mouth to say that he wasn't a *kid*, but then he closed it again.

'That's what the bucket's for,' Jude went on. 'Although sometimes I do pee straight out of the tree if no one's around.' He laughed again. 'It's not like anyone's using the park now.'

He dug into his pocket and pulled out a packet of tobacco, then swung himself round to sit on the branch. Gil watched Jude roll a cigarette carefully between his fingers. He licked the edge of the thin paper and pinched it together, then lit the end and took a big sighing suck of smoke. He looked as comfortable as if he was sitting in a deckchair. Another bus pulled up at Gil's bus stop, and after waiting a minute or two it drove off again.

'I know what you're thinking,' said Jude. 'You're thinking I shouldn't smoke.'

'Uh – I guess not,' said Gil, although the thought hadn't entered his head.

'It's a risk. I know that. But at least it's a risk I only take for myself. Pollution, now – that's far worse than smoking. If you drive a car you're poisoning the air for the whole planet. Anyway, life is full of risks. Falling out of a tree is a risk.'

Jude blew smoke through the bare branches. He didn't look for one second as if he was about to fall.

'Really though, don't start smoking,' he said. 'It's expensive, for one thing, and – oh, I'm sure you've heard all the other arguments . . .'

'Yeah,' said Gil. 'I have.' He stood up straight, folded his arms and gave his best impersonation of Dad delivering a lecture. 'Smoke from cigarettes damages the cells in your body, especially cells in the lungs. Or rather, it damages the DNA inside the nucleus of the cells. Scientific research shows it is this damage that leads to the mutations that can cause cancer.'

Scientific research . . . blah blah blah . . . Of course he knew that smoking was addictive and dangerous and stupid, but recently Gil had felt an overwhelming urge to try it just to wind Dad up.

26

Jude was staring, amused. 'Holy moly,' he said. 'Where was that from?'

'My dad,' Gil said. 'He sounds like that all the time.'

'Some kind of doctor, is he?'

'No.' Gil stopped. Was he a doctor? All his letters came addressed to *Dr Matthew Walker*. 'Actually I really don't know. He's a scientist now, but he might have been a doctor before that. He's always going on about cells and DNA and stuff like that.'

'Doesn't interest you, huh?'

'Not really.'

'He works at the university, does he?'

'Yes, I think so.'

'You should take more notice,' said Jude. His smile had gone, and his voice was quieter. 'Some of the stuff those scientists are doing – it's going to affect us all. It's going to hit us as hard as climate change.'

'What do you mean?'

'Oh, forget it for now,' said Jude. 'Let's concentrate on winning this little battle, shall we?'

Quickly he stubbed his cigarette out on the branch and dropped it into the bucket above him.

'Mustn't get done for littering,' he said brightly, jumping to his feet. The branch bounced and Jude balanced like a tightrope walker. 'Gil, would you do something for me?'

'Yes, of course!'

'You'd need to be careful. The police are finding just about any excuse to crack down on people who try and help me.'

'I'm not scared.' Gil waited with his heart thumping for Jude's instructions.

'Could you go and buy me a bottle of water? A big one?'

Was that it? Gil felt a flicker of disappointment. It didn't sound very subversive.

'Yeah, sure,' Gil said.

'You need some money?'

'No, it's fine, I've got plenty.'

The light was beginning to fade as Gil hurried up the road to the twenty-four-hour supermarket. It was crowded with people grabbing shopping on their way home from work and he stood in the queue for what seemed like hours, his arms aching under the weight of the two-litre bottle of water. When he got back to the park with the bottle in his backpack it was almost dark, and the police were nowhere to be seen.

'You're a total hero!' called Jude softly out of the tree. 'Wait a minute. I've got a bag on a rope somewhere.' He started ferreting around in the branches.

'You don't need to do that,' Gil said. 'I can throw it up to you.'

He heaved the bag off his back, pulled out the bottle and stepped over the low wall and on to the grass under the tree.

'Here! Catch!'

Gil swung the heavy bottle. It slipped out of his hands a fraction too soon and flew upwards into the tree. Jude made a snatch at it as it spiralled past him like an out-of-control satellite. Then the bottle dropped slowly, lazily, back to earth. It smashed on to the brown grass, the cap blew off, water exploded out of the bottle and soaked one of the placards.

'Aaaah!' yelled Gil in frustration.

Jude started to cackle, and after a moment Gil began to laugh too.

And then Gil felt a hand fall on his shoulder.

'I think you'd better come with me, laddie,' said the policeman's voice.

CHAPTER 4

As the policeman led him away, all Gil could think about was the hand gripping his arm so tightly it hurt. Far behind him, or so it seemed, Jude was yelling from his perch in the tree. 'Oi! Leave him alone! He's a kid! He hasn't done anything! You bunch of complete —'

Jude trailed off into a string of swear words. The policeman took absolutely no notice. He marched Gil into a side street where there was a police car waiting, and threw open one of the rear doors.

'Get in,' he said.

Gil crawled in, feeling sick. There was another policeman in the driver's seat who didn't even look round. The first policeman slammed the door on Gil, sat down heavily in the seat in front of him and immediately locked the doors.

There were no windows that Gil could open. The car smelt of other people's bodies. There was no way out.

'So,' said the policeman after a while, sounding almost friendly, 'how old are you?'

Gil wondered if he should lie. He was tall for his age, and might be able to get away with saying he was fifteen or even older, but it quickly seemed like a bad idea.

'Nearly fourteen.'

'Fourteen, eh? Not too young for an ASBO, you know.'

'Um . . . I'm not sure . . . what did I do, exactly? I mean,' Gil added hurriedly, 'I'm really sorry, but I didn't know I was doing anything wrong.'

'Well, there are several things we could get you on. Aiding an illegal protest, for example. Or littering.'

'Littering?'

'I saw you deliberately throw a plastic bottle into a public park. That constitutes littering. It carries a hefty fine these days.'

'I wasn't . . . I wasn't . . .'

Gil took a deep breath. The policeman was beginning to morph into Dad. He had to get a grip on himself. 'I was trying to help Ju— I mean, the man in the tree. He needed some water, that's all.'

'As I said,' snapped the policeman, 'aiding an illegal protest. After you'd received a formal warning.'

There wasn't anywhere else for the conversation to go, so Gil kept his mouth shut.

'I think we'd better take you home,' said the policeman. 'Have a little word with your parents. Or parent. Or whoever. Where do you live?'

Gil told him.

'Well I never,' said the policeman. 'Nice area, that is. I had you down for a yob off one of the housing estates. Put your seatbelt on.'

The police car purred off towards Gil's home.

Gil leaned his head against the window and flicked the seatbelt that pulled too tightly across his chest. *You idiot*, he told himself. *You total idiot.* OK, so he wanted to wind Dad up, but he hadn't meant to go quite this far. Not all at once, anyway.

But when he saw the look on Dad's face as he opened the front door, Gil began to think it might have been worth it.

The policeman started to explain to Dad why it had been necessary to give Gil a police escort. It took ages. Gil stood on the path, blinking in the light from the hall, saying nothing, even when the policeman made it sound as if Jude was some kind of dangerous child molester who liked to lurk in trees so that he could kidnap any young person who happened to wander too close. It was pointless contradicting the policeman. Gil knew he needed to save his energy for Dad.

'But as I say, we did formally warn your son not to go in the park,' said the policeman. 'In my view, if he's going to get up to this kind of thing in future, it might be wise not to let him go into the city centre on his own.'

'He's not allowed to do that anyway,' said Dad. 'I'm deeply sorry you've been put to this trouble. We'll try to make sure it doesn't happen again.'

Dad and the policeman nodded to each other stiffly like

a couple of penguins. Gil finally stepped inside, and the door closed behind him.

'So, what's for dinner?' Gil said, more brightly than he felt. 'I'm starving.'

He waited for the storm, but it didn't come immediately. Dad put a hand in the centre of his back and propelled him into the kitchen. Mum was sitting at the table. As Gil came in she pulled a tissue out of the box in front of her and pressed it to her face with both hands. There was no noise, but Gil could see she was trembling.

Oh, God. He hadn't thought about Mum the whole time he'd been in town. Maybe if he'd just made a quick phone call to say he was OK . . .

'I'm sorry, Mum,' Gil said. He meant it.

'Sit down,' said Dad. He sounded dangerously calm. Gil could hear a faint hiss in his voice, like the noise you hear when you put your ear to a can of fizzy drink that's been shaken violently. Any second now, when you lift the ring-pull . . .

Gil sat down. Dad began.

'So, putting aside for the moment the fact that you've just come home in a police car, let me tell you how things have been here for the last couple of hours. Your mother phoned me at half past four, frantic with worry. She'd already called Louis' house and found that you weren't there. Louis told her he'd seen you walk off towards the bus stop after school. He said he'd tried to stop you, but you'd taken no notice of him. And so we deduced that you had disobeyed us and gone somewhere on your own.'

Well, Louis would be over the moon, thought Gil. He'd stand there at skating tomorrow like one of those stupid little Mr Men, Mr Know-It-All, going, 'Told you it was a bad idea. Told you so.'

'I just —' Gil started to say, but Dad hadn't finished.

'As soon as your mother told me you were missing, I left a meeting – a very important meeting – and came straight home. We have spent the last hour and a half waiting for you to contact us or turn up. Your mother has been to hell and back. At the point where you arrived home we were considering phoning the police, which is pretty ironic, as you happened to be stepping out of a police car at the time.'

'I wasn't *missing*,' Gil said. 'I was totally safe.'

'Which is obviously why you nearly got arrested,' said Dad.

'Dad, the police were completely out of order. I wasn't doing anything wrong. I was just —'

'Where's your school bag?' interrupted Dad.

'I don't know. I must have . . . I probably left it at school.'

It was under Jude's tree. Gil saw it clearly, lying exactly where he'd dumped it while he threw the water bottle, just before the policeman had marched him away. And his wallet was in the bag. Crap.

Dad rolled his eyes. 'You didn't even have the decency to phone us to say where you were.'

'Yeah, I know, I'm sorry, but —'

'It's our fault because we won't let you have a phone? Is that what you were going to say? Well, there are still a number of public telephone boxes in the city centre, I

34

believe,' said Dad. 'But of course it would be beneath you, wouldn't it, to make a call from a grubby payphone?'

Gil rocked his chair backwards and gripped the edge of the table to steady himself. The table was bare apart from the box of tissues, which was just as well, Gil thought, because he wanted to throw something hard and heavy at Dad again. There was a pause. Mum took a deep, shuddering breath and finally peeled the tissue away from her face. She looked terrible. A tiny flame of guilt began to burn in the middle of Gil's chest, but Dad's next attack snuffed it out altogether.

'Your mother has spent most of the day at Oakwood, do you realise that?'

Dad paused again for effect. Here we go, thought Gil. Oakwood. That was really meant to guilt-trip him, because Oakwood was the nursing home where his granny lived. Mum went roughly once a week. Gil had never been allowed to visit. He'd given up asking to see his granny years ago, because the answer was always, 'No, she's not well enough.' If she'd been ill all that time, why wasn't she dead yet? It couldn't be cancer, so what was it? Whatever was wrong with her Gil didn't understand why he couldn't see her. It was just like the going-into-town-after-school issue. His parents had decided he wasn't allowed to, and that was that.

'That's Mum's choice, isn't it?' he said, swaying on two legs and looking at the kitchen floor.

'I beg your pardon?' Dad's voice was icy-cold.

You're the only one, said Louis' voice in his head. *That's why they're so protective.*

Gil dropped the chair forwards with a crash and went for it.

'You know what the problem is with you two?' he said. 'You're just so bloody over-protective. You don't let me go into town on my own, you won't let me visit my granny, you say I can't have a phone – you treat me like a baby, and it's all because I'm an only child, isn't it?'

'That has nothing whatsoever to do with it,' said Dad.

But Gil was gathering momentum, like a rock rolling down a hill. 'It's your fault. Why didn't you have more children? I never asked to be an only child. If there were more kids in this house at least you wouldn't be ganging up on me all the time. Oh, I know. You were just too *selfish* to have more than one child. You thought it would mess up your nice tidy lives, didn't you? You thought —'

Mum suddenly stood up, her eyes flashing like lightning, and Gil stopped.

'Oh, you have *no idea* . . .' she said, so fiercely that Gil was almost scared. She was staring as if she could see a ghost hanging in the air.

'That's right,' said Dad quickly, 'he has no idea. Let's leave it like that, Rachel. Gil, go up to your room, will you?'

Gil hesitated. He watched Mum sit down heavily in the kitchen chair and put her face back in her hands.

'What . . .?' he began to ask.

'Just go,' Dad said. 'Now.'

Gil got up slowly and started to go upstairs. Halfway up he stopped and listened. There was no sound coming from the kitchen, not even the sound of Mum crying. Gil tried to think of something that he could go back and say but his mind was empty, and in the end he just climbed the rest of the stairs to his room.

The room was still a mess. His homework desk stood right behind the door where he'd left it that morning. Gil squeezed past it and dropped on to the end of his bed. He ought at least to put the desk back where it belonged and pick a few things off the floor, but then Dad would notice he'd done it and say *I see you've obeyed me on something*, and even the thought of it made Gil begin to buzz with irritation. He sat for a long while gazing at the desk without moving it and wondering what the hell had just happened with Mum downstairs in the kitchen.

Oh, you have no idea . . .

No idea about what?

'Oh crap,' he said at last.

Somehow he'd stepped over a line that he didn't even know was there. In all the rows they had, Gil always knew exactly how he was winding Mum and Dad up, even if he didn't manage to make the argument go his way. He knew which rules he was breaking, and which buttons he needed to press to trigger a reaction. But this time it was different. The look on Mum's face had been awful in a way that he wasn't prepared for. He didn't have a clue what he'd done.

Maybe they hadn't *wanted* him to be an only child, thought Gil. Maybe they hadn't been able to have any more kids. But if that was true, why didn't they just tell him up front? Why did they hide together in corners and whisper things he wasn't meant to hear?

Mum and Dad were so wrapped up in themselves. They behaved as if life was one huge agonising problem that Gil wasn't grown-up enough to understand. They joined forces against him, all the time. He'd started to notice how Dad always spoke in the plural, like Queen Victoria. It was always 'we', and the word 'we' never seemed to include Gil. *We are not going to put up with this. We are not prepared to discuss it. We are not amused, Gil. We are not amused.*

Gil felt the anger begin to creep back into his guts. Dad hadn't let him tell his side of the story, about the way the policeman had jumped on him for practically no reason. Now he would probably never get the chance to explain himself. Nothing would change. Dad would come up with various punishments and life would wander along from day to day until he went insane with it.

Gil rolled over on to his back and looked at the window. The curtains were still open, though it was completely dark outside now. Gil thought about Jude. He imagined him lying in his hammock under the cold March sky, guarding the tree against the chainsaws and the bulldozers, not afraid of falling, not afraid of the police, not afraid of breaking the rules. Not afraid to leave his cosy bed and put himself on the line to fight for something he believed in.

How long was it, Gil wondered, before he turned eighteen and could go and live up a tree in a park if he wanted to? He did a quick calculation. Nearly fifteen hundred days. It was a life sentence.

CHAPTER 5

Dad produced his list of punishments first thing on Saturday morning. He'd typed the list up on the computer so there was no excuse for forgetting anything, and as Gil skim-read the page he quickly saw there was very little that Dad had missed.

No friends home after school or at weekends. No visits to friends' houses. No pocket money – well, that was obvious. No tuck shop money either. No ice-skating on Saturday mornings. No swimming. No going to school or coming home independently – it seemed as if Dad planned to reorganise his entire diary so that he could drive Gil to school and pick him up again at the end of the day. No Nintendo, no MP3 player – they were locked away immediately in one of the drawers in Dad's study. No sweets. No crisps. No favourite treats, like bacon sandwiches when Gil came home from school. A long list of chores to be fitted in around supper and homework. No going anywhere, even to the library round the corner, except with a parent. No television, no DVDs, no computer and no internet access unless Gil needed something for a piece of homework he was doing, and then Dad would have to supervise it.

'These punishments will last for two weeks,' said Dad. 'After that time, if you can prove to us that you are capable of behaving responsibly, you can expect to win back some of your privileges.'

Gil stared at the list in his hands and felt as if there was something very heavy pressing down on his shoulders. It was even worse than he'd expected. He'd never had a punishment as big as this before, and he wondered what he was being punished for. Was it because he'd nearly got arrested, or because he'd had a go at Mum and Dad for making him an only child?

'On the other hand,' Dad added, 'if we find you have broken any of these conditions, or if you manage to get yourself into any more trouble . . .'

He left the threat hanging in the air.

'We' again, Gil thought, even though Mum wasn't there to be included. She hadn't even got up yet.

Gil got a bowl of cornflakes from the kitchen and took it up to his room. He was still in his pyjamas, but it was pointless getting dressed if he wasn't going skating. While he sat and ate the cornflakes he read Dad's list of punishments again, until it occurred to him that this was a bit like going up a level in a computer game. You always ended the previous level on a real high because you'd got unbelievably good at whatever it was you needed to do to beat the enemy. And then you were faced with a new scenario that needed a totally different set of skills, and for a while you were out of your depth. Dad had just pushed the game up to a new level of difficulty, and it looked seriously daunting.

But as Gil read and re-read Dad's list, slowly his mind cleared and settled. Some of the punishments were things he didn't care about anyway. He only ever went to Louis' house these days, and he could do without Louis for two weeks, no problem, especially if Louis was going to insist on hanging around with Ben. Skating was something he did with Louis too, but recently it had begun to feel less and less of a challenge. There were always too many people at the rink to try anything really adventurous. Gil thought he could probably manage without pocket money; he wasn't allowed to go into town to spend it in any case. It wouldn't kill him to give up his MP3 player for a couple of weeks, and he was bored with most of his Nintendo games, so that wasn't a great loss either when it came down to it.

OK, thought Gil. What if he just made a conscious decision not to care about any of the other punishments? So Dad was going to be waiting for him at the school gates every day – so what? The morons in his year could say what they liked. No sweets, no crisps, no television – well, he wasn't addicted to them, was he? It would be good discipline to prove that he could do without them. Gil's mind drifted away again to Jude in his tree. Jude was probably living on bread and water. He wouldn't waste time longing for a packet of prawn cocktail crisps or wondering what was happening in *EastEnders*. He had more important things to do.

Gil traced over the pattern on his duvet cover while he considered his strategy. There must be something he could do to piss Dad off without actually breaking any of his rules. Something that would make a tiny crack in the solid wall that Mum and Dad put up in front of him. Right now Gil couldn't think of anything, but he knew when he did it would be like finding the secret power that makes your enemy crumble into a pile of dust. And meanwhile he would make a really good job of doing exactly what Dad wanted so that when he finally found the thing that was going to drive Dad crazy, Dad would be completely unprepared.

'Don't forget to look for your school bag,' said Dad as they drove off for school on Monday morning.

'Yeah, yeah,' Gil said, and then pulled himself up short. 'I mean yes, sure.' He was going to have to make an effort, otherwise he'd blow it before they got as far as the school gates. He rubbed his ear. It was hard, sitting this close to Dad without any possibility of escape. At home he could at least find an excuse to leave the room if Dad started to bug him, but he couldn't exactly throw himself from the car if Dad went off on one of those 'you-have-to-believe-that-we-are-acting-in-your-best-interests' speeches. Fortunately Dad seemed to feel in control, and he just talked about last week's maths homework and how early the cherry blossom was again this year. Gil didn't get the urge to put his fingers in his ears once. He felt pretty pleased with himself, especially as he'd managed to blag another three pounds off Mum for lunch without having to confess to losing his wallet.

'See you later, then,' said Dad as Gil climbed out of the car. 'Have a good day.'

Gil spotted Louis immediately, standing by the school gates. Even from a distance Gil could read all kinds of things in his face – relief, worry, curiosity. Louis was hopping from foot to foot as if he couldn't wait to ask what had been going on.

'Hi,' Gil said, as if it was just a normal Monday. 'Good weekend?'

'Yes. No. Gil, what happened to you on Friday? Your mum phoned and she sounded terrible. And then I never heard anything. You weren't at skating, and I phoned you on Sunday morning but your dad just said you weren't available.'

'I didn't know you'd phoned. Dad didn't tell me.'

But would he have bothered to phone back, Gil wondered, even if Dad had given him permission? He hadn't really thought about Louis at all over the weekend. Louis had become just another item on Dad's list, one of the many things he was no longer allowed.

'So . . .?' said Louis eagerly, making a hurry up gesture with his hand.

'So what?'

'What happened on Friday?'

'Oh, that,' Gil said. 'I went into town, I did some stuff, I was about to come home and then . . .'

He waited a split second before finishing, to create the maximum impact.

' . . . the police nearly arrested me, just for dropping a plastic bottle.'

Louis' eyebrows shot up in horror. 'The *police*? You're joking!'

'It wasn't a big deal.' Gil grinned, enjoying Louis' reaction, until he remembered the smell in the police car, the smell of other people's bodies, and he had to swallow quickly to stop himself feeling sick.

'What do you mean, it wasn't a big deal?' Louis peered at him closely. 'I'd have been cacking it.'

'Yeah, that's because you're such a wuss. Anyway, I knew I hadn't done anything wrong, so they couldn't arrest me. They took me home in a police car, though, just to try and scare me.'

Louis stopped in the playground with his mouth open.

'You can guess what Dad said,' Gil went on.

'I *told* you it was a bad idea, didn't I?' said Louis.

'Oh, wow, what a surprise. I so didn't expect you to say that. And by the way, thanks a lot for dumping me in it when my mum phoned to see if I was at your house. That was *really* helpful.'

'What was I supposed to tell her? You told me you didn't care what I said,' Louis fired back at once. 'You know I'm rubbish at lying. You should have given me something to say if you wanted me to cover for you. Anyway, as soon as the police brought you home it would have been pretty obvious

I wasn't telling the truth. Then I'd have got a load of grief for lying, wouldn't I?'

'God, Louis, what are you getting so angry about?'

'What am *I* angry about?' Louis was starting to sound squeaky. '*You're* the angry one. You've been getting worse and worse for ages now. It just sort of leaks out of you all the time. It's like sitting next to a bloody nuclear meltdown sometimes. You never laugh about anything any more. And now you're showing off about nearly getting arrested!'

'I'm not showing off!'

'You are! It's so stupid! You never used to be like this!'

'Yeah? Well, you know what, Louis? I can do without a lecture from you. I get enough of that kind of crap at home.'

Gil spun round and walked off in the opposite direction.

'You're doing it again!' Louis yelled after him.

Gil stopped and turned back, very slowly, as if he was having second thoughts. He stood gazing at Louis until the anger left Louis' face and was replaced by a look of complete uncertainty.

'Maybe you'd like to come over to my house sometime this week,' Gil said.

'Um . . . yes, I would,' Louis said. 'I haven't been for ages.'

'So you'd really like to come, would you?'

'Yes, sure. Look, I'm sorry I got annoyed. It's just that sometimes . . .' Louis looked down, and Gil didn't wait for him to finish.

'Well, tough,' Gil said.

Louis' head snapped back up. 'What do you mean?'

'I mean you can't come to my house. I'm grounded. I'm

45

not allowed to see anyone. And you know something else? I don't care. I don't want to see you anyway, so it's not exactly a punishment, is it? The joke's on Dad for once. And you.'

Louis opened his mouth but nothing came out. Gil walked away rapidly, and when it became obvious that Louis was going to spend the rest of the day avoiding him Gil made no effort to try and approach him again. Louis was a prat. He was a moron like Ben, like all the other morons at school. The only surprise, Gil thought, was that it had taken him so long to notice it.

CHAPTER 6

'Bag?'

Dad was standing inside the school gates, waiting.

'What?'

'Where's your bag? Did you even look for it?'

'Uh – no, I didn't.'

That was true, anyway, Gil thought. There was no point looking for it at school when he knew he'd left it under Jude's tree.

Dad wrinkled his nose in disapproval. 'Well, you'll have to look tomorrow. I haven't got time to hang about now. I need to get back to work.'

When the car pulled up outside the house, Dad didn't get out. He waited just long enough to see Gil walk up the path and Mum open the front door, and then he was off again.

'Hello, darling,' said Mum.

As usual, the way Mum said *Hello, darling* made Gil's

heart sink. She made it sound as if Gil had been away for weeks instead of hours, and she looked so happy to see him he could hardly stand it. Mum was *always* at home these days. Not for the first time, Gil remembered how he'd spent all those years at primary school going to an after-school club he hated because Mum was at work full-time, and just at the point where he was finally looking forward to getting a front door key so he could come home to an empty house, Mum had suddenly given up her job and announced that she'd be there for him. Every day. It was like walking into a house where the central heating was up way too high.

'Hi,' Gil said, squeezing past Mum. He went straight into the front room, fell on the sofa and was just picking up the remote to flick on the television when he heard Mum behind him.

'Gil . . .'

She was hovering in the doorway.

'Oh.' Gil suddenly realised. 'I'm not allowed, am I?'

'No,' said Mum. 'I'm afraid not.'

The house was so quiet that Gil could hear the pulse in his ears. If he couldn't watch television, what was he going to do to fill the silence?

'Did you have a good day?' asked Mum. She didn't quite come into the room.

'Um – not bad.'

Silence.

'How about you?' Gil said.

Mum stared. 'Sorry?' she said.

'Did you have a good day?'

'Oh. Yes. Thanks. I didn't do much really. Just pottering, you know.'

Pottering. That was what old people did, Gil thought. Pottering in the garden. Pottering in the kitchen. There was something about it that didn't feel right. Surely Mum had never spent so much time doing so little? She'd always wanted to be out and doing things. And now – pottering. Doing nothing. Hanging about the house waiting for Gil to come home. Why didn't she get a job again, like other people's mums, and get off his back?

Gil couldn't think of anything else to say to Mum, except all the things he knew he mustn't say. *Did you go and see Granny again? How is she? What's wrong with her? Is there something wrong with you, too? Is that why Dad's started to treat you as if you were about to break any minute, like a bubble? Is that why you spent most of the weekend in bed? Is that why Dad's the one picking me up from school, even though he hasn't got time and it puts him in a bad mood?*

'How about a bacon sandwich?' said Mum. 'You're probably hungry.' Then her face fell. 'Oh,' she said.

'That's on the list too, isn't it?' Gil said.

'Yes.' Mum looked uncomfortable. 'Sorry.'

'Well, I won't tell Dad if you don't.'

'Oh no, I really think . . .'

You really think I deserve to be punished like this, Gil nearly said, but he stopped, because Mum was looking as if it was just as much of a punishment for her.

'Don't worry, I'll have some cereal,' he said instead.

Mum went ahead into the kitchen and quickly got out a

bowl and the milk. Gil always preferred taking his after-school snack up to his room, but today he sat and ate the cereal at the kitchen table, wondering if it was too late to say sorry for Friday. The problem was that he didn't really know what to say sorry *for*, and he couldn't think of a way to apologise without risking upsetting Mum again. He gave up. It was safer to leave it as it was.

'How's Louis?' asked Mum.

'Oh – fine.'

The conversation crashed again. It was too complicated to talk about what had happened with Louis, and anyway Mum would only give herself a hard time for phoning Louis in a panic on Friday.

Slowly the week staggered past. Now and again Mum would remind Gil about something he wasn't allowed to do, but always really gently. Dad did the school run every morning and afternoon, his head so full of work he barely spoke. Louis carried on avoiding Gil, and Gil went on obeying every single item on Dad's list of punishments. The only thing that mattered for now was staying in control.

On Wednesday evening Gil came down to get a dictionary from the front room. Dad was watching the news, and Gil hadn't seen any television for days. The story was something boring to do with banks, but he looked at it anyway while he pretended to leaf through the dictionary. After the news there was two minutes of sport, and then the jingle that started the local news programme.

'And there were angry scenes in the city centre today as environmental protesters clashed with police over plans to cut down trees in Stanmore Park,' said the presenter cheerfully.

The camera panned over the little park with the two big trees, and Gil suddenly started to pay attention. There was a shot of Jude's hammock flapping in the branches, and then a mass of bobbing heads and waving placards, and a screaming woman being dragged away feet first by two policemen. Gil's heart thumped as Jude's face filled the screen, his hair blowing wildly in the wind. He looked magnificent, like the hero of a disaster movie.

'There has been no consultation of any kind about this redevelopment,' he said. 'We want to draw people's attention to the council's total hypocrisy on environmental matters. It is appalling that these trees —'

Dad flicked the button on the remote and the television pinged off.

Turn it back on, Gil wanted to shout. *I want to see Jude.*

'Is that where the police picked you up, then?' said Dad, glancing round.

'What? I wasn't watching,' Gil said. 'How do you spell *Palaeolithic?*'

'Ah,' said Dad. 'Early Stone Age. Interesting. What did you want to know?'

'Just the spelling, Dad, thanks.' Gil was tempted to add *I know you were born in the Stone Age, Dad, but I really don't need you to tell me all about it.* He thought better of it.

After Gil had managed to escape back to his room, he went over and over the tiny bit of news he'd seen. Jude had looked smooth, polished, powerful. He wasn't just a bloke up a tree, smoking a roll-up. He was a leader. He was in charge.

He was the one the television cameras focused on, the one everybody wanted to interview, and Gil longed to be there in that crowd of pushing shouting people, linking arms with Jude as the bulldozers roared towards them.

The next day at school, Gil's bag reappeared. It arrived in the classroom without any explanation. There was nothing missing. Even Gil's wallet was still inside, holding the cash that Gil hadn't managed to spend in town.

If it was Jude who brought it back, Gil thought, then it means the police didn't get him. He's free.

He searched the bag for some trace of Jude – a twig, a cigarette end, anything to prove that it had passed through his hands. The bag did smell a bit of smoke, which was something. But it was only when Gil got home and pulled everything out of his wallet that he found the note, folded up neatly and slipped in behind a five pound note.

Gil, I hope this finds you OK. I hope the police didn't frighten you too badly. The first time is always the worst. After that you get used to their bully-boy tactics. You tried to help me – I appreciate that. You're a true friend. Maybe you've seen us on the news. Maybe by the time you read this they'll have bulldozed the park, but the struggle will go on. There are so many battles to fight, Gil. Perhaps you'll join us some day. Remember – the revolution will not be televised! I'll see you around, brother!

Jude felt like clean air, freedom, defiance. Jude had leapt out of the cage, and this was a clear invitation to follow him. Gil folded the note again carefully and hid it right at the back of the drawer under his bed.

CHAPTER 7

On Saturday morning Dad woke up in a horribly good mood.

'Well, Gil, you've done fairly well this week,' he announced over breakfast. 'We're not going to abandon the punishments just yet, so you can't go skating, I'm afraid, but we think you're due for a bit of a treat.'

Gil didn't like the sound of it.

'I'm going to take you into town,' said Dad. 'I want to go to the market, but then there's a special exhibition on at the Natural History Museum. I thought we could go there together.'

He waited. Gil couldn't think of a reply, except for 'Thanks, Dad, but I'd rather spend the day cutting my toenails', which probably wasn't the answer Dad wanted.

'Don't look so enthusiastic,' said Dad, raising his eyebrows. 'Anyone would think it was another punishment.

Anyway, you don't really have a choice. Your mother's going to the hairdresser's and we don't want you to stay at home on your own.'

So there it was, thought Gil. A compulsory reward. *You are going to enjoy yourself whether you like it or not.* Another of Dad's specialities.

They went into town on the bus and Gil wandered slowly round the market behind Dad for what felt like hours. Dad pored over the food stalls, buying watercress, a bag of tiny apples and some smoked eel. The eel looked revolting, like a piece of rotting rope. Then it was on to the butcher's stall, where Dad chose some lumps of blackish-red meat that looked as bad as the eel.

'What *is* it?' Gil asked.

'This one's venison,' said Dad. 'Deer meat. It's just like steak. We had it at Christmas, remember?'

'You made me eat *deer*?'

Dad laughed. He was still in a good mood. 'And this one's rook,' he said. 'Wild rook.'

'Rook? You mean those big black birds that look like crows?'

'Yes, that's right.'

'Dad, how *can* you?' said Gil, pulling a face.

'How is it different from chicken, exactly?' asked Dad.

'Well, it's . . . I don't know, but . . .'

'It's better than chicken, if you think about it,' said Dad. 'Chickens live cooped up on farms, in pretty unpleasant conditions a lot of the time. These rooks spent their lives flying around, free as a bird.' He chuckled. 'My personal

54

view is that you shouldn't eat anything you wouldn't be prepared to kill yourself. Agreed?'

Gil said nothing. He tucked the comment away in his memory in the hope that a smart answer would occur to him later.

Gil had to admit the museum wasn't so bad. As he looked up at the huge grin of the Tyrannosaurus skeleton that almost filled the entrance hall, he even felt a little flicker of excitement. When he was six it had been his favourite thing in the whole world, even though it scared him half to death. He'd pleaded with Mum and Dad to take him to look at it again and again and again. In those days dinosaurs had walked in his dreams and he'd really believed they were more than just heaps of bones. Today the special exhibition was fossils, too, and Dad leapt about from cabinet to cabinet as if there were springs in his shoes.

'*Tiktaalik* . . .' he murmured. 'Oh, this is so amazing. Do you see, Gil, how it's exactly halfway between a fish and a reptile? The head is flat, like a crocodile, and it's got teeth, but it's also got scales, and the fins are turning into prototype limbs, so it can walk about in shallow water. Do you see?'

He stood there, breathing misty patches on the glass, while Gil watched him.

'This is the moment where life began to leave the sea,' Dad whispered. 'We evolved from a creature like this. Extraordinary. And it's still all there – it's all there in our genes. All the information that built *Tiktaalik*.'

It was weird, thought Gil, to see Dad fizzing with excitement about what was basically just a fish-shaped lump of old rock.

When they left the museum they headed back towards the bus stop by the little park. Gil had always known they would end up here, but as the park got nearer his heart started to thump hard against the inside of his ribs. His arms hurt, and he had to concentrate on his breathing. It was just like his terrified excitement about the Tyrannosaurus all those years ago. Gil couldn't work out what he was so scared of. Seeing Jude? Not seeing Jude? Dad's reaction when he saw Jude? Dad paused to look in a shop window. Gil carried on walking, too nervous to stop, but as he came down the street past the last few shops he saw it was all over. The park was completely boarded off, and poking up over the top of the high fencing was the shovel of a bulldozer. Jude's tree had vanished, and so had the other one. Gil stared at the gap where the trees had been, trying to remember how the branches had fitted into the space. He was nearly at the bus stop before he saw the really important thing.

Jude was still there. Not in the park, but outside the fence, right next to the bus stop. There were two tables on the pavement, with a big display board leaning on the fence. The tables were piled with leaflets and books, and Jude was standing behind one of them. He was showing someone a leaflet and talking with the same bright confident look on his face that Gil had seen on the television. He looked up for a moment at Gil, shook the hair out of his eyes and sprang over the table.

'Gil! Gil, I'm so glad you're OK! That whole thing with the police was ridiculous. Did you get your bag back? I got someone to bring it into school for you.'

'Yes,' Gil said. 'Thanks. I saw you on the news.' He felt suddenly stupidly shy and he could hardly get the words out of his mouth.

Jude looked at him, grinning, nodding. 'Yeah, we got some good publicity out of that,' he said. 'Even though we lost the trees.'

'I was worried you'd be arrested,' Gil said. Oh crap. He was talking like a total moron. But Jude shook his head slowly, still grinning.

'That would have been a terrible waste,' he said. 'It was all a bit of a side-show for me, really. I was doing a friend a favour because they didn't know anyone else who had the time to spend a week living in a tree. Don't get me wrong, I think climate change is a pretty big issue, but personally I'm saving myself for a greater cause.'

He waved a hand at the tables behind him. Hanging along the front was a banner that read *CLOSE DOWN THE LABS – PROTECT ANIMAL RIGHTS*. The display board propped against the fence had an enormous poster of a ginger-brown monkey with huge sad eyes and what looked like a tangle of wires around its ears. Gil's head was still so full of trees that he couldn't make sense of the picture for a while.

'Well,' said a voice, so unexpectedly that Gil jumped. It was Dad, standing right at his shoulder. Gil had completely forgotten that Dad was with him, but it was too late now to do anything about it. Dad moved a step closer so that he was face-to-face with Jude. There was a long moment where they stood and gazed at each other, like two stags before they charge and smash heads. It was long enough for Gil to notice that the two of them were about the same size and both had very blue eyes.

'So you must be the young man who nearly got my son arrested,' said Dad, as if it was a totally normal thing to say to someone he'd never met before.

'And you must be Dr Matthew Walker, torturer of defenceless animals,' said Jude, showing his teeth. It didn't look like a smile. 'Delighted to meet you.'

Dad didn't move. He just stared Jude down.

Gil's head began to whirl. How did Jude know Dad's name? Why was he calling him a 'torturer'?

'I don't believe you know anything at all about what I do,' said Dad at last.

'Oh? Really? There's quite a lot of interesting information on your website. Of course, it doesn't actually say how many animals you've butchered over the past year, but if you read between the lines . . .'

'You know, if you didn't twist the facts so much I might have more time for people like you,' Dad interrupted. He stabbed a finger at the giant monkey, and Gil could see his chest rising and falling quickly. 'That picture you have up there, for example, has nothing whatsoever to do with our labs. It's a photo from America, and it's at least twenty years old. You know that perfectly well. You just like to wheel it out to prop up your pathetic sentimental arguments.'

The monkey gazed down sadly. Its face reminded him of Mum, Gil realised, and then he saw that the wires weren't wrapped around the monkey's head. They were poking out of its skull. The photograph clearly showed slots in the monkey's head where the wires had been plugged in, as if it was going to be connected up to an electrical circuit.

'You scientists are the ones with the pathetic arguments,' said Jude calmly. 'So, if you're not prepared to discuss monkeys, are you going to admit what other dumb creatures you torture? Mice? Frogs? Guinea pigs? Or are you going to try and tell me you only experiment on lettuces?'

'Our research does not involve any form of torture. Torture is what human beings do to each other. What we do is very carefully monitored, and it's far more humane than farming. We look after our animals.'

'What kind of an excuse is that? How does that justify messing about with animals as if they were just bits of computer equipment?'

'I have never killed an animal needlessly,' said Dad, so quietly that Gil could hardly hear him.

'Oh, but you've killed them, haven't you? You've killed them. When they've stopped being useful to you, when you've cut out so much of their brains that they might as well be vegetables anyway, when you can't cure the diseases you've given them – you kill them then, don't you?'

A tiny bit of spit flew out of Jude's mouth and landed on Dad's cheek. All at once Gil's feeling of confusion began to turn into fear. What if Dad hit Jude? Was Dad capable of hitting someone? Gil couldn't remember ever seeing him like this. Dad never lost an argument, and if he lost his temper he always calmed down quickly. But now, facing Jude, Gil saw him so angry he could hardly speak, and trapped in a corner that he didn't seem able to escape from.

'Dad,' said Gil. He pulled Dad's arm, but Dad didn't move. Neither did Jude. At one of the tables Gil could see a woman tidying piles of leaflets, her eyes fixed on Dad and Jude as if she was getting ready to step in the second either of them raised a hand.

Then very slowly Dad dropped his eyes and let his body relax. He took a step away from Jude, like a cat backing away from a fight it knows it can't win.

'Oh, this is crazy,' he said, running a hand over his mouth. 'I'm wasting my time.'

Jude was silent. He stared at Dad a little longer, as if to make absolutely sure he was defeated. Then he took a deep breath and turned to Gil.

'I'm sorry, Gil,' he said. 'I know this is your dad, but I feel so strongly about this. I can't pretend I don't care just to protect your feelings.'

Instantly Dad sprang to the attack again.

'Leave my son out of it,' he said. 'Leave him alone. Keep your damn ideas to yourself.'

'Don't you think he's old enough to make up his own mind? You can't brainwash him for ever.'

'Brainwash.' Dad tried to laugh. 'Oh, that's funny. Gil, tell this man what I do.'

'Um – you're a scientist,' Gil said.

'Bravo. What kind? What do I actually do?'

'I'm not really sure, Dad. I don't think you've ever told me.'

'Where do I work? I mean in which building?'

'In the university somewhere?'

'You see?' Dad turned back to Jude. 'He hasn't got a clue. How is that brainwashing, exactly?'

'He's got a right to understand the arguments,' said Jude.

'I don't really know what you're arguing *about*,' Gil said. 'Not properly, anyway.'

Jude grabbed a booklet off the table behind him. 'Read this,' he said, handing it to Gil.

'Over my dead body,' snapped Dad. 'It's a load of inaccurate propaganda.'

'So you're going to ban him from reading it, are you? You're going to tell him that science is a wonderful journey towards knowledge and progress and all that garbage? You don't want him to know about the kittens with holes where their eyes should be, and the two-headed mice, and the rats with tumours as big as your fist – all the monsters you scientists have deliberately engineered in your glorious quest for the truth, do you?'

A bus had pulled up at the bus stop. Without another word Dad put a hand on Gil's shoulder, and Gil allowed himself to be marched away. He rolled up Jude's booklet and stuffed it in his back pocket.

The bus was halfway home before Dad said anything.

'So,' said Dad at last, 'what on earth possessed you to pass personal information about me to a complete stranger?'

'What?'

'He knew my name, and he knew what I did. What did you tell him?'

'Dad, I didn't tell him anything. Well, I might have told him *my* name, but that was it. We were talking about smoking and —'

'You mean he was encouraging you to have a cigarette.'

'No! He was telling me how stupid it was! I just said some of the stuff you've told me, about the damage smoking does to DNA, and he asked if you were a doctor. And I said no, you were a scientist. That's all. He must have found the rest out himself. Maybe he Googled you, I don't know. What *do* you do, anyway?'

'Oh, you heard the man back there. I torture small animals for fun. Just for the sheer hell of it.' Dad stopped for a moment. After a pause he went on. 'Let's hope the house doesn't get fire-bombed.'

'Dad, what are you talking about?'

'Some of those animal rights protesters are insane. They love animals, but they hate people. They wouldn't think twice about trying to hurt us.'

'You're crazy. He's not like that,' said Gil.

'What's his name?' asked Dad.

'I don't know.' Gil looked out of the bus window. 'He didn't tell me.'

'Well, whoever he is you're not to talk to him again, Gil, do you hear me? He's dangerous. And he's also wrong.'

CHAPTER 8

When they got home Mum still wasn't back from the hairdresser's. It was late, and Gil was hungry. Dad made sandwiches, and then took his own plate and went and shut himself in his study.

Well then, Gil thought. He sat in the kitchen, stripped the crusts off his sandwich and ate it quickly. Then he went up to his room. By the time he got to the top of the stairs he was exhausted, as if he'd swum thirty lengths at the pool.

The booklet that Jude had given him crackled in his trouser pocket as he sank on to the end of his bed. Gil wondered why Dad hadn't taken it off him and thrown it in the bin the moment they'd got home. Maybe he didn't care if Gil read it or not. Gil knew he probably *ought* to read it, but it was too soon. He felt as if he'd just stepped off a rollercoaster ride that had lasted most of the morning, and his head needed some time to return to normal. Gil keeled over sideways on the bed and gradually let his mind begin to sort out the tangle of things he had discovered that morning.

Dad worked in the labs where they did experiments on animals.

Jude wanted to close down the labs where Dad worked.

Dad hated Jude and everything he stood for.

Jude hated Dad and everything he stood for.

Dad thought Jude was a dangerous nutter who wanted to kill him.

Jude thought Dad was an evil scientist who tortured animals.

And me? thought Gil. What am I supposed to think?

Of course he knew that people did experiments on animals. But he knew it in the same way that he knew Beijing was a city in China – it was a fact that lived in a corner of his mind somewhere, filed away with lots of other facts. It had never made him *feel* anything. He hadn't ever wondered about what sort of experiments they were, or what kind of animals they used, or who actually carried out the experiments.

Now he'd discovered it was his *dad* who carried out the experiments.

And Dad had never told him.

Gil had a vision of Dad in a white doctor's coat, bending over a cat that was pegged to a table, belly-up. A razor blade flashed. Blood spurted on to the clean white coat.

Was that what he did all day at work?

Gil urgently needed not to think about it. He went downstairs, checked that Dad's study door was closed, went into the front room and put the television on quietly. Then he sat and channel-hopped until he found what he was looking for – *Fireman Sam*, baby television, the kind of stuff he always liked to watch when he was ill.

There was a tap on the front room window which made Gil leap off the sofa as if something had bitten him. It was Mum, peering through the glass, smiling and waving. He went to the front door and let her in.

'I locked myself out,' she said. 'Silly of me, wasn't it? Have you eaten?'

Dad was there instantly. Gil didn't even hear the study door open. It was as if Dad had beamed himself down out of the Starship Enterprise.

'I was getting worried,' he said to Mum. 'I've just tried to phone you.'

Mum smiled, but she looked cold and tired. 'I left my phone here somewhere. And my keys. Sorry.'

The *Fireman Sam* theme tune drifted out of the front room, and Mum looked at Dad. 'Did you say Gil could . . .?'

'Forget it,' said Dad. 'The television doesn't matter, in the scale of things. Let me make you some lunch.'

They both went into the kitchen, and Gil went back to *Fireman Sam*. He watched him rescue Bella's cat Rosa from the top of a tree while he weighed up the choice he needed to make.

Dad or Jude?

It was simple, really, Gil realised – as simple as Fireman Sam plucking the cat out of the tree. He didn't need to know whether animal experiments were right or wrong. He didn't need to know anything about them at all. The only thing that mattered was that Jude had pushed Dad to the limit. They'd gone head to head, and it had taken Jude less than five minutes to defeat him completely.

It was suddenly clear to Gil that he had found the thing he was looking for, the secret power that could make your enemy crumble into a pile of dust. Animal rights – this was the issue that made Dad froth and fall apart like a piece of chalk dropped in acid. If Gil joined Jude's campaign against the labs it would drive Dad crazy. It was even better than taking up smoking, because it wasn't illegal for a thirteen-year-old and it wasn't likely to kill him.

Gil's first step came at lunch on Sunday. Dad had roasted the venison he'd bought from the market. It smelt good, but Gil had already decided what he was going to do. He watched Dad carve slices of meat and pile them up on the dish, while steam rose from the bowls of roast potatoes and parsnips and peas and broccoli and carrots. Gil waited until Dad was about to put the meat on his plate before he made his announcement.

'Actually, you know what?' he said. 'I really don't want any meat.'

'What?'

Dad stopped with the meat in mid-air.

'I've been thinking about becoming a vegetarian,' Gil went on. 'I might as well start now.'

'Gil, are you sure?' said Mum anxiously. 'You're growing like mad at the moment. It might not be good for you.'

Dad didn't move.

'Is this a result of all that animal rights nonsense yesterday?' he said at last.

'No, of course not,' Gil said, innocently. 'Actually it's a result of what *you* said, Dad.'

'What are you talking about?'

'When we were at the market you said you shouldn't eat any animal unless you were prepared to kill it yourself. Well, I agree with you. I wouldn't be prepared to kill the deer this venison came from. So I'd better not eat it, had I?'

'It's organic,' said Mum. 'And RSPCA-monitored.'

'You mean it was happy before it was murdered? No thanks. I'll just have the veg.'

Gil went to help himself to roast potatoes, but Dad moved the dish before he could get to it.

'Sorry, Gil,' he said. 'You'd better not have those. They've been cooked in the meat juice, I'm afraid. And that means you can't have the parsnips, either. Or the gravy.'

As Dad whisked away the potatoes, a gorgeous meaty smell wafted up Gil's nose and all at once he had a vivid glimpse of what he was letting himself in for. No meat. No chicken, no pork, no bacon, no ham, no beefburgers, no sausages. It was going to be really hard. He shut his eyes briefly. He was going to need every gram of willpower he possessed.

'I think I'll just have some bread and cheese, then,' Gil said.

Mum started to get up, but Dad put a hand on her arm.

'I think you'll just go and get it yourself, then,' he said to Gil.

As Gil came back to the table with bread and butter and

cheese he was aware of Dad watching him intently.

'You know, Gil, if you're going down this route, you might want to consider doing it properly,' Dad said through a mouthful of meat.

'What do you mean, *properly*?'

'You shouldn't be eating cheese either,' said Dad. 'Do you know how they make cheese? They mash up dead calves' stomachs and use it to break down the milk.'

'Matt, please,' said Mum, putting down her fork. 'Not over lunch.'

'I'm just telling him the facts,' said Dad. 'That butter you've got there – it's a direct consequence of killing animals for their meat. Cows start to produce milk only when they have calves. The female calves are allowed to grow up to have more babies, but the male calves end up on the dinner table as beef. Milk is just a useful by-product of the meat industry. So you see, Gil, if you're not going to eat meat, the only logical choice is to become a vegan and not eat anything at all that comes from an animal.'

Gil swallowed a lump of cheese with an effort. Jude would know how to argue back, he thought. Jude would be able to smash Dad's stupid facts to a pulp and wipe that self-satisfied grin off his face. He was still considering how to reply when, to his complete surprise, Mum stepped in.

'Don't give him such a hard time,' she said. 'Let him make up his own mind. He needs to think these things through for himself.'

Dad looked as surprised as Gil felt.

'I'm helping Gil to think things through, that's all,' he said.

'No, you're not. You just want to win the argument. Look, he's allowed to have principles, Matt. After all, we did. We stood up for what we believed in. I was a vegetarian for years. Ten years, at least. Just – let Gil have a bit of space. Even if you don't agree with him.'

There it was – a tiny crack in the wall. Gil couldn't believe it. Very gently, like a butterfly stamping, Mum was putting her foot down. She was disagreeing with Dad.

'I never knew you were a vegetarian,' Gil said. 'Why did you give up?'

'Well,' Mum said. 'I suppose there was a point in my life where it no longer seemed terribly important.'

Dad suddenly looked up at Mum. On his face was another of those expressions that Gil knew he wasn't meant to notice, let alone understand. Mum just concentrated on her dinner, and a silence settled over them.

Gil finished his bread and cheese first, but for once he didn't try to get away from the table as quickly as possible. He waited until Dad had put his knife and fork neatly on his plate and leant back in his chair, and Mum looked as if she was about to get up, and then he jumped up and started to clear the table without even being asked. He ferried plates and dishes and cutlery to the dishwasher and passed them to Mum for stacking. Mum thanked Gil for every single plate – as if he was handing her ten pound notes, Gil thought. He was impressed at how easy it was. If he worked at it a bit he might be able to get Mum on his side, and then Dad would be out on his own in the cold.

There was just the big meat plate left on the table.

'Let me get that,' said Mum.

'No, it's OK,' said Gil. 'I can do it.'

He carefully lifted the oval plate that was as big as a tray and passed it to Mum. She took it from him, smiling. And immediately – Gil saw at once what was going to happen, but he could not stop it – her fingers buckled and it slid out of her hands.

Gil felt the crash of the heavy plate smashing into the tiled floor like a physical shock, but it was Mum's scream that really scared him. It was a scream like feedback through a microphone. It hurt his eyes and the inside of his skull as well as his ears. And it didn't stop. Dad sprang up from the table and looked at the smashed plate, the meat splattered on the tiles. Then he looked at Gil.

Gil shook his head. 'I didn't . . .' he started to say, but he couldn't make himself heard above Mum. She was screaming, screaming, screaming, her hands hanging at her sides, tears pouring down her face. Dad stepped over the mess of meat and crockery and put his arms around her. She didn't move. She went on screaming.

'Shhh, shhh,' whispered Dad. 'It's all right, it's all right, it's all right.'

Mum's scream gradually turned to sobbing. She howled into Dad's chest. *Please, make her stop*, begged Gil inside his head. It was horrible to watch, like one of those news reports with women wailing because their whole village has been wiped out by some catastrophe. He wanted to run away but he was pinned to the spot.

'It's all right,' Dad said, over and over again. 'It's all right.'

'I – I dropped – dropped it,' she sobbed at last. 'I dropped it, Matt. Oh God, I'm so scared. I'm getting so clumsy. And I forget things now – I forget things all the time. Like yesterday, locking myself out. I'm so scared. I don't think I can stand it. What am I going to do?'

'It's just a plate, Rachel,' said Dad. 'Everybody drops things sometimes. It's completely normal.'

'It was my mum's plate.' Mum started to cry again.

'Look, perhaps it wasn't you. Gil passed you the plate, didn't he? Perhaps it was his fault.'

Dad turned his head towards Gil, and at once Gil opened his mouth to deny everything. But then he read Dad's face properly and stopped, bewildered. Dad wasn't accusing him of anything. He was pleading with Gil to take the blame away from Mum.

'Yeah, I wasn't very careful, Mum,' Gil said at last. 'I'm sorry.'

He felt sick, as if he'd been blindfolded and spun round in a room he didn't know. It was impossible to tell what was going on. Half an hour ago Dad had been stalking him like a lion looking for a chance to pounce on its prey. Now he seemed to be begging Gil to join in with some kind of weird game to make Mum feel better. And there was Mum, crying like a baby in Dad's arms, when at lunchtime she'd stood up to Dad and told him to leave Gil alone.

What the hell were they doing to him?

Dad took Mum out of the kitchen. Gil listened to her

sobs growing fainter as she went up the stairs. He knelt on the floor and began to pick up chunks of broken plate and put them in a carrier bag one by one. After a while Dad came back and tapped him on the shoulder.

'Leave it, Gil,' he said. 'I'll do it later.'

Gil watched him go to the little medicine cupboard high up on the kitchen wall and take out a packet of tablets.

'What's wrong with Mum?' Gil said.

'She's just upset, that's all.'

'Dad, it was a plate. She screamed like someone was trying to kill her.'

Dad fiddled with the tablets and didn't reply.

'Is she ill?' asked Gil.

Nothing.

'Dad, please tell me. I can handle it.'

'No, I think she's all right,' said Dad at last. 'Honestly, Gil, it's nothing you need to worry about.'

'So what are those tablets for?'

'It's just something to calm her down a bit.' Dad slipped the little box into his pocket and turned away, but Gil had already seen the label.

'It's Valium, isn't it?' Gil said. 'I know about Valium. We did it at school, in drug education.'

Dad didn't look round. 'Yes, it's Valium. But Mum's not taking it because she's ill. She's just got herself into a bit of a state and she needs a sedative. I'll be down in a while.'

Valium. People who were mentally ill took Valium. If you took it for more than a few weeks you could become addicted to it.

72

So was Mum having a breakdown? Was she going mad? Why was Dad trying to pretend she was fine when it was obvious she wasn't?

Gil stared at the dishwasher. He could start the wash cycle, that might cheer Mum up.

Was any of this *his* fault? he wondered.

Why did they never tell him anything?

CHAPTER 9

Gil lay on his bed for a long time, twisting Jude's booklet in his fingers. There was a picture of the sad ginger-brown monkey on the booklet's cover, and Gil could hardly bear to look at it.

His head was filled with a mess that was like the smashed plate and meat and gravy that had covered the kitchen floor. Suddenly he was terrified that Mum was ill. It had been coming for a while – little hints here and there that she wasn't quite the person she had been before, the way she hung about the house and seemed to rely on Dad so much – things that irritated Gil more than anything. But now she had fallen apart so badly that he couldn't ignore it any longer. There was something really wrong with Mum. If he did anything to upset her it might make her worse.

And of course that was the perfect way for Dad to keep him in line. *Don't argue, Gil, it'll upset your mother. For your mother's sake, please try to sort yourself out. Blah blah blah blah blah.* It's Dad's fault, thought Gil furiously. It's all Dad's fault. But his anger fizzled out as quickly as it had started. There was too much to be scared about, all the things that Gil was now certain Dad didn't tell the truth about, the things that he and Mum deliberately kept hidden from him. Without warning, Gil found himself staring right at the terrible thing he'd discovered the previous day.

Dad experimented on animals.

Dad experimented on animals, and *he had never told Gil.*

The shock of it made the inside of Gil's head clang like a gigantic bell.

After a while Gil sat up and smoothed out Jude's booklet. He had to read it. He needed to know exactly what Jude was accusing Dad of. But the booklet was so hard to get through that he nearly gave up.

It told Gil about people who squirted toilet cleaner in rabbits' eyes to see if it made them go blind. People who shaved the fur off guinea pigs and then dripped bleach on their skin to see how badly it burnt them. Researchers who fed monkeys cocaine and cannabis to make them into drug addicts, who infected monkeys with AIDS and then tried to find ways to cure them. People who made dogs eat lipstick to see if they got cancer. Scientists who fiddled with the genes in embryos and made mice with two heads, or with half their head missing altogether, or with no legs, or with too many legs. People who grew eyes on creatures where eyes were never meant to grow. Scientists who put electrodes deep into chimpanzees' brains and then ran electricity through them to see how the chimps twitched.

People like Dad.

Some of these procedures, the booklet said, were now banned. Animal rights movements had fought long and hard to achieve this. As a result, no UK experiments were permitted on chimpanzees or gorillas any more. The use of animals in the testing of cosmetics and household chemicals had been reduced.

But it had not stopped. Millions of animal experiments were carried out every year in Britain alone, and millions more in the rest of Europe and in the USA. Millions of animals that could not speak for themselves, that needed people to stand up and speak out for them.

The pictures were awful. When Gil closed the booklet he felt sick and upset. He didn't want to feel like this, he thought angrily. He wanted to be able to make *Dad* feel sick and upset, while he stayed in control just like Jude had.

Jude was right. It was torture. Dad took part in the torture of animals.

The thought was too big to fit inside his head properly. The rollercoaster feeling swept over him again and for a while the ground and the sky switched places. Gil lay back on the bed with his eyes closed, trying to picture Jude the way he had looked on the television news. He very badly wanted to see Jude again. He needed Jude to appear out of nowhere to rescue him, crashing through the ceiling on a rope dangled out of a helicopter.

There was a knock on the door and Dad came in before Gil could say anything.

'I'm making tea,' he said. 'What would you like?'

'Uh – maybe just a cheese sandwich.'

'You had that for lunch,' said Dad.

Gil looked up at Dad as he stood in the doorway, with the W-shaped crease between his eyebrows, and black hair flopping over his face. He looked so ordinary, and he was talking about ordinary things. Could the people who did the things in Jude's booklet really seem so normal? It was hard to make sense of it. The idea came into Gil's head that Dad might be like one of those *Doctor Who* monsters that look exactly the same as human beings, until the moment when their skin splits open and the alien inside bursts out and starts to devour people.

'OK then, pasta,' Gil said.

'Are you OK?' said Dad.

'Yeah,' said Gil. 'Fine.'

Dad nodded, and then he frowned. He'd seen the booklet.

'Have you read this?' he said, picking it up and leafing through it quickly.

'Mmmm.'

Dad hesitated. 'It's not . . .' he started. 'It's not the way they make it sound, Gil. This is deliberately written to shock people. It's propaganda. There is another side to it, you know.'

'Oh,' Gil said. 'Really.'

'For one thing, they've lumped everything in together. I can see that at once. They don't make any distinction at all between different kinds of animal testing.'

Was there a difference? Gil didn't see how.

'Maybe we can talk about it sometime,' said Dad, after a short silence.

No, you mean *Maybe I'll give you a lecture on why you should see things exactly the way I do,* Gil thought, but instead he said, 'Why did you never tell me you did experiments on animals?'

'Well . . .'

Dad looked at the floor and didn't answer for a while. He flicked a corner of Jude's booklet.

'Safety, partly. Some of my colleagues have had their property attacked. Car tyres let down, brakes damaged, fireworks through the letterbox, even occasional death threats. When you're in that situation, the fewer people who know what you do the better. And it's a difficult subject, I acknowledge that. I was going to tell you when I thought you were old enough to cope with it.'

'And when would that have been, exactly?'

'Gil, I didn't want you to be upset or frightened.'

'It's pretty frightening to suddenly find out that my dad's a . . .'

'A what?'

Torturer. Gil opened his mouth but he couldn't say it. Dad looked serious and a bit impatient, the way he always looked during this kind of discussion. But behind him Gil could see the shadow of another Dad, a man in a white coat with a knife in his hand, grinning like a madman.

'Gil, listen. I am a respected scientist who makes tiny genetic changes in mice in order to try and bring about massive improvements in the health of thousands of people. I do not hurt animals for fun. I don't believe in fox hunting. I don't approve of factory farming. I don't support the use of animals in testing cosmetics and chemicals. I certainly don't agree with using animals to test weapons of any sort. But what we're doing in our labs – it's different, Gil. It's critically important research.'

'Oh,' said Gil. 'Right.' *Argue back, you moron,* he told himself, but Dad was off again before he could put a sentence together.

'And even if I didn't disagree so profoundly with their views,' Dad went on, waving Jude's booklet, 'I really wouldn't want you getting mixed up in this animal rights stuff. It's too confrontational. Believe me, I've seen enough demonstrations outside my building in the last few years to know how violent and nasty it gets. It's not something that a boy of your age should be involved in.'

'Dad, you haven't got a clue. Like sitting in your office and watching demonstrations through the window makes you an expert, does it?'

Dad looked at Gil with a strange expression on his face, as if he was listening to music from very far away.

'I know a lot more than you think,' he said. 'From experience as well as observation.'

'Yeah, sure.'

'In fact, I met your mother on a demonstration. We were both members of the Campaign for Nuclear Disarmament, and we took part in a mass attempt to break into a military base where nuclear weapons were held. It got pretty unpleasant. We were arrested for criminal damage and trespass and ended up sharing the back of a police van.'

Gil stared at Dad. He didn't look as if he was joking.

'I don't believe you,' Gil said.

'We had to go to court for it. We both got fined – well, so did a lot of people. Then some of them, including your mother, refused to pay the fine and went to prison.'

'Prison? Mum?'

That was even harder to imagine than the idea of Dad on a demo. Mum, who drifted about the house and screamed with terror when she broke a plate – how could she ever have been tough enough to survive prison?

'For about a fortnight, yes.'

'And what about you?' said Gil.

'I paid the fine at the last minute,' said Dad. 'I had an interview for a very important research post. If I'd gone to prison I might have missed my chance altogether.'

'So you let Mum go on her own?'

'Gil, we hardly knew each other then. Anyway, we wouldn't have been together. There are separate prisons for men and women. I did visit her, though.'

Dad gazed through the bedroom window and Gil saw the faraway look come over his face again.

'If you've been arrested yourself,' Gil said, 'how come you gave me such a hard time when I came home in a police car?'

Dad immediately snapped back into the room. 'That was completely different,' he said sharply. 'I was arrested for something I believed in passionately. We were trying to prevent crimes against humanity. You were picked up by the police for littering in a public park.'

Gil bit the tip of his tongue so hard that it hurt. 'Why aren't you still out there, then, demonstrating, or breaking into nuclear bases, or whatever it was you did, if you thought it was so important?'

'Things changed,' said Dad. 'I grew up. I discovered that not everything is as straightforward as it seems when you're young. You will too, some day.'

He walked out of the room, still holding Jude's booklet.

So this was what growing up was about, was it? thought Gil fiercely. You started out with principles. You had things you really believed in, things you would fight for and shout about. And then, slowly, they started to fade. They shrivelled up and became unimportant. And eventually you turned into people like your parents – people who couldn't be bothered to stand up for anything any more, people who had terrible secrets that they hid from you for years, people who told you to do one thing and then did the opposite themselves.

At that instant, Gil decided it was never going to happen to him. He was going to join Jude and stand shoulder to shoulder with him until they achieved something huge. It was a waste of time waiting for the world to change. Gil would change the world with his own hands.

CHAPTER 10

But just finding Jude, Gil knew, might be a task in itself. When Gil had met him he'd been living in a tree, and now even the tree didn't exist any more. How did you track down someone like that?

After tea, Dad went up to see Mum again. Gil didn't feel like asking if he could come too. Instead he sat in the front room looking at the silent television set and wandered around in his thoughts.

He had no phone number for Jude, no idea where he lived or worked, not even a surname. Maybe, though, there would be a contact number for the local animal rights group on the back of Jude's booklet. That would be something. Gil jumped up, and then flopped down again. It was pointless looking in his bedroom. Dad had walked off with the booklet. He could have put it anywhere. But at least Gil had a bit of time to poke about while Dad was safely shut away upstairs with Mum. He got up again and began quietly to move around the house.

The booklet didn't seem to be in the front room or the kitchen. Gil peered in the bin. Right at the bottom was the carrier bag full of broken plate that Dad had cleared up. Gil lifted it carefully, but there was nothing underneath. So unless Dad had taken the booklet upstairs, it was probably in Dad's study. Gil stopped for a moment. Dad's study was completely off limits. Now that Gil was beginning to get an idea of what Dad did at work, it was obvious why Dad would want to ban him from the study. There was probably all kinds of sensitive stuff in there that he wanted to keep secret.

But it's my house too, Gil thought. It's my life. I've got a right to know. He slipped off his shoes and padded up the hall to the study door. As he stood with his fingers on the handle, listening carefully for any sound from upstairs, he felt his heart thumping uncomfortably. *Don't be stupid,* he told himself. *It's just a room.* But it was a room he knew he shouldn't enter, in the same way that he knew he shouldn't steal things or hit anyone even if they hit him first. It was hard to break a rule that had been in your head for as long as you could remember.

He pushed open the study door. It felt as heavy as a slab of rock.

Most of the house had wooden floors but Dad's study was carpeted, and the small room seemed soft and muffled. One whole wall was lined with bookshelves, and there were several filing cabinets and an armchair, and then Dad's big desk with everything laid out neatly – pens and trays of papers, a holiday photo of the three of them, Dad's laptop and a notebook. Above the desk was a big fossil fish in a glass box. In the middle of the desk was Jude's booklet. Gil pounced on it with relief. Quickly he tore a page out of Dad's notebook and copied the phone number from the back of the booklet. He stuffed the paper in his pocket.

Then Gil stood and listened again. He should leave now, before Dad caught him. But the study was out of sight of the top of the stairs. If he got out as soon as he heard a sound from above he would still be safe.

Without knowing exactly what he was looking for, Gil's hand went to the top drawer of Dad's desk. The drawers were locked, of course, but his hand moved again as if it had a mind of its own. *Look,* his fingers said, *Dad's forgotten to take the key out of the lock.* The key turned smoothly, with a little click. This was probably where Dad had put his Nintendo, Gil thought as the top drawer slid open. Maybe he could remove it without Dad noticing.

He poked through the items in the drawer. It was mostly paper clips and scissors and envelopes and Dad's headed notepaper and cartridges for the printer – but there was also a box with a set of keys and a funny black pendant with a silver button on it.

Right at the back was a rusty badge that said *Scientists against the Bomb,* with a small piece of wire twisted into the safety pin. The middle drawer had piles of printed emails and other papers. Sure enough, his Nintendo and MP3 player sat on top of the pile. Gil hovered over them for a minute and then left them where they were.

But in the bottom drawer Gil found something different. It was a photo album.

For a split second he hesitated. A photo album, in a locked drawer, in a room that he wasn't supposed to be in. All their other photo albums were on a shelf in the front room. There were albums full of holidays, school shows, skating galas, friends – photos that made them all look happy and normal. If this one was locked away then Gil wasn't meant to see it, for sure.

Put it back, right now, said the voice in Gil's head. He stared at the plain black cover of the album. Whatever secrets it held, he had to face up to them sometime. He let the album fall open in his hands.

There was no blood, no dying animals, in fact nothing at all that made much sense to him. He found page after page of photos, all nearly identical, all labelled neatly. Each photo was a smudgy picture of a cluster of blobs, like a spoonful of frogspawn. A few of the pictures were labelled with dates and names. *Thomas. Imogen. Anna. David.* Gil flicked through, mystified. The dates seemed to be from before he was born, and the photos were going brown at the edges.

There was a tiny noise from upstairs. Gil jumped as if a balloon had suddenly popped in his ear. He slid the album back in the bottom drawer, closed it gently, turned the key and slipped out of the study, scudding hurriedly back to the kitchen.

No one came.

Gil took the stairs two at a time and dived into the safety of his bedroom.

He waited. When nothing had happened for another ten minutes, he went downstairs to the front room with the phone number from Jude's booklet.

He knew he had to act quickly, but he was so agitated that he stood and stared at the phone for a stupidly long time while he got up the courage to dial the number. It took him three attempts to get it right because his fingers kept missing the numbers. And then the phone just rang and rang and rang. Gil shut his eyes and listened to the dial tone buzzing in his ear. The strange blobs from the photos floated behind his eyelids, like the after-image you get when you've stared at a bright light for too long. At last there was a little click and a woman's voice said, '*Hi, thanks for calling. There's nobody here right now, so please leave your number and a message after the tone and we'll get back to you.*'

Gil hung up immediately and tried the number again to check he hadn't made a mistake. When he got the same answerphone he bottled out of leaving a message and put the phone down well before the bleep began. He sat and gazed at the dead screen of the television again.

The blobs must be something to do with Dad's research. They were probably photographs of cells, tiny fragments of the animals he experimented on in the labs. What was so important about them to make Dad put them in a special album? Maybe he'd poked about inside them, changing their DNA, trying to create the kind of monsters Jude had accused him of making.

And why did all the blobs have names? Weird names, too. More like names of people than something you would call a mouse or a frog or even a monkey. Surely scientists didn't bother to name all the creatures they experimented on? Gil shivered. It was freaky enough to think of Dad creating a two-headed, four-eyed mouse and calling it 'Imogen'. It was even worse to think he could do that and then come home and pretend to be a normal dad by making cheese on toast.

The phone rang very suddenly and loudly next to his elbow. Gil grabbed it, convinced that Jude must be on the end of the line somehow, even though there was no logical reason why he would be, and sent the phone crashing to the floor.

'Hello?' Gil said, scooping up the phone. 'Are you still there?'

'You nearly blew my bloody ear off,' said a familiar voice. 'What are you trying to do, smash the phone up?'

It was Louis.

'Oh,' Gil said. 'It's you.' He made no effort to hide his disappointment.

'Look, I want to say sorry about last week, that's all.'

Gil couldn't be bothered to think of a reply.

'Gil?'

'Yeah, I'm still here,' Gil said in a bored voice.

'So is that OK, then? Can we just go back to normal?'

Back to normal. Where was 'normal', exactly? Normal was ages ago, before Gil had discovered Dad's horrible secret, before he'd met Jude, before he'd broken Dad's rules and gone into town and nearly got arrested. Normal was before he'd read Jude's booklet, before his head had filled up with pictures of suffering animals, before Mum had screamed so terribly about so little that he knew there must be something seriously wrong. It was like looking through binoculars the wrong way round. Everything normal was very small and far away and Gil knew he couldn't go back there even if he tried.

'OK,' Gil said. 'If you want.' He didn't care much one way or the other. Louis probably only wanted to make up so he could get Gil to help him with maths and science.

'I'll see you tomorrow, then,' said Louis.

Gil put the phone down. He had plans for tomorrow, or at least he wanted to have plans for tomorrow. He sat in the dark in the front room waiting for inspiration. By the time Dad found him sitting there and sent him to bed, Gil knew that he had to do *something* tomorrow, but he still hadn't worked out what the something was.

Before he went to bed, Gil was allowed into Mum and Dad's room to say goodnight to Mum. He almost didn't want to see her in case it really was his fault that she'd got so hysterical at lunchtime and the sight of him set her off again. But she was sitting propped up in bed with a book, and looked up brightly as Gil came in.

'Night night, darling,' she said, as if nothing at all had happened.

'Come on, then,' said Dad, before Gil could decide if he wanted to ask Mum how she was. 'Bed.'

When Dad had gone, Gil packed his school bag as if he

was preparing for an expedition. He spent twenty minutes digging about in drawers and cupboards, looking for things that might be useful, but since he wasn't sure what he was preparing for it was difficult to decide exactly what he needed. A torch? A penknife? String? A compass? A city street map? In the end Gil threw everything into his bag, together with the animal rights office phone number and his wallet. He could only hope that on Monday he would wake up with a clear idea of what he was supposed to do.

CHAPTER 11

When Monday morning arrived it was so grey and foggy that Gil couldn't even see the apple tree from his bedroom window, though it was only a few metres away. Mum didn't appear at breakfast, and it felt wrong. Dad moved silently and efficiently round the kitchen making porridge and toast and coffee, hardly speaking, and Gil tried to attract as little attention as possible, like a mouse hiding from the hawk circling above him.

'How's Mum?' Gil asked as they left the house.

'Still asleep,' Dad said. That was it.

The car crawled to school through the thick fog. Gil watched the fog lights of oncoming cars as they appeared in pairs and disappeared again in the gloom. Dad dropped him at the school gates and was gone again at once. The distance from the gates to the school building seemed to have doubled, and shapes loomed up in unfamiliar places. Gil didn't like it much. But at least it meant Louis didn't manage to find him until they'd both got into the classroom.

Louis was chattering excitedly before he was even close enough for Gil to hear him properly.

'Man, that was weird,' he said. 'I waited for you at the gate but I couldn't see a thing. Then I got completely lost coming across the playground and ended up in the sixth-form block. Do you reckon this is what it's like to be almost blind?'

Gil shrugged.

'God, I'd hate to be blind,' Louis rattled on. 'That fog is so bright it hurts your eyes. It's given me a headache already. Hey, do you think there's such a thing as fog blindness? You can get snow-blind, can't you? I remember, you told me about it, when we used to play that brilliant game you came up with, about being Arctic explorers, and we hid in the freezer, and —'

'Yeah,' Gil said. 'I remember.'

'That was cool.'

'No it wasn't. It was a stupid kids' game.'

'I thought you wanted to be an explorer.'

'Well I don't, OK?'

'Why not?'

'Because it's boring, like everything else.'

'Oh. Well, anyway, do you think they'd let me off PE if I said I was suffering from fog blindness?'

It was a whole week since Gil had spoken to Louis, and Louis was already driving him crazy. It had taken less than five minutes.

'Louis, you're talking crap,' Gil said.

'Oh.' Louis stopped, but only for a second. 'So, are you still grounded? You weren't at ice-skating again.'

'Yeah . . .'

'So you can't come over to my house, then?'

'No.'

'What's the problem?' Louis was looking at Gil with a frown.

'Nothing.'

'You look . . .' Louis shook his head. 'You just look like you're not really *here*.'

'Oh, for God's sake,' groaned Gil. 'Give me a break.' But there was a little pinging noise in his head that told him Louis was right. He felt as though he was hundreds of miles away, marooned on a floating island in the middle of a vast sea, waiting for something to break the surface.

'Did your dad say —' began Louis, but broke off as Mr Montague sprang into the room.

By the time Mr Montague had got halfway through the register, an idea had arrived in Gil's head out of nowhere. He waited until his name was called, right at the end.

'Gil Walker?'

'Here, sir. Um – excuse me, sir . . .'

'Yes?'

'I've got to go to the dentist this morning. I've got a note somewhere from my dad.'

Gil pretended to look in his school bag while he waited for Mr Montague to become restless, which as usual took all of five seconds.

'OK, Gil, just take your note down to the school office,'

said Mr Montague briskly. 'They'll let you go.'

'What a pain,' said Louis, tracking Gil out of the classroom. 'I'd rather do PE than go to the dentist. Is your dad picking you up? Are you missing the whole of maths? God, if you're not back for science I'm in trouble. How long are you going to be?'

Gil managed to shake Louis off on the way to maths and locked himself in a toilet cubicle to forge a note from Dad. He wasted several sheets of paper trying out different styles of handwriting before deciding it would be safer just to print the letter as neatly as possible, but when he got to *Yours sincerely* he stopped. He couldn't for the life of him remember what Dad's signature looked like. In the end, he did a big swirling tornado of scribble and wrote *Dr Matthew Walker* in brackets underneath it.

At the office the secretary fiddled with her glasses as she studied the note.

'Your appointment's at ten,' she read, not looking at Gil. 'That's over an hour away.'

'Yes,' Gil said. 'I know.' Idiot, he thought. Why hadn't he put nine-thirty?

She slid the glasses to the end of her nose and peered at Gil through the security window.

'Where's your dentist?' she demanded.

'Brogan's Hill.'

'And how are you getting there?'

'Um – walking.'

'Even at snail's pace that'll only take you twenty minutes,' she said, disapprovingly.

'But it's foggy. I'm worried about getting lost. And . . . and . . . I really *hate* the dentist. If I don't go now I'll bottle out completely. And my dad will be furious. Please.'

Gil could hear real desperation creeping into his voice. If he couldn't blag his way out of the school building he couldn't put the next part of the plan into action, and now the plan was filling his head he badly wanted to get on with it.

'All right,' said the secretary, relenting.

The door clicked open and Gil was out into the safety of the fog.

He was so grateful for the fog. It was like a huge invisibility cloak. It meant he didn't have to look behind him all the time for fear that someone would read his mind and drag him back to school, and it made the fog inside his head feel less oppressive. It was only after walking for ten minutes that he realised the next part of the plan required a phone, and he didn't have the faintest idea where to find a phone box. He couldn't see more than a few metres in any direction. Slowly the fog wrapped itself tighter around him, making it hard to breathe. *Ha ha*, the fog whispered. *Gotcha.*

Suddenly a colourful shop front appeared, and Gil pushed the door open. A bell tinkled, and a man turned from behind a counter.

'We not open,' he said. 'Later. Twelve noon. Sorry.'

It was a Chinese takeaway.

'It's OK, I don't want to buy anything,' Gil said. 'I just need a phone. Do you know if there's a phone box anywhere round here?'

'We have payphone,' said the man. He pointed to the end of the counter. 'You need make call?'

'Oh. Yes. Thanks.'

Gil had to tip most of the contents of his bag out on the floor before he found the animal rights number. The man watched him all the time.

'You OK?' he said at last. 'Why you not in school?'

'I've got an appointment,' Gil said. 'I just need to phone someone. I'm not sure where I'm going.'

The man half-nodded, but didn't move.

'Dial first,' he said. 'Wait for answer. Then put money.'

The phone rang and rang and rang, just as it had the night before. Gil stood with the receiver pressed too tightly to his ear, clutching a fifty pence piece, ready to drop it into the slot. Then with a little click the answerphone message cut in again. The payphone began to bleep frantically. Crap, thought Gil. There's still no one there. Now what do I do?

'Hello?' said a woman's voice suddenly.

Gil pushed in the fifty pence piece just in time.

'Hello?' said the voice again.

'Hi,' Gil said. 'I'm sorry to bother you, but I need to speak to – to . . .' He swallowed, trying to make his tongue feel less like a potato in his mouth.

'Who?'

'Jude. A guy called Jude.'

'Jude? Are you sure? I don't think I know anyone . . .' The woman's voice trailed away into silence. The payphone started to bleep again and Gil shoved in a pound coin.

'You must know Jude,' Gil said. 'He gave me a booklet

with this number on it. He does the animal rights stall in town. Have you got a phone number for him?'

'Who *are* you?' The woman sounded suspicious.

'I'm a – a friend of Jude's. I met him last week. Please, I really need to talk to him.'

'I don't give out people's personal phone numbers,' the woman said sharply. 'You could be anybody.'

'I'm not anybody, though.' Gil cast around in a panic for something he could say to stop the woman putting the phone down on him. 'Can you – would it be all right if you called Jude and asked him to call me back? It's really important.'

'Just a minute.' The woman was sounding very irritated now. Her voice was muffled for a while, as if she had her hand over the mouthpiece. Then without warning she snapped, 'Name?'

'Sorry?' said Gil.

'Name. Your name.'

'Oh, sorry. Gil Walker.'

'Number?'

'Um – just a sec,' Gil said, searching every available surface of the phone. He couldn't see a number written anywhere. When he picked up the phone to look underneath it, the takeaway man silently pointed to a piece of paper sellotaped to the counter. Gil read out the number and the woman hung up immediately.

'They're phoning me back,' Gil said to the takeaway man, more confidently than he felt. The man moved up the counter to stack menus, but he still looked suspicious, as if he expected

Gil to pull a knife on him and raid the till. What's the problem? thought Gil grumpily. I'm in school uniform, for God's sake. It's not like I'm even wearing a hoodie.

The wait seemed endless. Maybe Jude was asleep. His phone might be off. Or he might be busy doing something heroic and impressive. Or maybe Jude wouldn't remember anything about him. *Gil?* he might say. *I don't think I know anyone called Gil. Must be a hoax.*

No, of course Jude would remember him. It was only two days since he'd had the showdown with Dad in town. But what if Jude didn't want to see him? And what if the woman that Gil had just spoken to didn't even bother to pass on the message?

Gil felt dizzy. He shut his eyes and immediately a parade of wounded animals appeared in his head, marching slowly and painfully. Dad was behind them, forcing them to go faster, and scattering little white blobs on either side of him as if he was sowing seeds. 'Live,' he said as he flung a handful of blobs to the right of him. 'Die,' he said as he threw blobs to his left.

The phone rang and Gil snatched at it, praying it wasn't an early customer for the takeaway.

'Hi,' he gulped. 'It's Gil. Is that . . .?'

'Gil! It's good to hear from you!' Jude's voice was cheerful and comforting. A great flood of relief washed over Gil. 'Are you at home?'

'No, I'm not. I need to come and see you. Now, if possible.'

'Oh. Is this about what happened on Saturday?'

'Yes.'

'Oh, God, I upset you, didn't I?' Jude sounded concerned. 'I'm sorry, I should have kept my bloody mouth shut. I'm really sorry.'

'*You* haven't upset me,' Gil said. 'Jude, can I just come and talk to you? I need to sort a few things out. In my head, I mean.'

'All right. Come to my place. Where are you now? Somewhere near your school?'

'Yes.'

'OK, I'm on the other side of town. It's a bit of a trek – you need to get yourself on a number fifteen bus, and get off just past Tesco on the Chesapeake Road. Do you want me to meet you?'

'I've got a street map,' Gil said. 'If you just give me the address.'

Jude dictated his address slowly, then his mobile number.

'If you can't find me,' he said, 'give me another call.'

'I haven't got a phone,' said Gil.

'There's a call box in Tesco. Give me a call from there. See you in a bit.'

'Thanks,' Gil said.

The man from the Chinese takeaway watched him all the way back out into the fog.

CHAPTER 12

As the bus bumped across town the fog started to clear. The sky became whiter and whiter until it was too bright to look at, and then the sun appeared like a ghost, even paler than the sky. By the time Gil reached Tesco on the Chesapeake Road there was enough sunlight to cast faint shadows.

Gil had never been here before. There was no reason to come to this part of town. He didn't know anyone who lived here, and if he and Mum went to Tesco it was always the giant superstore at the retail park. This Tesco was smaller and scruffier, wedged between little shops with goods that spilled out on to the pavement – greengrocers selling vegetables he couldn't identify, and discount stores with piles of plastic boxes and cheap toys.

Gil pulled out his city map again to make sure he knew where he was going. Albert Street, second on the left. He walked past a pub with hundreds of cigarette ends trodden into the pavement outside, past a mobile phone repair shop as small as a telephone box, then a kebab shop, and a place that looked like a jeweller's with a sign in the window that said, *Cheques cashed. Offers made on all jewellery.*

Albert Street was a short road of houses with a big brick church built right across the bottom of the street. A couple of the small front gardens were piled full of old sofas and mattresses. Rubbish trickled out of people's gates. There was no one around, but the street made Gil nervous. It was a dead end, and Jude lived all the way down at number thirty.

He counted houses to calm himself down. Sixteen. Eighteen. Twenty. Twenty-two. Nearly there now. Look, there was Jude's house, behind a low wall. The curtains were still closed in the downstairs window, and the gate swung open into the street.

Gil was on the path that led up to the front door before he properly noticed the body lying in the garden.

She was face down, with her legs across the path. She didn't move. The front door was open, but Gil would have to step over her to get to it. Oh God, was she dead? What was he supposed to do? There was a groan from somewhere underneath the body, and one of the arms jerked a bit. It was too much for Gil. He raced back to the main road and dived into the safety of Tesco. It was a few minutes before he could get it together enough to phone Jude.

'Jude here.'

'Jude, it's – it's me. Gil.'

'Hey, Gil! Where have you got to?'

'I found your house,' Gil said, 'but – but —' He had to swallow hard after every word, as if they were marbles in the back of his throat. 'There's – someone – lying – on your – path. A wo–woman. I – can't – get to the – door.'

'Oh, it's Sally again, is it? Don't worry, I'll sort her out. You're in Tesco, are you?'

'Yeah.'

'Come back, and I'll meet you outside.'

When Gil got there, Jude was kneeling on the path. The woman had her head in his lap. She was sobbing in a way that reminded Gil of Mum the day before, when she'd broken the plate in the kitchen. It sounded as if she would never be able to stop. Jude reached across and took a can out of her hand, and then tipped the contents away at the side of the path. A small river of golden liquid ran down towards Gil's feet.

'She'll be all right in a minute,' Jude said, looking up at Gil. 'Can you get up, Sally?' he said to the woman.

She got herself to her knees and then Jude held her arm while she struggled to her feet. She stood, leaning on him, swaying a bit. Her hair was stuck to her wet face.

'It's in my head,' she whispered. 'They've put something in my head. Something – I don't know what it is. It's growing in there. It's telling me what to do. It hurts.' She started to cry again.

'Sally, there's nothing in your head,' said Jude. 'I promise you. They don't do that to human beings. Only to animals.'

Sally suddenly turned to gaze at Gil with eyes that stared too widely, and he wanted to run away.

'You're a nice boy,' she said wonderingly. 'What are you doing here?'

'He's my friend,' said Jude. 'He's come to see me.'

'Don't let them put anything in your head,' said Sally. 'They did experiments on me. They're trying to turn me into a dog without my permission.' Without any warning at all she barked at Gil, so loudly and fiercely that he began to back away out of the gate, and then she started to laugh.

'Stop it,' said Jude firmly. 'You're scaring him. Have you taken your tablets?'

'I don't know,' said Sally. 'I'm sorry. Sorry,' she said again to Gil.

'Come on,' said Jude. He ushered Sally through the front door. Gil hung back in the gateway, wondering whether it was safe to follow.

'Come on,' said Jude again. 'You're not going to get eaten. Sally's a vegetarian dog, you know,' and he and Sally both laughed much more than Gil thought there was any need for, but he followed them into the darkness of the house.

'Just go in my room,' said Jude, pushing open a door. 'I'll be back in a minute.' He began to help Sally up the stairs.

It was dark in Jude's room too, but there was a narrow slice of daylight falling through the back window. The room was shabby but extremely tidy. In a funny way Gil felt it looked like a faded version of Dad's study – the desk, the bookshelves, the filing cabinets, the single armchair – but it was a room that Jude obviously lived in, because there was also a bed and a wardrobe.

Above the desk, in the same place that Dad had his fossil

fish, there was a framed photo of someone holding a beagle puppy. Gil went closer to look at it. The dog was cute and cuddly, but the photo wasn't, because the person in the picture was wearing a black balaclava and Gil couldn't see anything of their face except two shadows where the eyes must be, and a hole for the mouth. He – or she – was dressed like a terrorist, but they were carrying a puppy instead of a gun. It looked completely wrong.

Several minutes went by, and Jude didn't come back.

There was a smell of stale cigarette smoke and damp. Gil sat on the edge of Jude's neat bed and began to wish he'd never come. If only he hadn't been able to come up with a plan. If only he were like Louis, too thick to have ideas of his own, the sort of person who always said, *Wow! I wish I'd thought of that!* He ought to run back to school while he had the chance, Gil decided, standing up quickly. Louis would just be coming out of maths and making his way to the science block. Double science – it suddenly seemed the most wonderful thing in the world, as appealing as a big roast dinner with all the trimmings. *Which I'm not going to eat any more*, Gil reminded himself. *You stupid, stupid, stupid . . .*

But before he could escape Jude came through the door, carrying two more cans which he dumped on a table.

'Poor old Sally,' he said. 'I'm sorry I took so long. She couldn't find her tablets. I suppose I shouldn't encourage her to take them, really, seeing as they've all been tested on animals. She freaked you out, didn't she?'

'Um – yeah, a bit,' Gil said.

'She wouldn't hurt you. She's more likely to hurt herself,'

said Jude. 'She's got schizophrenia and she drinks as well. It's not a good combination. There're things going on inside her head that you wouldn't wish on your worst enemy.'

Gil thought of Mum again. If Mum was going mad, would she end up like Sally, lying face down in the front garden with a can of lager? Was there any way he could stop it?

'Sit here,' said Jude, patting the armchair.

Gil sat down carefully, feeling the springs creak. The chair was covered in green velvet, but there were bald patches and cigarette burns on the arms. Jude plonked himself on the old office chair at his desk and sat twizzling from side to side. He pulled the tobacco out of his pocket and started to roll a cigarette. Gil watched him for a minute and suddenly felt better. Why had he wanted to run away? Jude was safe. There was nothing to worry about. He allowed himself to relax into the chair.

'That stuff Sally was talking about – the experiments,' Gil said. 'That isn't really happening to her, is it?'

'Not in quite the way she imagines,' said Jude. 'But yeah, it's happening all right. Sally's convinced someone's been fiddling with her DNA, trying to turn her into an animal. But it's not so far from the truth. You know about genetic modification, I guess?'

'Not a lot,' said Gil.

Jude looked down at the flimsy cigarette paper in his fingers. His voice was clear and soothing. 'It's a massive issue. All kinds of plants and animals that we use for food have had their genes altered without us knowing, and nobody really knows what impact it's going to have. Strawberries, for example – well, they've created a strawberry that's got a gene from an Arctic flounder spliced into it to make it more resistant to frost. Half-fruit, half-fish. Creepy, eh? But if you ate it you'd never know. They've probably got them on the shelves over at Tesco. So Sally's not quite as crazy as she sounds. It's the science that's mad. And the scientists, who think they've got a licence to do whatever they want in the pursuit of knowledge and money.'

'Like my dad, you mean,' Gil said.

'Yes,' said Jude seriously. 'Like your dad.'

'I know it sounds stupid,' Gil said, 'but I never knew . . . I never knew . . .'

Gil's throat closed up and to his complete horror he realised he was going to cry. His stomach rose, squeezing the space inside his lungs and demanding that he took a breath. But he didn't dare breathe. If he breathed he would sob like a baby. He couldn't let Jude see him cry. Instead he shut his eyes and heard Jude say in the darkness, 'You never knew what your dad did, huh?'

Gil shook his head.

'He never told you he worked in the labs,' said Jude. 'Doing all that stuff to animals.'

'No,' Gil managed to say.

'And I was the one who dumped it on you without warning, wasn't I?'

Gil opened his eyes. Jude was fiddling with his cigarette. He looked unhappy.

'I should have considered your feelings before I laid into

him,' he said. 'I'm really sorry. It's a shock for you, isn't it?'

'It would have been a shock however I found out,' Gil said. 'It's not your fault.' He found he could breathe again, as long as he did it carefully. He watched Jude put the cigarette between his lips and light it, then inhale deeply and blow the smoke out into the room, just the way he had when Gil had first seen him in the tree.

'The problem is . . .' Gil went on, and then stopped, distracted. Jude had whipped the cigarette out of his mouth and was stubbing it out furiously on a corner of the desk. 'You don't have to do that,' said Gil. 'I really don't mind if you smoke.'

'Nah,' said Jude. 'I shouldn't inflict it on you. I can wait. Go on.'

'It's just – I don't know what to do now. Now I know about all the stuff in that booklet you gave me, I want to *do* something. I want to tell Dad he's wrong, for a start. But talking to him is . . .' Gil shook his head. 'It's impossible. He's always got an answer. I mean, yesterday I decided I'd become a vegetarian, and he even had an answer for that.'

'What did he say?' asked Jude.

'He said it was pointless being a vegetarian because things like milk and butter all lead back to meat in the end. So the only logical thing was to become a vegan and give up animal products altogether.'

'He's right, actually,' said Jude. 'Clever git.'

'So are *you* a vegan?'

'Yep.'

Gil didn't know what to say. He'd been a vegetarian for

less than twenty-four hours and already it felt difficult. How did anyone have the willpower to be a vegan? What on earth did you eat if you weren't allowed cheese or butter or eggs?

'Giving up meat is a fantastic start,' said Jude, gently. 'Meat production is almost as sickening as the stuff your dad's involved in. Don't give yourself too hard a time if you can't do everything at once.'

'So what else can I do?'

'Well, don't argue with your dad, for one thing. It's a waste of time and it'll wear you down. You'll never convince him. It's like trying to convince a dog not to eat its own sick – it'll just keep going back to it once your back is turned. Your dad's whole reputation is built on animal experiments. He won't give it up just like that. But you can talk to other people – your friends at school, people on the streets – tell them about the reality of animal experiments. People don't know half of what's going on, and they need to know. I can give you leaflets to hand out if you like. You can boycott products that are tested on animals. You can write to shops and manufacturers and tell them you'll stop buying their goods unless they change their policy on animal testing.'

'Is that what you do?'

'Amongst other things, yes.'

Gil saw Jude glance up at the photo above his desk, and then immediately look away as if he'd been caught spying.

'That's you, isn't it?' Gil said.

'Yeah,' said Jude.

'What were you doing, in that picture?'

'Liberating a dog that was used in experiments.'

'Where from?'

'Can't tell you. Sorry,' said Jude.

'If I wanted to do that too, would you let me help you?'

Jude shook his head. 'It's too dangerous, Gil. If I got caught I'd go to prison. I can't drag you into that.'

'So are you planning to shut down the labs where my dad works?' asked Gil.

Jude nodded.

'How?'

'I can't tell you that either.'

'But you're really going to do it?'

'If we can work out a strategy,' said Jude quietly. 'It's a tough one. The place is probably as well-defended as Buckingham Palace, for one thing.' He grinned suddenly. 'I reckon you've got a bit of a revolutionary streak, haven't you? Just like your namesake.'

'Who's my namesake?' Gil didn't have a clue what Jude was talking about.

'Gil Scott-Heron. When you first told me you were called Gil I thought you might be named after him.'

'Who is he?'

'*The revolution will not be televised*,' said Jude, in a really bad American accent. He leapt up, pulled a CD off the bookshelf, and slid it into a tiny music system. 'Listen.'

Gil listened. It was like a rap poem, but it was full of names he didn't recognise and he only understood bits of it. He looked at the face on the CD cover, a black man with big afro hair and a beard, bellowing into a microphone. You could see the veins in his head and neck standing out with the effort.

'*You will not be able to stay home, brother.*
You will not be able to plug in, turn on and cop out . . .
Because the revolution will not be televised.
The revolution will not make you look five pounds thinner,
Because the revolution will not be televised, brother . . .
There will be no highlights on the eleven o'clock news . . .'

Jude bounced around in his office chair in time to the beat, and then joined in with the words.

'*The revolution will not be televised, will not be televised,*
will not be televised, will not be televised.
The revolution will be no re-run, brothers.
The revolution will be LIVE.'

Gil tried to imagine Dad at the desk in his study, chanting along to Gil Scott-Heron. It wasn't easy, even when he remembered what Dad had told him about being arrested and nearly sent to prison.

'I don't think I was named after him,' Gil said, as Jude flicked a switch on the music system.

'Jude?' Sally was calling from outside the door. 'I'm hungry.'

'Oh, I forgot,' said Jude. 'I promised her breakfast in exchange for the cans.'

'I'd better go anyway,' said Gil. 'I need to get back to school. They think I'm at the dentist.'

'Will you be OK?'

From the way Jude looked at him Gil knew he meant more than, 'Will you be OK getting back to school?' It was eleven o'clock in the morning and already Gil was worn out. Jude's room was safe, but it could only be a temporary hiding place. Gil knew that he had to venture back out into the world again, and that later he would have to face Dad and decide what part he was going to act.

'I think I'm OK, yes.'

'Take some leaflets.' Jude took a big stack out of a box under his desk. 'Phone me any time, if you need to. And do what you can, Gil. Just do what you can.'

CHAPTER 13

Gil dawdled as much as he dared on the way back to school but still got there too early, more than half an hour before the end of morning lessons. Even after he'd spent five minutes explaining to the secretary on the front desk exactly why his visit to the dentist had taken so long, he still couldn't avoid joining the tail end of the science lesson.

He sneaked quietly into a room full of chatter, with everyone clustered in small groups around microscopes. Gil reckoned he had a good chance of blending in without being noticed, until he saw Louis look up from the other side of the room and beckon him over enthusiastically.

Crap, thought Gil. Why did Louis always notice him? Did he beam out some kind of radio signal that went straight to Louis' brain? And Ben was with him again. Reluctantly Gil began to make his way across the room.

'You've got to help us,' said Louis loudly. 'We can't do this stupid thing. Look.'

Louis pushed Ben away from the microscope. Ben shoved him back, hard, and the microscope wobbled.

'Ask Mr Montague,' said Gil. 'I haven't been here, have I? I don't have a clue what you're trying to do.'

'We're supposed to be drawing a cell, dummy,' said Ben. 'But we can't even *see* it.'

'So?' Gil shrugged. 'Not my problem, guys.'

'Oh, stuff this,' said Ben, pushing the microscope away roughly. 'You're no help, are you, Jillian?'

'What did you say?' said Gil, faking a smile.

'I said, *Jillian*, that you're no bloody help. Have you got a problem with that?'

Gil stared at Ben's face. Maybe he should just punch Ben hard, right between his stupid piggy eyes. Or kick him right between his stupid fat legs. But it would get him a week of detentions at least. It probably wasn't worth it. As Gil stood considering, he became aware of Louis leaning closer to him.

'Where have you been?' said Louis suspiciously.

'At the dentist,' said Gil. 'Where do you think?'

Louis sniffed. 'You smell of cigarettes. And you've been gone ages.'

'Yeah, well, it took ages.'

'So why do you smell of cigarettes? Dentists don't smoke. Not at work, anyway. Did you sneak out of school to smoke or something?'

'Jillian wouldn't try a cigarette,' sneered Ben. 'Might get into trouble with Daddy.'

Gil turned away so he couldn't see Ben's face.

'I probably stood next to someone smoking at the bus stop, that's all,' Gil said.

'What, you went on the bus?' Louis frowned.

'Yes. So what?'

'I thought you were supposed to be grounded. If your dad won't even let you come to school by yourself, how come he let you go to the dentist by yourself?'

'So you don't believe me?'

'Not really,' said Louis.

'That's your problem, then, isn't it?'

'If you've been to the dentist, what did you have done?'

'A filling,' said Gil. 'A big one.'

'Show me.'

'Oh, yeah!' said Ben enthusiastically. 'Let's see! Did it make you cry, Jillian?'

Gil walked away, right over to Mr Montague's desk, and as soon as the bell rang he headed straight for the door. Louis managed to catch him up in the corridor on the way to the canteen.

'Are you hacked off with me or something?' he puffed.

'Yeah,' said Gil. 'For hanging out with Ben again.'

'I wasn't hanging out with him. You weren't there, remember? Mr Montague put me with him. I didn't have much choice. God, I hate science.'

'So do I,' said Gil. He thought of Jude's booklet, and the pile of leaflets in his bag. 'The whole thing's sick.'

'But you're *good* at it,' said Louis, looking puzzled.

'That doesn't mean I like it, does it?'

They had reached the canteen. Hardly anybody else was there yet, and Gil headed straight for the usual counter. So it would be sausages, chips and beans again. Gil picked up a sausage with a pair of tongs and then remembered with a jolt that he wasn't supposed to be eating meat any more. What was he meant to have for lunch at school if he didn't eat meat?

Louis watched in astonishment as Gil held the sausage above his plate for several seconds.

'What are you *doing*?' he said.

'Thinking,' Gil said sharply.

After all, he thought, gazing hungrily at the sausage, Dad couldn't control everything he did at school. He could be vegetarian at home and carnivorous here and Dad wouldn't know any different. Unless someone told him. Like Louis, the blabbermouth. But then Jude was a vegan, and that was really something to look up to. Gil had told Jude he was a vegetarian now, and if he wanted Jude to take him seriously he ought to stick to his promise. In any case, who knew what suffering the pig had been put through before it was turned into school dinners?

Gil dropped the sausage on to Louis' plate and moved on.

'You're weird,' said Louis as they slid into the plastic canteen seats. 'Why have you only got chips and beans?'

'I'm a vegetarian,' said Gil.

'Since when?'

'Since yesterday.'

'Don't you like meat any more?' Louis speared a sausage

with a fork and waggled it under Gil's nose. 'Look – meat! Lovely meat!'

'That's not the point,' said Gil. 'I just think it's wrong to kill animals for food.'

'Why?'

'Because it is, you loser.'

Gil never bothered coming up with proper answers for Louis. Louis wasn't Dad. He never really argued. He agreed with pretty much anything anyone told him.

'I don't think I could give up meat,' said Louis thoughtfully through a mouthful of sausage. He watched Gil eating chips for a while and then said suddenly, 'You can chew all right, then? With your massive filling.'

'What?' It took Gil a moment to remember his imaginary dentist's appointment. 'Oh, yeah. It's fine.' He patted his cheek.

'Wow! That's great!' said Louis, his voice full of fake relief.

Gil waited until they were in the playground after lunch before he showed Louis the leaflets Jude had given him. He had a pretty good idea of how Louis would react, and he wasn't disappointed.

'Oh my God, Gil!' Louis howled. 'What are you trying to do, make me throw up?'

There was a picture of another monkey on the leaflet, but this one looked as if the top of its skull had been sliced right off. A drop of blood oozed down its forehead.

'This is one of the reasons I'm a vegetarian,' said Gil.

'It's gross,' said Louis, studying the photo with a frown. 'Is it real?'

'Why wouldn't it be?'

'Oh, I don't know. Sometimes they make these things up to shock you, don't they? Or they make it look worse than it is, anyway. Hey, I read about this horrible thing they do with monkeys! I can't remember where now. It's some place where they like to eat monkey's brains, but they like them really fresh. So they get a monkey, and they saw the top of its head off, so you can see the brains – just like the one in this picture – and then they give you a spoon. Like you were going to eat a boiled egg. And the monkey's still *alive*. How gross is that?'

'You just made that up.'

'No, I didn't. It's true.'

'Look, forget about all that rubbish,' said Gil. 'This monkey is from a lab where they do animal experiments. Don't you think *that's* horrible?'

'What sort of experiments?' Louis looked interested. 'Why do you think they've taken the top of its skull off?'

'Just to torture it, probably.'

'There must be a reason. They wouldn't do it for nothing. I wonder what they were trying to find out?'

'It doesn't matter, does it? The monkey's in pain. It's horrendous.'

'How do you know it's in pain?'

'Oh, for God's sake, Louis! How would you feel if you had the top of your bloody head cut off and someone was poking about in your brains?'

'That depends what bit of the brain they were poking about in,' said Louis seriously. 'I saw a programme about it.

You can stimulate loads of different bits of the brain, even really deep inside it. But it only hurts if you stimulate the pain centres. The rest of it doesn't hurt at all.'

'You mean you don't *care* that animals get randomly chopped up like this?'

Louis wiggled his head. 'I don't know, really. I mean, what if you find out something important – you know, something that's going to cure AIDS or cancer or whatever, and save millions of lives? I think it's kind of fifty-fifty for and against. It's complicated, isn't it?'

'No. It's not complicated at all. It's incredibly simple. Animal experiments should be banned.'

Gil waited for Louis to give in and agree, but he didn't say anything.

'So are you going to help me hand out these leaflets or what?' Gil said after a while.

'What are you on about?'

'I've got a whole stack of leaflets.' Gil thrust a hand into his bag and pulled some out. 'I'm going to give one to every single person in this school.'

'Where did you get these from?' asked Louis. 'Is this what you were up to this morning?'

'Oh, yeah,' Gil said, sarcastically. 'There was a big pile of them at the dentist, so I just helped myself.' He offered a handful of leaflets to Louis but Louis didn't take them.

'I don't know about handing them out,' said Louis. 'I'm sure we're not supposed to do stuff like that. We'll get into trouble, won't we?'

'Oh, come on, Louis. It's not a big deal. The most we'll

get is a detention. You don't really care about that, do you?'

'I don't want to get a detention for handing out stupid leaflets.'

'So you're not going to help me.'

'No.'

'Look, just do it.'

'Make me,' said Louis, folding his arms.

'What the hell is wrong with you today?'

'Oh, it's me that's the problem, is it?' said Louis crossly. 'As usual.'

Gil gave up, and walked across to the other side of the playground to hand out the leaflets by himself.

It didn't take long to get rid of them. Some of the girls took one look and ran away, but others gathered into groups and stood around shrieking about the 'poor little monkey'. The boys made less fuss, but Gil thought they seemed much too entertained by the leaflet, calling their mates over to look at the monkey as if it wasn't a real creature at all but just a bit of CGI from the latest computer game. Why didn't it bother them the way it bothered him? Gil sighed, and then saw Ben coming towards him with a leaflet.

'Now this,' said Ben, waving the leaflet, 'this is *cool*. It's really sick.' He laughed loudly and went to slap Gil's hand, but Gil avoided him. 'Nice one, Jillian.'

Most people glanced at the leaflet and dropped it where they stood. By the end of lunchtime the playground was carpeted with paper. Hundreds of pairs of monkey eyes stared up into the sky.

Gil looked at the playground and a feeling of gloom

settled over him. What would Jude say? It hadn't been a great success. As he turned to go inside he saw that Mr Montague was waiting at the door. He was holding one of the leaflets.

'Just come with me for a minute, Gil,' he said, opening the door of an empty classroom. He sat on the edge of a desk, and waved Gil towards a chair.

'Now, Gil,' he said, tapping the leaflet with the back of his fingers. 'I admire your commitment, and I'm sure this is an issue you feel strongly about. But you know, don't you, that it's against school rules to hand out this kind of literature on school premises. It's not political, exactly, but even so we can't allow it. Some of these animal rights groups are pretty extreme, and it would make things difficult for the school if we were seen to be encouraging young people to join them. Do you understand that?'

He said it kindly, with no hint of a threat that Gil could hear.

'Yes, sir,' Gil said.

'Do your parents know about your interest in this?'

'Um – kind of.'

'Your father's a genetic scientist at the university, isn't he?'

'Uh – I think so, yes.'

'You're an intelligent young man, Gil. You don't plan to follow in his footsteps, then?'

Gil thought that he would rather shovel crap for the rest of his life than have anything to do with what Dad did for a living, but of course you didn't say that sort of thing to a teacher.

'I don't know, sir,' he said.

'And is everything else OK? There's nothing you want to talk to me about?'

Gil looked down. Mr Montague's eyes were searching his face, and it made him intensely uncomfortable. He really didn't want to be having this conversation. It was way too personal.

'I'm fine,' he said, looking at the floor. He waited until Mr Montague started to speak again.

'Well,' he said at last. 'I don't think there's any need for me to take further action. Just – well, be careful, Gil. Be careful about what you get mixed up in. And I really don't want to see any more of these leaflets. I'd like you to clear the playground before you go up to registration, please.'

Gil saved as many leaflets as he could, but most of them were ruined – ripped in half or screwed up, or trodden on repeatedly.

It was harder than Gil had expected, changing people's minds. How many thousands of leaflets would he have to give out to make just one person think again? Even Louis didn't want to listen, and he was supposed to be Gil's friend. The rest of them were a bunch of brainwashed, mindless sheep.

'You got into trouble, didn't you?' whispered Louis, as Gil slipped late into registration.

Gil didn't answer. He knew Louis would only say, *I told you so*.

CHAPTER 14

'I could really do without this,' muttered Dad. He wriggled his shoulders irritably and Gil shut one eye so he didn't have to see him. It was after school on Monday, and they were stuck at some roadworks. Ahead, a small machine crawled noisily over the surface of the road, chewing up the tarmac and spitting it out into the back of a truck. This is going to take for ever, Gil thought, and he slid down as low in the seat as he could to try and make himself invisible.

It didn't work.

'Sit up properly,' said Dad. The words whined in Gil's ears like mosquitoes.

'What for?'

'Just sit up. You look like a slob.'

'I'm bored. I want to be at home.'

'And I'd rather be at work. This is the last thing I want to be doing.'

'So let me out. I can walk from here.'

'No. That privilege will be returned to you next week, if you're lucky.'

'I suppose you're desperate to get back to work to murder a few more animals, aren't you, Dad?'

'Don't be so utterly childish,' said Dad coldly.

Gil tried to remember Jude's advice. *Don't argue with your dad. It's a waste of time.* But it was so hard to keep his mouth shut. The air inside the car was thick and hot and Gil could feel his brain squeezed and pummelled like pizza dough every time Dad spoke. He buzzed the window all the way down to give himself the illusion of escaping. Cold air streamed in, together with the juddering noise of the road resurfacer and the stink of car exhaust and burnt tarmac.

'Stop it,' said Dad. 'Shut the window.'

'I'm hot.'

Dad pressed the button at his side that controlled the passenger window, and the window slid upwards. Gil jammed a finger on his button and the window stopped again. Then he faked a yawn, and tipped his head sideways to rest on the edge of the half-open window. It really wasn't very comfortable but Gil had already decided he didn't care. He could sense Dad's eyes boring into the side of his head.

I dare you, he thought. *I dare you to close the window now and trap my head in it.*

The car crept towards the roadworks. Dad didn't say another word, but the tension twanged like a guitar string.

They arrived home late, and Mum was waiting at the entrance to the driveway looking anxious.

122

'Everything all right?' she said as Gil stepped out of the car.

'Splendid,' said Dad, sounding totally over-the-top. 'Roadworks. Couldn't be better. I'll see you about seven, OK?'

He drove off.

'How was school, darling?' said Mum. She put a hand on Gil's shoulder. Then she frowned. 'You smell of smoke,' she said. 'Gil, please tell me you haven't been smoking.'

'I have not been smoking, Mum,' said Gil, glad to be able to stare her in the face and tell the absolute truth. 'Smoking is stupid.'

Mum looked pleased. 'Let me make you something to eat.'

Gil followed Mum into the house and through to the kitchen. As she got things out of the fridge he had a feeling that she was building herself up to say something. He wondered what it was. He thought about all the things he'd done that day that Mum would be horrified about and he hoped he wouldn't have to lie too much if she asked questions. Lying was tricky. It was so easy to forget what you'd said, and if he told Mum one thing and Dad another there would soon be a showdown.

'Gil,' Mum said at last, 'I want to apologise for yesterday. You know, when I . . . when I dropped the plate.' She was buttering a piece of bread with great concentration. It seemed to be taking her longer than usual.

'Oh,' Gil said. 'That.'

'Dad was quite cross with me. He said I'd frightened you.'

'Um – a bit. I thought you were ill.'

Mum looked at Gil with a big deliberate smile. 'I'm not ill, as far as I know. I just worry too much, that's all. I got myself into a terrible state about nothing, Dad said. I'm sorry. He's quite right, it wasn't fair on you. You mustn't feel any of it was your fault.'

Gil wanted to believe her, but he wasn't sure he did. Mum's smile looked too artificial. Maybe she was lying to protect him, it was hard to tell. Gil studied the conversation like a chess board, trying to decide how to move.

'I don't understand why you were so upset about breaking a plate,' he said finally. 'Is it because it belonged to Granny?'

'Well, partly, yes.'

'Are you worried about Granny?'

'Not worried, exactly. Sad, I suppose.'

Gil took another step into the unknown. 'What's wrong with her, Mum? You never talk about it.'

Mum was silent.

'Why don't you want me to visit her?'

'It would upset you,' said Mum, looking away. 'And it would be pointless. I don't think she'd know who you were.'

'That's because you never let me see her.'

Mum shook her head. 'No, it's not that,' she said quietly. 'Sometimes she doesn't even seem to know who I am, any more.'

'So why do you visit?'

'Because she's my mother. She brought me up. She loved me. She still loves me, I think, or she would if . . .'

'If she knew who you were.'

'Yes.'

'Has she got Alzheimer's?'

'No,' said Mum. 'It's not Alzheimer's.'

Gil heard an edge in her voice that warned him to stop. He knew he'd gone far enough down this road for one day. There was no point pushing Mum to the limit. He looked for a way to change the subject completely.

'Mum, why did you and Dad call me Gil?' he asked.

'Oh,' said Mum, brightening up at once. 'Well, you were named after Gilbert White. He's one of Dad's heroes.'

'Who's Gilbert White?'

'He was a vicar in the 1700s who studied nature in his spare time. He wrote a book called *The Natural History of Selborne*. It's a classic. He was one of the first real biologists.'

Oh, great, thought Gil. Typical. He should have guessed he'd be named after a dullsville English vicar instead of a revolutionary black American.

'And then of course *Gilbert* means *bright promise*,' said Mum, smiling, shiny-eyed. 'You were our bright promise. You still are, you know.'

Gil cringed at the comment and took a large bite of sandwich to avoid having to reply. As he munched, he watched Mum tidy up a kitchen that already gleamed like a catalogue photo. He wondered if she had any idea at all what Dad did at work. Then he wondered whether to try and talk to her about it. He was still trying to find a way to start the discussion when Mum launched into something else that was clearly on her mind.

'There's another thing, Gil,' she said. 'I know this is

difficult for you, but I'd really like you to stop fighting so badly with Dad.'

'So you think it's my fault we argue all the time.'

'No, I wasn't saying that. I know he needles you sometimes. But if you could try not to get so angry about little things, like not having a phone . . .'

'That's not a little thing to me.'

'Just try, Gil, please. It would help so much.'

'He drives me crazy,' Gil muttered.

'You'd had another row in the car today, hadn't you? I could tell. Honestly, it seems to be getting worse and worse.'

'Tell him to get off my back, then,' Gil said. 'He listens to you. He never listens to me.'

'Yes, he does. That's not true.'

'What about yesterday, then, when he had a go at me for deciding to be a vegetarian? He clearly thought it was a crap idea.'

'He thought you were doing it to annoy him,' said Mum.

'Is that what *you* think?'

'Of course not. It was a bit sudden, but I really respect your decision. I think it's important to have principles.'

Gil suddenly saw his chance, and jumped in with both feet before he could have second thoughts.

'Well, what about other principles, then? What about animal rights, for example?'

'Oh, God.' Mum groaned. 'Please, please don't get into that one with Dad.'

'Mum, do you *know* what Dad does at work?'

'Yes, of course,' said Mum.

'So why didn't you tell me?' Gil demanded.

'Well, Dad thought it was. . . I just didn't . . .' Mum trailed off, looking uncomfortable.

'And you think it's OK? All that horrible stuff with animals?'

'It's not horrible,' said Mum, with sudden energy. 'Gil, your dad is a good man. A really good man. He showed me the booklet you got from that stall in town. He told me what happened with that protester who got you into trouble with the police. It upset Dad dreadfully to be accused of torture when he's working so hard to do things that benefit people. Animal rights is an emotive issue, I know, but you do have to try and see it from Dad's point of view as well.'

No, I really don't, Gil wanted to say. But he kept the thought to himself.

And a couple of days later at teatime, as Gil tried to work up some enthusiasm for eating the beanburgers that Mum had made specially, Mum quietly dropped a stunner of an idea into the silence.

'I've been thinking, Matt,' she said. 'Why don't you take Gil to work with you one day?'

It took a moment for the idea to detonate. Then the shockwaves hit Gil, and Dad erupted. '*What?* Rachel, what are you talking about?'

'Well, Gil's read a few things about animal experiments and it's bothering him. You know what the reality is. You know you've got nothing to hide. So why not take him to the labs, and put his mind at rest?'

Take him to the labs. The labs that Jude had said were as

hard to get into as Buckingham Palace. Gil almost stopped breathing. He was going to be given a free entry ticket to the labs. If he could just keep himself under control long enough not to mess it up.

'You've got to be joking,' said Dad. 'I'd never get security clearance.'

Gil forced another chunk of beanburger into his mouth and mashed it to a gritty paste between his teeth. He clutched his knife and fork tightly to stop his hands from trembling.

'He's a boy, Matt,' said Mum. 'He's your son. He's read one booklet about animal rights, that's all. He's hardly a dangerous undercover agent, is he?'

Dad looked at Gil for a long time, thoughtfully. Gil gazed back, as wide-eyed and innocent as he could manage, but it felt as if Dad had a hand inside his skull, rummaging through his thoughts. Any minute now he would seize on a memory of Gil's forbidden meeting with Jude on Monday. *Don't find it,* Gil pleaded silently.

He didn't find it.

'What do you think, Gil?' Dad said.

'Do you think I'd be allowed?' said Gil.

'It's not usual to allow visitors, for obvious reasons. But I think I could probably persuade the powers that be to let you in.'

Gil could see the wheels turning in Dad's mind, the logic kicking in – yes, of course, show Gil the labs, that'll sort everything out, he'll see how reasonable it all is, he can't possibly argue about anything then.

Mum was nodding, smiling, pleased with her peace-making efforts.

'It would be interesting to see what you do, Dad,' said Gil. 'Honestly.' It was easy to sound genuine because he meant it, though perhaps not in quite the way Dad had in mind.

'Oh, Gil, you always used to be so keen on science,' said Mum. 'All those trips to see the dinosaurs. This could be a new start for you.'

'All right,' said Dad. 'Maybe it's not such a crazy idea. I'll see what I can do. We could go on Saturday, perhaps.'

Gil excused himself from the table as soon as he'd swallowed the last bit of beanburger on the grounds that he had a pile of homework to do. He went up to his room, shut the door and lay face down on the bed. It felt as if someone had punched a hole right through the middle of his ribcage and replaced it with a skin stretched as tight as a drum. He could feel the vibration of every emotion in his body, but still it was hard to tell if he was scared or excited. Perhaps he was both. What would Jude say if he told him he was going into the labs? What would he ask Gil to do?

This is my big chance, Gil told himself. It was a chance to do something a bit more dramatic than handing out stupid leaflets. But what was he supposed to do? Plant a bomb? It wasn't exactly going to help if he blew up a building full of animals that were already suffering. What then? What would Jude do?

Gil lay with his face pressed into the pillow until his hair was damp with sweat. He had to let Jude know somehow. He was *desperate* to let him know, to hear Jude's confident voice. *OK, Gil, this is the plan. Here's what we're going to do . . .*

At last Gil rolled off the bed and slowly made his way back downstairs. In the doorway to the front room he paused. Mum was there, curled up on the sofa reading. There was no way he could sneak in and use the phone to call Jude.

'How's the homework?' Mum asked, looking up. 'You look a bit flushed. Are you feeling OK?'

'Yeah, I'm fine.'

Gil went on standing in the doorway, and after a minute Mum closed the book and put it down next to her.

'What is it, then?' she said.

'I need to use the phone.'

'Of course. Go ahead.' She didn't move.

Gil hesitated. 'It's kind of private, Mum.'

Mum looked puzzled, and then a look of understanding spread across her face.

'You mean – a girl?'

Gil nearly laughed out loud. He couldn't have come up with a better lie if he'd tried all evening. He was aware of a stupid grin spreading across his hot face. It was perfect. It would tell Mum everything she thought she needed to know.

'Well, if you want to be private,' she said, jumping up, 'you can borrow my mobile and go and hide yourself away somewhere if you like. Just this once.'

Gil took Mum's mobile and ran out of the back of the house, ducking under the apple tree and into the shed at the bottom of the garden. The shed smelt of winter, even though the flowerbeds outside were splashed yellow with daffodils. He unfolded a creaky garden chair and sat down to phone Jude, shuddering with more than just the cold.

As he waited for Jude to answer he noticed something in a corner of the shed – the old cage where once upon a time he had kept a series of pet mice. He hadn't thought about them in ages. The last two, Turbo and Minky, had died months ago, and he'd buried them under the apple tree. Now he wondered where Dad had got them from in the first place. Dad experimented on mice, didn't he? Had his pet mice come from the labs?

'Jude here,' said the voice. He always sounded the same, thought Gil – decisive, alert, ready for anything.

'Hi, it's me. Gil.'

'Hi, Gil! How's it going? Do you need more leaflets already?'

'No, I – I've got something I need to tell you.'

'What's that, then?'

'I think my dad's going to take me into work. To the labs. It was Mum's idea but he's really gone for it. I think he might take me on Saturday.'

Far away, so far away he could have been speaking from the moon, Gil heard Jude swear softly under his breath, and then there was silence. In his mind Gil could see him clearly, twirling on his office chair in front of the picture of himself with the liberated beagle.

'Jude, say something,' Gil said at last. 'I'm on my mum's phone. I can't be too long.'

'Bloody hell, Gil, I don't know what to say. Are you

serious? You can't be serious, surely. Would your dad really do that?'

'I don't know,' said Gil. 'I think so. I mean – he doesn't know I saw you on Monday. He doesn't know I'm phoning you now. Mum thinks I'm phoning a girl. They don't know anything. So if you can tell me what to do, if I get into the labs . . .'

'Oh my God . . .' There was a long hissing sigh, like a dragon breathing in its sleep. 'Gil, I can't tell you what to do. I can't. You're only a kid. It's not right.'

'I am not —' Gil had to stop for a moment. 'I am not a *kid*. Jude, I really want to do this. You told me it was impossible to get inside the labs, but I've actually got a chance to get in there and do something. Maybe it's the only chance. So are you seriously saying I can't do it because I'm just a *kid*?'

Jude was quiet, and when he spoke again his voice had the crisp, clean bite that Gil wanted so much to hear.

'OK, Gil, you're on. Let's go for it. Here's the plan.'

Listening to Jude's plan was like watching a magician do a clever card trick. It unfolded so quickly and easily that Gil knew he must have done this kind of thing hundreds of times before.

'You'll be a mole,' said Jude at the end, and laughed.

'What do you mean, a mole?'

'You know, a double agent. Everybody thinks they're on one side, but secretly they're working for the enemy, too. That's what moles do – they dig hidden tunnels into places they're not supposed to go. And then they pop their heads up and make a real mess.' He laughed again. 'So, I'll see you tomorrow morning?'

'Yes, OK. If I can get out of school again.'

'We need to crack on with this,' said Jude. 'Don't want to miss our golden opportunity, do we?'

Gil sat in the shed for at least five minutes after the call had ended, checking the call register obsessively to make absolutely sure he'd deleted Jude's number and that no trace of it remained on Mum's mobile.

He didn't sleep much that night. He lay in the dark with his eyes open, running over every detail of Jude's plan, and trying to visualise the building Dad worked in, although he had never seen it. It would have high blank concrete walls, Gil reckoned, and heavy doors, like prison doors, and bars on the windows, if there were any windows at all. He imagined the rows and rows of tiny metal cages where Dad's victims sat injured and terrified, waiting for death.

Gil's entire body buzzed and hummed with anticipation. He was determined to make Jude proud of him. He was going to be a hero.

CHAPTER 15

'Last couple of days, then,' said Dad as they drove to school on Thursday morning.

'Huh?' said Gil.

'I mean we're coming to the end of your period of sanctions. I don't think I'll need to take you to school next week. You've done pretty well, on the whole. Your mother and I are proud of you.'

'Oh.'

He was going to have to be extra-careful. If he got caught today it would wreck everything. He'd have to slip out of school in a way that drew as little attention as possible. And today there was no fog. It was brilliantly sunny, the first real taste of spring.

'So, are you still interested in coming to see the labs?' said Dad, glancing sideways.

'Uh – yeah.' Gil tried not to sound too excited in case

it raised Dad's suspicions.

'You don't sound terribly enthusiastic. Are you sure?'

'Dad, of course I'm sure. It'll be a real experience.' Gil remembered what Mum had said. 'It'll be good for me, to try and see things from your point of view.'

He saw Dad's eyes widen in surprise and pleasure, and knew he'd pressed exactly the right button.

'Ah,' Dad said, nodding his head very slightly, just like Mr Montague did when someone gave the answer he wanted to hear.

As Gil got out of the car near the school gates he saw the crowds of people surging down the hill towards school, and decided at once that it would be much easier to disappear before school started than to try and escape later. As soon as Dad had driven off he began to battle his way uphill through the streams of kids, away from school. But suddenly there was Louis, bowling happily down towards him, and there was no time to dive out of the way.

'Hi, Gil! Where are you going?'

'Just – coming to meet you, actually.' Oh crap, thought Gil. Why hadn't he got some excuse ready? Any old lame thing would have done for Louis.

'Oh, great! Have you been here long? I've been rushing the whole way, thinking I was going to be late, but I'm not, am I? God, it's really warm, isn't it? Too warm for this time of year, my mum says. Oh, hang on a minute, I've got to get this sweatshirt off before I melt . . .'

Louis chattered on, the usual waterfall of nonsense gushing out of his mouth. Gil followed him reluctantly back down the hill, knowing that if he tried to disappear now Louis would stick to him like chewing gum. He'd ask a load of questions about where Gil was going and what he was up to and then go all suspicious and silent again.

It would have to be lunchtime, then, thought Gil.

The morning crept along much too slowly. By the time Gil came out of the last lesson with Louis he had almost lost his nerve. It was a stupid idea anyway, he told himself. It would never work. But he made himself say to Louis, 'I'm going out to get lunch.'

'We're not allowed off site at lunchtime,' said Louis immediately, just as Gil had expected.

'So? Who's going to notice? Oh, unless you grass me up, of course.'

'Oh.' Louis looked hurt. 'I wouldn't do that.'

'You'd better not.'

'Why do you need to go out, anyway?'

'I'm sick of chips and beans. The canteen's vegetarian food is rubbish. I want to get a takeaway.'

'Oh.' Louis looked envious. 'Could you get me one?'

'No. If you're too much of a wuss to come with me you can just eat the canteen crap.' Gil held his breath and hoped Louis wouldn't find it in himself to be brave. Louis gazed at him plaintively and said nothing.

'See you later, then,' Gil said, and walked away to the school gates without him.

The bus ride to Jude's house was much quicker than Gil expected. The fog three days ago had made it seem like a journey halfway across the world, full of mysterious twists and turns and sudden stops. In sunlight it didn't feel that far. Gil hadn't bothered to bring the map this time. He knew what Albert Street looked like and just how far down Jude's house was. He was even prepared to find Sally sprawled across the path again. But the little garden was empty and quiet, and the front door was shut.

The doorbell rang somewhere deep inside the house. Gil stood on the broken tiles of the path in a bubble of warm sunshine and waited. Jude was a while coming to the door, but then he whisked Gil inside quickly without a word as if he feared someone was snooping on him. After the spring sun the house was as chilly and dark as a cave.

'I thought you might have changed your mind,' Jude said quietly, when his door was safely shut. 'I thought you'd be here earlier.'

'I didn't want anyone to suspect anything, so I had to wait till lunchtime.'

'Oh. Right.'

'I've only got about twenty minutes.'

Jude stood with his heels just off the ground, like an animal getting ready to run. He looked tense and serious, quite unlike the relaxed figure Gil had seen hanging out in a tree two weeks ago. Gil began to feel nervous, and he wondered what there was to be nervous about. After all, he wasn't going to do anything really dangerous, was he? No break-ins, no weapons, no bombs, no direct confrontation. Just a bit of spying, that's all.

'You do know what you're letting yourself in for, don't you?' said Jude.

'Um – I think so.'

'You're almost certainly going to be breaking the law. I don't know what the rules are for kids – sorry, I mean people of your age – but if I did this I could end up in prison.'

'But you've done it yourself, haven't you? And it wasn't a problem then. You didn't get found out.'

'No, but I'm just concerned for you,' said Jude. 'All you need is for one tiny thing to go wrong. They might have a body scanner, like the ones they have in airports. They might even frisk you, I don't know.'

'I'm going to do it, OK?' Gil's heart was banging so loudly he wondered if Jude could hear it.

'You don't know how much help this could be to us, if you can carry it off,' said Jude very softly.

'Could you just get on with it,' said Gil, 'before you freak me out completely?'

A hint of a smile crossed Jude's face and was gone again at once. He pulled a small bunch of keys out of the pocket of his jeans and unlocked a drawer in his desk. Then he took out a big metal cash box and unlocked that too. Inside, Gil could see something wrapped in a tea towel. And when Jude unfolded the tea towel, there was a tiny square thing.

'This is the camera,' said Jude. It was so tiny that Gil couldn't believe it would really work.

'It's got a button stuck to it,' Gil said, puzzled.

'Yeah, that's why it's called a buttonhole camera,' said Jude, rolling his eyes ever so slightly. 'The button's clipped to the camera lens, which is just a pinhole. You put the button through your jacket, or whatever, with the camera hidden behind it, and no one suspects a thing.'

'What if I haven't got any clothes with the right sort of buttons?'

'What about that shirt you've got on?'

'This? It's a school shirt.'

'It's perfect.'

'But I never wear this sort of thing at weekends,' said Gil.

'Wear it,' said Jude. He poked about in the cash box and pulled out a small white button, almost identical to the buttons on Gil's shirt. Jude snapped it on to the lens, and then dropped the camera into Gil's hand.

'Slip it inside your shirt,' he said. 'Let's have a look.'

The camera felt cold against Gil's skin as he buttoned the lens cover into his shirt. A thin wire trailed back over his shoulder. Jude took a step away and inspected him carefully.

'You'll need to put something dark underneath to disguise the camera,' he said. 'A T-shirt, maybe. Then you can run the lead down to the recorder in your pocket. It'd be a good idea to tape it in place so it doesn't get tangled or pop out of your collar.'

Jude came closer and touched the button with the tip of his finger, gently pressing the camera against the place where Gil's ribs met, and a sudden weird feeling flooded Gil's head. It was as if everything he had ever felt in his life was squeezed into the tiny space under Jude's fingertip, like the invisible speck that contained all the matter in the universe in the instant before the Big Bang. Time didn't exist. Everything was waiting, and Gil waited too, his mind as light as dust. He felt that Jude's finger might burn a hole into his chest and right out the other side.

Jude stood there, frowning, thinking. His voice, when it came, sounded as loud as thunder. 'The best thing would be to take the real button off altogether, and make a slit in the material. Then you'll be able to button the camera through both layers. It'll be better hidden that way.'

'OK,' Gil said, with some difficulty. Jude was still fingering the button in the centre of his chest.

'And put it a bit higher up, just in case they make you wear a lab coat or something.'

Jude bounded away to his desk so unexpectedly that Gil nearly fell over, as if the fingertip had been the only thing holding him upright.

'See how well this fits in your pocket,' Jude said. The recorder that went with the camera was about the size of a mobile phone. Gil's trouser pocket swallowed it whole. 'Feed the lead down under your shirt and we'll do a dummy run. Remember, the main thing is not to get too close to your subject, otherwise you'll just get a big messy blur.'

Gil tried hard to concentrate while Jude ran through how to operate the controls by touch while the recorder was hidden in his pocket.

'Now film me,' said Jude.

'Is that a good idea? I mean, what if I got caught with a shot of you on the camera?'

'We'll wipe it afterwards, don't worry.'

Gil pressed the record button and tried to angle the camera towards Jude as he leaned back against his desk, grinning.

'Say something, then,' said Gil.

'*The revolution will not be televised,*' said Jude. 'At least I bloody hope it won't.' He cackled loudly.

Gil pressed stop, and Jude played the footage back through the tiny LCD screen on the back of the recorder. Gil was surprised at how good the picture was. He'd managed to cut the top of Jude's head off, but it didn't seem to bother him.

'Whatever you do, don't walk like this trying to point the camera higher,' said Jude, strutting about the room with his chest puffed up. 'You'll be rumbled in no time.'

'You look like a chicken,' Gil said, and Jude immediately began to flap his elbows and make clucking noises, jerking his knees nearly up to his chin as he pranced around. Gil started to laugh and found he couldn't stop. He laughed and laughed, hysterically and stupidly, until his face ached and his stomach hurt. It was horrible, like being drowned in laughter.

Then there was a knock at the door and Jude froze. 'Who is it?' he said casually, as Gil quickly stuffed the video recorder back in his pocket.

'It's me,' said a quavering voice.

Jude opened the door a crack, and Gil could see a little piece of Sally's face.

'I want to come in,' she said firmly.

'Not now, Sally, we're busy. I'll come and see you in a bit.'

'You're laughing at me, aren't you? I could hear you. Why are you laughing at me?' She was beginning to sound upset.

'Of course we weren't laughing at you,' said Jude. 'I was

141

being silly and it made Gil laugh, that's all. You remember Gil. You met him on Monday.'

'Oh, it's that nice boy again,' said Sally, almost managing a smile as she caught sight of Gil through the crack. 'You all right?'

'Yes, I'm fine.'

'I'll come and see you in a minute,' said Jude again. 'We're nearly finished.'

'All right, then.' Sally vanished without a sound.

Gil pulled the recorder out of his pocket and unbuttoned the tiny camera from his shirt.

'Wrap it in this,' said Jude. He handed Gil the tea towel. 'The camera's the bit you need to be careful with. It's really delicate. We don't want you to go through with this and then find the bloody thing didn't work because it was damaged, do we?'

Gil carefully put the wrapped equipment into the bottom of his school bag.

'Now, let's just run through it one more time.' Jude repeated the main points of the plan. The camera battery would last about four hours. Gil's job was to film everything from the moment he got to the labs to the moment he left, because even if it seemed boring to him it would give Jude valuable information about what was going on in there. To be on the safe side, he shouldn't phone Jude again from home, or even from Mum's mobile. And then Gil would bring the camera back first thing on Monday.

'You're a total hero,' said Jude as he showed Gil to the

door. 'There aren't that many people who've got the bottle for this kind of thing. I think you're amazing.'

Hero. Amazing. It was everything Gil had wanted to hear. He stepped out into the sunny street and Jude's words felt warmer than the sun.

On the bus ride back across town, Gil fantasised about what Jude had asked him to do. He was going to make a film that would expose what went on in the dark heart of the animal labs. Perhaps Jude would put the film on a website for the whole world to see. Or perhaps he would turn it into a television programme. It would be just like all those fly-on-the-wall documentaries where dangerous criminals secretly got filmed doing outrageous things. Of course Gil knew he would never be able to put his name to it, but there would be a huge outcry when people saw the terrible things in his film and then they would have to close the labs. Dad would be beside himself, but he would never know that he'd led the enemy into the building himself. He would never know it was Gil who had more or less single-handedly shut down his place of work.

Gil wandered back into the school playground at the tail end of the lunch break, still submerged in his spying adventure, and Louis latched on to him at once.

'Nice lunch?' Louis said, spikily.

'Yeah, not bad.'

'What did you have, then?'

Slowly Gil started to rise out of the deep place that his daydream had taken him to. Lunch? He hadn't even thought about lunch. He was absolutely starving.

'Um – a kebab,' he said. 'Actually it wasn't that nice. I feel a bit crap now.'

'Right. A kebab. Perfect food for a vegetarian.'

'I don't mean a *meat* kebab, you moron.'

'What other kind of kebabs are there?'

'Well, it had – uh – peppers, I think, and some kind of cheese . . .'

'Oh, for God's sake, Gil, just shut up, will you?' Louis interrupted. 'I'm getting sick of this.'

'Sick of what?'

'Sick of you lying to me the whole time. I'm not stupid. I don't know what's going on, but I'm getting to the point where I don't believe anything you say to me any more.'

'I'm not lying!'

'Yeah, sure, Pinocchio. I can see your nose growing from here.'

'God, some bloody friend *you* are,' Gil said. He turned away and tried to step back into his daydream, but Louis wasn't about to stop.

'You want to know what sort of friend I am? I'm your *only* friend. Because nobody else will put up with you, will they? And I can't say I blame them. Half the time you just use me, like when you wanted help handing out those stupid leaflets, and the rest of the time you treat me like a piece of dog poo. I mean, when was the last time we actually *did* anything together?'

'I've been grounded for the last two weeks, remember?'

'And when are you going to be ungrounded?' Louis demanded.

144

'This weekend. Probably.'

'So you'll be coming skating on Saturday, then?'

'Uh – I don't think I can, actually,' said Gil.

'Oh. What a surprise.'

'My dad wants me to go into work with him on Saturday.'

'Liar.'

'It's true!'

'That's the kind of excuse *girls* come up with,' said Louis, spluttering with anger. 'It's like, "Sorry, I can't see you tonight, I'm washing my hair." You're *pathetic*. Why haven't you got the guts to tell me you don't want to go skating any more? At least then I could ask someone else.'

'Fine. Ask someone else. Do you really think I care?'

Gil stared Louis down. Louis' face was so furious it was almost funny. On one of his hands the fingers were twitching as if he might even be thinking of throwing a punch. Just try it, thought Gil. Louis was such a wimp he'd be able to hold him off just by blowing on him.

'God, you're unbelievable,' said Louis finally. 'When it all goes wrong, don't expect me to help you get out of it, that's all.'

'When what goes wrong?'

'Whatever it is you've got sucked into. It's bloody obvious there's something going on. Are you dealing drugs or something?'

'Why, do you want me to get you some?' said Gil. 'What do you want? Weed? Crack, maybe?'

There was a long silence. Gil just waited.

'Oh, forget it,' said Louis. He shrugged and walked quickly away.

Result, thought Gil. Maybe he'd even shaken Louis off for good. He needed Louis less than ever. Jude was his friend now. And Jude thought he was a hero.

CHAPTER 16

'Nearly there,' said Dad. The car purred along the road past the Natural History Museum. 'In fact we could stop here and walk, if it weren't for that little lot.' He nodded his head forwards.

A short way down the road Gil could see a group of people on the pavement. 'Who are they?'

'Animal rights protesters, of course. They've got a more or less permanent presence opposite our building. They're not allowed to demonstrate right outside the entrance any more because there were several scuffles with our staff and the police moved them on. But they didn't go far, as you can see, and there's not much we can do about it. In fact, it's one of the main reasons I drive to work.'

Gil looked up at Dad's building as they drew closer. He had imagined it as a blank prison, but the reality was confusingly different. The walls were made of yellow stone, soft and expensive-looking, and there were two sets of curving steps leading up to a huge smoked glass entrance. It looked more like a hotel.

'What would the protesters do if they saw us walk in there?'

'They'd shout at us, or throw things, perhaps. Eggs and tomatoes are popular missiles. It's more of a nuisance than anything, to be honest, although the shouting can get —'

There was a terrific crack, as if something had suddenly snapped inside the car, and Gil jumped in terror. The seatbelt pulled sharply across his shoulder and he felt the hidden camera dig into his chest.

'Well, well,' said Dad calmly. He didn't either slow down or speed up. 'That was predictable.'

Yellow slime slid down Gil's side of the windscreen. One of the demonstrators had thrown an egg. Gil listened to the shock echoing through his body and was finally forced to admit to himself that he was terrified.

All morning he'd made himself concentrate on the preparations. He'd retrieved the school shirt from the drawer under the bed where he'd stuffed it on Friday so they didn't all end up in the wash. He'd removed the button as Jude suggested and cut a small hole to let the camera lens through. He'd dressed and undressed several times, trying on different T-shirts to see which one hid the wires best, and different trousers to see which ones had the biggest pockets. He'd taped the wires to his skin with thick black carpet tape stolen from the shed. He'd even made an extra hole through the back of the trouser pocket so the lead from the camera was completely invisible. Then he'd posed like a girl in front of the mirror, sticking his chest out to see if there was a bulge that gave the camera away, and patting his body to check that none of the wires sprang out. He'd had his desk wedged against the bedroom door the whole time just in case Mum or Dad tried to come in, though neither of them did.

As he'd followed Dad from the house to the car, Gil had congratulated himself for being so cool, calm and professional. And now suddenly he was rigid with fear. Belly-gripping, heart-hammering fear. What the hell was he doing? How exactly did he think he was going to get away with this?

Dad glanced at Gil. 'That frightened you, didn't it?' he said sympathetically. 'There was a time when it frightened me too, but I'm afraid I'm used to it by now. You can see why I didn't want you getting involved with those people.'

The car turned a corner and drove slowly down a narrow road between high buildings. There was an electronic barrier across the road. Dad slipped a card into a slot, the barrier rose silently, and they crept through into a car park.

'Here we are, then,' said Dad, getting out of the car and stretching.

Gil's hand shook as he opened the car door. Dad seemed so relaxed. It really didn't sound as if he suspected anything, so maybe that meant Gil could pull this off after all. But as Gil followed Dad away from the car he spotted a security guard walking around the edge of the car park with a big Alsatian pulling at the lead, and immediately he felt his stomach gurgling unhappily. Then he realised he still had his hoodie on. Crap. If he pressed the record button now, all he would do was film the inside of his clothes.

'Sorry, Dad,' said Gil. 'I need to take this off. I'm a bit hot.'

'Leave it in the car if you like,' said Dad. He opened the passenger door again, and then began to mop the egg off the windscreen with a tissue.

Gil pulled the hoodie over his head with hands that didn't seem to work properly. When he finally wriggled out of it, he saw Dad looking at him in astonishment.

Oh my God, thought Gil. I've ripped the wires out. He can see the camera. He can see everything. But before the panic had time to take hold of him Dad gave a wide smile.

'Good grief, Gil,' he said. 'You look a bit smart for a Saturday.'

'Oh, well, I thought I'd better make an effort . . .' Gil mumbled. He fiddled with the fake button on his school shirt. He couldn't get rid of the impression that it was buzzing, bleeping, flashing out a message loud and clear. *Hey! I'm fake! I'm a camera lens pretending to be a button! Look at me!* Then he slipped a hand into his pocket and pressed 'record' before he could think any more about what he was doing.

'It's a shame we're not going in at the front,' said Dad. 'It's such an impressive building. But this entrance is much safer, and it means we can avoid some of the more extreme security measures.'

He didn't say what they were. Gil wondered if Jude had

150

been right about the body scanner. It didn't help his nerves much.

The back door was just an ordinary-looking metal door, like the back of a fire exit. It took two keys to unlock it. The door opened outwards, Gil stepped in behind Dad, and the door swung shut again with a clunk.

They were in.

Where were the animals? Gil strained his ears, half-expecting to pick up their cries of distress through the thick walls. But the building was huge. They could be anywhere, even underground.

Dad paused and glanced at the wall beside him. Gil glanced after him, and saw a panel with a keypad and several small lights. Dad checked it briefly, then turned and double-locked the back door behind them.

A little way up the corridor was a door which Dad opened with a third key. Once they'd both gone through he locked it behind him again. There was yet another door beyond that, and here Dad pulled something out of his pocket and hung it round his neck. Gil recognised it as the pendant that he'd found in the drawer in Dad's study. Dad leant forwards and put the silver disc against a pad that was next to the door. The door whirred open automatically.

'You've got a lot of doors,' Gil said.

'We need them,' said Dad. 'To keep out the egg-throwers.'

At the end of the short corridor was a flight of stairs leading upwards. Dad took the steps two at a time, humming under his breath. The stairs went round and round for ages. Gil panted after Dad, worrying again. What if the camera wasn't working, or there was something blocking the lens?

'Haven't you got any lifts in this building?' puffed Gil as he got to the top.

'Good Lord, I never use the lift,' said Dad cheerfully. 'They're terribly bad for you. Using the stairs keeps you fit.'

'Is there a toilet somewhere?'

Dad nodded towards a door, which for once wasn't secured in some way.

Was it likely they'd have CCTV in the toilets?

Gil went into a cubicle and fiddled with his clothes for a while. Then he went out and looked in a mirror. Nothing seemed out of place. He would just have to hope.

Forget the camera, forget the camera, Gil told himself over and over again as he stared in the mirror. *Be natural. Be yourself. Relax.*

Relax-relax-relax-relax-relax, thundered his heart.

As Gil came out of the toilet he found Dad leaning against a wall, still singing softly to himself. He was already sick with anxiety, and this glimpse of Dad unnerved him completely. Here was Dad looking utterly at home, as if home was really a prison and this was the place where he felt set free. *Who are you?* thought Gil. He barely recognised this Dad. He was like someone Gil had met only in passing.

'So first of all I thought I'd show you a bit of the new work I'm doing,' said Dad, setting off down the corridor so fast that Gil had to trot to keep up.

There were two more doors that Dad opened with the

pendant, and then they entered a room that seemed entirely white and silver. It gleamed like the inside of a spaceship. There were no windows, but the lights were white-hot. There was no one else there, and Gil couldn't see any animals either.

'This is where I make mice,' Dad announced.

'You *make* them?' Gil was so surprised he briefly forgot his worries about the camera.

Dad laughed. 'It's not as science fiction as it sounds,' he said. 'We use IVF techniques, that's all. You know about IVF, don't you?'

'Um – you mean making babies artificially in test tubes?'

'Yes, that's right. We harvest eggs from female mice and sperm from male mice, and then we make mice embryos here under the microscope.' He pointed at a big white cabinet with a glass front.

'But Dad, why do you have to *make* mice? Why don't you just let the mice have babies normally?' Gil was aware he was beginning to sound like the voice-over in a nature documentary, but Dad didn't seem to notice.

'Well, we do, usually. But sometimes we want to try something new, and with IVF we can control so many things. We can engineer mice with specific features to help us in our research. Look. I'll show you.'

Dad bounded across the room and slipped on a white doctor's coat that was folded over the back of a chair. Then he washed his hands quickly at a sink in the corner, and pulled a thick pair of gloves out of a drawer. He went to a big silver door that ran from the floor almost up to the ceiling and pressed down a lever-shaped handle. A curl of something that looked like steam sneaked out of the opening and dropped to the floor.

'This is the freezer where we keep eggs, sperm and embryos until we're ready to use them,' said Dad, pulling out a small round dish and shutting the door immediately. 'What we do, inside that cabinet, is to pick up a single egg with a pipette, and inject it with a single sperm using a fine syringe. It's difficult and time-consuming because the eggs and sperm are so tiny – but, if it works, you've got an embryo.'

Dad stood cupping the tiny dish carefully in his clumsy gloves, his hair flopping over his face, his eyes shining as he looked at Gil.

'Gil,' he said, 'have you any idea at all how extraordinary life is? How utterly astonishing it is to see a creature build itself from virtually nothing?'

'I've never really thought about it,' said Gil, trying to keep his voice ordinary. Dad looked as excited as a boy who's found a really spectacular bug in the playground, and it made Gil feel old. He stood watching Dad, filming him, concentrating on keeping still and keeping his distance so that the picture would be as clear and steady as possible.

'When the sperm fuses with the egg you have a single cell. And after a few hours the cell divides. And then those two cells divide again, and again, until you have a tiny ball of eight cells. The embryo's still microscopically small, just a speck. But that ball of cells . . .' Dad stopped for a moment, breathing fast with excitement. 'It contains all the information you need to build a mouse. Can you imagine that? It's like putting eight bricks in a field, and watching them slowly turn themselves into a house . . .'

Dad was fizzing with so much energy that Gil almost thought he could see him glowing. It was just like the day when they'd gone to see the fossilised fish at the museum. Gil tried to remember when he had last felt that excited about anything, but it seemed years ago. Then he noticed that Dad had stopped, waiting for him to say something.

'Wow,' said Gil. Even he could hear that it didn't sound very convincing.

A flash of irritation crossed Dad's face. 'Look, do you want to know what I do or not?' he said. 'It wasn't the easiest thing in the world to set this visit up. The least you can do is show a bit of interest.'

'Sorry, Dad. I *am* interested, really. Just go on.'

Dad looked at Gil, frowning slightly, and Gil put his hands behind his back to stop the urge to fiddle with the fake button on his shirt.

'So what do you think I do this for?' Dad said.

'What do you mean?'

'Why do I go to all this trouble? As you pointed out, it's an awful lot easier to let the mice get on with making their own babies.'

'I don't really know,' said Gil.

'Do you know what *transgenic* means?'

'I don't think so.'

'If a creature is transgenic it means it contains genes from a different kind of organism. So the mice we make here —'

'Oh, OK,' Gil interrupted. 'I've heard about this. I heard they've made a strawberry with a fish gene spliced into it.'

'Yes.' Dad had started to fiddle with the big microscope cabinet, and he didn't sound remotely bothered.

'Isn't that really dangerous?'

'No, of course not. Putting a single fish gene into a strawberry doesn't turn it into a fish. It doesn't even make it *half* fish. Look, think about a toaster and a car. They're both made of largely the same materials, aren't they, although they're entirely different? So if you used part of the car to mend the toaster – a bit of wire, say, or a nut and bolt – it wouldn't turn the toaster into a vehicle, would it? It'd still be a toaster. It's exactly the same with living things. They all have remarkably similar DNA, and much of it is interchangeable.'

'Oh,' Gil said. But in his head he had a picture of a big flabby flatfish-shaped strawberry with slimy eyes, and he couldn't get rid of it. He stood and waited for Dad to finish whatever it was he was doing with the glass cabinet. It took ages, and slowly the fear in his stomach transformed itself into impatience. Here he was, wasting valuable battery time filming Dad doing something completely irrelevant. *For God's sake hurry up*, he said silently.

'Here,' said Dad. 'Look.' He stepped away from the microscope cabinet and waved Gil forwards.

When Gil put his eyes to the microscope he had to blink a bit before he could bring anything into focus. Then he saw it. A clump of little spheres like frogspawn, just like the pictures in Dad's secret photo album. It was impossible to tell how big the spheres were, and for a second Gil had the bizarre feeling that he was gazing through a telescope rather than a microscope, and that the spheres were as big as stars spinning across the galaxy.

'What is this thing?' said Gil.

'It's a mouse embryo. I've introduced a sequence of human DNA that will give this mouse a genetic disease.' The words hummed in Gil's ear. 'The next step is to put the embryo back into a female mouse and let her grow it for me.'

'But you said it's got a disease.'

'Yes.' Dad's voice was calm. 'I guess you don't like the thought of that, do you?'

'What kind of disease?'

'Well, in this case, a peculiarly dreadful genetic condition that gradually destroys the brain.'

'What?' Gil jerked away from the microscope, genuinely revolted. 'That's *horrible*. So you're going to let this mouse grow until its brain just disintegrates? How can you *do* that deliberately to a mouse?'

'It's far more horrible for people than it is for mice, I can tell you that.'

'How do you know?'

'Because the mice we make don't know that they're ill. Mice can't think about themselves in the way that people do. And we don't let them suffer physically. As soon as they become unable to do the basic things that make mice happy, we put them out of their misery. But human beings who have this disease have to live for years with the knowledge that their brain cells are slowly and irreversibly choking to death. Every single day they have to face the fact that they will end up unable to do anything at all for themselves, even think. It takes an unbearably long time. It destroys lives, Gil. It destroys whole families. Because it's a genetic disease, you see, so parents often pass it on to their children.'

Dad was quiet. All his excitement had evaporated. Gil stepped down from the microscope, and Dad bent over it again. He was there for a long time, while Gil hopped impatiently from foot to foot and fretted about the camera battery.

'Sorry,' Dad said at last, straightening up. 'I was miles away. Do you want another look?'

'No, I want to go and see the animals. Especially the ones you've given diseases to.'

'All right.'

Dad scanned Gil's face for a while. His eyes were serious. 'Think about it,' he said. 'Think about it very carefully, that's all I ask. Don't be too quick to dismiss what I do because you assume it's cruel.'

They left the room and Gil began to follow Dad through the maze of corridors and stairs and doors that led to the animals. They went deep into the heart of the building, inwards and upwards, as if they were heading for the canopy of a rainforest. Everything was very clean and bright, although Gil noticed they didn't pass a single window. Dad was silent. There was nothing for Gil to hear except the tapping of their feet on the polished floors, and his own heart thudding in his ears.

CHAPTER 17

Gil tried not to think what he might find at the end of the journey. In fact he tried not to think at all, but he could not prevent a really hideous thought that bubbled up from somewhere. What if Dad had lured him to the labs to experiment on *him*? What if he needed a human subject, and Gil happened to be convenient?

Don't be stupid, he's my dad, Gil told himself. But he couldn't squash the thought completely, and as they climbed the final flight of stairs it trailed behind him like a Halloween balloon.

There was one last automatic door, and then a loose curtain of clear plastic strips across the corridor. Dad pushed the strips aside to let Gil through, and he found himself in a space that looked like a changing room, only it was as spotless as the kitchen at home and there was no smell of stinky trainers.

'We need to clean ourselves up first,' said Dad, steering Gil towards a washbasin.

'What for?'

'This isn't a zoo. We don't want the animals exposed to any more germs than they have to be.'

'I thought you said they had diseases anyway?'

'All the more reason to protect them. They're vulnerable enough as it is. Here, put this on.' Dad handed Gil a blue boiler suit made of some very light material. As Gil struggled into it, Dad pulled it up over his back and then did the Velcro fastenings right up to his chin.

'It tickles,' Gil complained, pulling at the Velcro. *Crap*, he thought. The boiler suit completely covered the camera lens, even though he'd put the camera as high as possible, just as Jude had suggested. Before he had time to do anything about it. Dad shoved a plastic cap on Gil's head, pulling it down over his ears, and passed him a pair of thin rubber gloves like the ones dentists wear. Gil pulled them on quickly and then turned away from Dad so that he could pull apart the Velcro strip on the front of his boiler suit without Dad noticing. It was a fiddle because the gloves made his fingers feel tight and fat. By the time Gil looked round again, Dad had put on his own boiler suit and cap and gloves. He looked ridiculous, like a giant baby, and Gil started to laugh.

'I suggest you take a look at yourself before poking fun at me,' said Dad. 'Now we need a shower to hose off any remaining microbes.' He pointed Gil towards a square cubicle set into the wall.

'A shower? But . . . but . . .' Gil protested.

It didn't look like a shower. It looked like a portal to another universe. As Dad pushed Gil inside he pressed a button and big jets of air suddenly blasted them on all sides. It was like being on top of a mountain in a high wind, and when it stopped Gil couldn't speak for a minute or two.

'Air shower,' said Dad with a small smile. 'Bet you've never had one of those before.'

They stepped out of a door on the other side of the air shower and walked towards another of the plastic curtains. We're here, Gil thought. This was it. He closed his eyes and plunged through the curtain behind Dad.

'So, this is where we keep some of our torture victims,' said Dad softly.

Gil couldn't open his eyes. They felt glued shut. All sorts of pictures of sad and damaged animals crowded his head, and now he'd got this far he couldn't bear to see any real ones, not even if it was going to make Jude think he was a superhero. He wanted to turn and run.

He felt Dad nudge him.

'Open your eyes,' he said. 'I thought this was what you wanted to see. You look as if you're expecting someone to hit you.'

Gil opened one eye a crack, just enough to let in a blur of light between his eyelashes. There was daylight coming from somewhere, the first daylight he'd seen since they'd entered the building. The room smelt of straw. Gil realised that he had his arms folded tightly across his chest, as if he really did think someone was going to attack him. He dropped his arms to his sides, opened his eyes properly and looked around, shaking.

He saw a room full of hutches stacked two high – normal-looking hutches with chicken wire and straw, each one about two metres long and a metre deep. They were arranged around a big enclosed square that looked like a sandpit, and each hutch had a tunnel or a sloping wooden ladder leading out into the sand.

There were white rabbits everywhere. Gil did a quick count. He could see about thirty of them, stretched out in the straw on the floor of their cage, or hopping about, or washing themselves, or digging in the sand. Occasionally there was a snuffle and the thump of a rabbit's hind legs.

It was weird, thought Gil. It reminded him of the petting area in a zoo, except it was cleaner and quieter. It was only the clipboards attached to the cages that told him these rabbits were not pets. Dad was silent, and Gil moved closer to a line of cages, acutely aware of the camera burning a hole in his chest. Not too close, Jude had said, otherwise the film would be useless. He shuffled round slowly, examining the rabbits one by one. None of them looked like the pictures in Jude's booklet, as far as he could see. There were no visible wounds, no dreadful injuries.

A feeling of unreality washed over Gil and for a moment he lost track of where he was and what he was supposed to be doing. It was a long time since he'd had a pet, he thought. Maybe a rabbit would be good. He'd never had one before. Then he jumped as a woman burst through one of the plastic curtains, wearing a boiler suit and cap and carrying a portable cage. She glanced at Gil in some surprise before she spotted Dad.

'Oh, hi, Matt,' she said. 'I didn't know you were in today.'

Dad dipped his head with a smile. The woman inspected the clipboard on one of the hutches, opened the door, lifted out a huge floppy rabbit, popped it in the portable cage and marched back out through the curtain.

'What's she going to do with the rabbit?' Gil asked Dad after the woman had disappeared.

'I'm not sure, exactly. This isn't my project. Most of these rabbits are being used to study reproductive disorders – problems in pregnancy, that sort of thing.'

'But it doesn't look as if there's anything wrong with them.'

'Are you disappointed? What were you expecting, blood and screaming?'

Gil didn't answer. Suddenly all his terror had soaked away and he felt completely flat. It was impossible to imagine that Jude would be interested in a bunch of ordinary rabbits sitting quietly in their cages. Gil put his hand down to where the recorder sat in his trouser pocket, buried under the boiler suit. If he could have reached it he might even have switched it off altogether. It felt like a huge risk to have taken for so little.

'Do you want to come and see my mice?' asked Dad.

Gil followed him, pushing through another plastic curtain into the next room. It was like a room full of filing cabinets, except that the drawers were made of transparent amber-coloured plastic. There were over five hundred drawers, Gil calculated, in stacks of eight. Each one had a miniature clipboard attached to it.

Gil walked along the rows of cabinets and looked in the drawers. They all had mice living in them. Some held one mouse, some two or three, which meant there must be roughly a thousand mice altogether. There was sawdust on the floor and piles of shredded paper for the mice to burrow in, and toilet-roll tubes and home-made exercise wheels and boxes to hide in. The mice looked like – well, mice. Gil examined the drawers carefully, half hoping to find a mouse with some kind of appalling deformity, like the cancerous rat he'd seen in Jude's booklet, carrying a huge tumour on its back like a snail shell.

'So – what are they all for?' asked Gil after a while. 'Why are there so many of them?'

'Pretty much all of these mice are being used for genetic studies,' said Dad. 'They've had their genes manipulated in some way, and then we study the results and extend our understanding of how genes work. Or if the result of the genetic manipulation is a disease we try to find ways to make the mice better.'

'Are there any that look . . .' Gil tried to find a way of asking the question that wouldn't sound too obvious. 'I mean, I've read about experiments that made . . . well, you know. Mice with two heads, or something like that.'

'Ah, yes. The notorious two-headed mouse,' said Dad. 'And the five-legged frog. And of course the three-winged chicken. The thing is, Gil, those so-called monsters were made mostly by accident by people studying the development of embryos. So no two-headed mice here, I'm afraid. We have *nude* mice. That's about as bizarre as it gets.'

He pulled out a drawer, and Gil looked in. Two pink, wrinkly, shiny mice blinked up at him. They had no hair at all, except for a fringe of fine whiskers around their eyes and under their chins.

'Yuk,' said Gil under his breath. The mice looked repulsive. He hung over the drawer a little longer, wondering if the camera angle was right. 'Why are they bald?'

'They've been bred like that,' said Dad.

'What for?'

'I think these ones have lymphoma,' said Dad, studying the clipboard. 'It's a disease that's a bit similar to leukaemia.'

'You mean they've got cancer?'

'Yes, they're probably trying to find a new kind of treatment that will —'

'Someone's actually given these mice *cancer*?' Gil stared at the nude mice. They looked shivery and pathetic, and too delicate to handle. He felt sorry for them. 'It's not fair.'

'Perhaps not, but neither is lymphoma. And there'd be very few ways of treating it unless we did this kind of research on animals first.' Dad pushed the drawer back in and turned away without waiting for Gil to reply.

'These are mine,' he said, running his hand down a stack of mouse drawers right at the end of the row.

Drs Walker and Patel, it said in neat handwritten letters on every clipboard. *Gene IT-15, CAG expansion*. Then there were dates, and a lot of scientific words that Gil didn't understand.

These were the mice that Dad had condemned to a lifetime of illness, Gil reminded himself. They would live only until their brains turned to mush. He pulled out a drawer and looked at the two mice scurrying around the box, popping in and out of the toilet-roll tube. They were going to die a slow and dreadful death. Possibly they were in pain right now. Gil poked and prodded himself with the thoughts, trying to provoke a reaction, but nothing happened. He just felt numb.

'Do you want to pick one up?' said Dad.

'Um – OK,' said Gil.

He reached into the box with fingers that still felt tight and awkward inside the rubber gloves, grasped the tail that was poking out of the tube and pulled. The mouse wriggled and came out backwards into mid-air, its feet spread out as if it was doing a parachute drop. One of its back legs had a tiny identification tag on it, and Gil was just turning the mouse to get a better look when there was a sharp cry from Dad.

'Put him down!'

'Why?' Gil lowered the mouse back into the box. It ran away immediately and hid in the shredded paper. 'What's the problem?'

'Have you any idea how much stress you were causing that mouse? Didn't you notice his body language, for goodness' sake?' Dad sounded really cross.

'I didn't think it mattered how you picked them up,' Gil mumbled.

'Mice are prey,' said Dad. 'To them, we are gigantic

predators. If you pick that mouse up by the tail he thinks you're going to eat him. I really thought you knew better than that. You had pet mice for years.'

'I forgot,' said Gil defensively. He remembered with a flicker of guilt that it had always amused him to pick Turbo and Minky up by their tails so he could watch them wriggle and squirm in mid-air, trying to clamber back up their own bodies.

Dad put his hand palm-up on the bottom of the mouse drawer, and after a minute or two the mouse came out of the shredded paper, sniffed his hand and then crept on to it. It didn't seem bothered about Dad's rubber glove.

'Hello, little fellow,' said Dad.

'Is that one ill?' said Gil. 'What's going to happen to him?'

'This one? No, he's a control mouse. There's nothing wrong with him. He's just one of the normal ones that we do exactly the same tests on as we do for the diseased mice. Then we have something to measure our results against.'

'What sort of tests?'

'Do you want to see one?'

Gil remembered the camera again, and felt a little flutter of nervous excitement. A test would be good. A real live experiment. What would it be like? A joke tumbled into his head from nowhere, one of Louis' all-time favourites. *What's green and turns red at the touch of a button? A frog in a blender!* It was enough to make Gil feel sick.

Dad was opening one of the cupboards on the wall. He took out a small plastic container no bigger than a sandwich box, and carefully popped the control mouse into it. Then he pulled out another drawer and let a mouse clamber on to his hand before placing it in the little box too.

'So, now we have one diseased mouse and one healthy one,' Dad said. 'Let me show you one of our standard tests.'

He led the way into a bigger room, almost as white and shiny as the room downstairs. In the middle of the room was something like a paddling pool, filled with a blue-green liquid that looked like a disgusting kind of soup.

'This is a memory experiment,' said Dad. He put the mouse box on a workbench and lifted out a mouse. It sat crouched in the palm of his hand, and Dad scratched the top of its head with a finger. 'Watch what happens to the healthy mouse.'

He slipped the mouse into the coloured water and let go. The mouse swam. Its little nose twitched above the surface, and its legs paddled invisibly underneath. Within a few seconds the mouse had found a place which must have been shallower, because it stopped swimming and sat up on its hind legs, washing its face.

'These mice have done this test dozens of times,' said Dad. 'As you can see they've learnt that there's a small underwater platform, and the healthy mice can find it pretty quickly.' He scooped out the mouse and patted it dry with a piece of kitchen paper. 'Now for the other one,' he said.

He put the diseased mouse into the pool. It started to swim. It swam and swam and swam, round and round, backwards and forwards, patiently and hopelessly.

'She can't find it,' said Dad after a while. 'She used to

know where the platform is, but now she can't remember. That's because the disease is clogging up the brain cells that are used for memory.'

'So are you going to let her drown?' asked Gil. The mouse was still swimming. It was hard to tell if she was getting tired or not. How long could mice swim for, anyway? He badly wanted to rescue her before she gave up.

'Don't be silly,' said Dad. 'What would be the point of that? We need them alive. We want to be able to measure changes in the mice, so we can tell if any of our attempts to affect the disease are working.' He carefully grasped the mouse from behind and lifted her out of the water.

'So – is this it? You spend your whole day doing this?'

'This kind of thing, mostly, yes.'

'It just seems a bit . . .'

'Boring?' said Dad with a smile. 'Low-key? Repetitive?'

'Yeah, I guess so,' said Gil.

'You're right. It is.'

'Don't you ever . . . well, cut them up or anything?'

'Only when they're dead,' said Dad.

'So you do kill them?'

'Yes, of course, when we have to.'

'How?'

'It depends,' said Dad. He was still holding the diseased mouse, stroking her absent-mindedly. 'If we need to analyse the brain tissue, we give them a lethal injection, like you would for putting down a sick cat or dog. Otherwise . . .'

He paused.

'Otherwise what?'

'Well, we'd use another method. But they're all humane. None of them causes the mouse any suffering, I promise you that.'

Gil looked at the mouse in Dad's hand. What was going on in the mouse's head? he wondered. Did she really have no idea she was ill?

'You know, I once found a pigeon in the garden,' Dad said. 'It'd had its wing almost ripped off by a cat. It just lay there, thrashing about on the path. I had to wring its neck, because it would never have survived. That was worse than anything I've ever done to any creature in this building.'

There was a little silence.

'So,' Dad said. 'Tell me, Gil. What do you think about all this?'

'I don't know,' Gil said. His head felt full of a sticky liquid, like the blue-green soup in the pool.

'Can you see now that the lives of a few hundred mice might help us find a cure for a disease that destroys the lives of thousands of people?'

'I don't really understand why it's so *difficult*,' said Gil. All at once he wished he'd never come here. He wanted to go home. 'To find a cure, I mean. If there's something wrong with the gene, why don't you just replace it, or cut it out, or something?'

Dad shook his head. 'You can only do that at the embryo stage, when a creature is still a single cell. Once an animal is fully grown it becomes impossible. There are around a hundred trillion cells in the human body. If you have a disease caused by a faulty gene, that gene is in every single one of those trillions of cells. Think of a field of sunflowers. Imagine there are about ten sunflowers in every square metre of the field. Now imagine the entire United States of America, every single bit of it, planted with sunflowers. That's what a hundred trillion looks like. Finding and removing a gene from every cell would be like gathering a single grain of pollen from every one of those sunflowers. For a cure to work, it has to have an effect on the faulty gene in every cell in the body. It's not easy to achieve that.'

Gil tried to follow what he was saying but the scale of it was huge, too huge for him to get his head round.

'What else do you want to see?' said Dad.

'Uh – where are the monkeys?'

'There are no monkeys here,' said Dad. 'We don't use them for genetic research.'

'Oh.'

'Do you want a drink?' asked Dad after a while.

Gil nodded.

'Let's go along to my office.'

They went back through the mouse room, where Dad put the mice in their drawers, back through the rabbit room, back through the changing room where Gil had been blasted by the air shower. He took off his protective clothes and Dad led him out between the strips of the plastic curtain. They turned left down a corridor, and left again, and there was a door with a name plate saying *Dr Matthew Walker*. Gil stood looking up at it, and then he put his hand in his pocket and switched off the camera.

Dad unlocked the door and ushered Gil in. The office

had a proper window that you could look out of. Gil went across and looked through the smoked glass. Dad must really be quite important, he thought, if he had a room with a window in a building that had almost no windows at all. There wasn't much to see, though, just more buildings made of cream-coloured stone and a slice of the road they had driven down past the museum, and a little patch of garden far below. Gil pressed his face against the glass to see if he could glimpse the animal rights protesters they'd driven past, and managed to bang his knee on a big metal box just under the window. 'What's this thing?' he asked.

'Fire escape,' said Dad. 'We can't have a proper fire escape on this floor for security reasons. So all of us who work up here need to have a fire ladder next to the window, just in case we ever have to flee a burning building.' He grinned. 'Makes climbing out of your bedroom on to the conservatory roof look pretty tame, doesn't it? It's quite a long way down there.'

Gil sat in an office chair while Dad took a can of Coke out of a tiny fridge. Dad didn't really approve of Coke, and Gil couldn't imagine him drinking it himself. He wondered if Dad had put it there specially as a reward for the end of their visit. Dad stood quietly leafing through papers while Gil sat and slurped, looking around the office. There was a huge photo above the desk, a cluster of spheres blown up thousands of times bigger than life size. At least now he knew what they were.

'Is that one of your mice?' Gil asked finally, pointing at the picture of the embryo.

Dad was busy with something and took a while to reply.

'It's not a mouse at all,' he said. 'In fact, it's a human being.'

'How can you tell?'

'Well, the embryos do look virtually identical. But I happen to know this one is human, that's all.'

Gil drained the last mouthful from the can, and then they made their way down through the building to the car park. Dad hadn't quite got all the egg off the windscreen and it had dried like glue. He tutted in annoyance. The security guard was still patrolling the car park with his dog, and when they drove out on to the main road, Gil saw the animal rights protesters were still there. Dad turned the car smoothly away from them and soon they were out of sight.

At home Mum opened the door, smiling expectantly. Gil noticed the way she exchanged looks with Dad, and how Dad nodded his head as a way of indicating to Mum that he thought it had gone well.

'Well, you've had a long morning, both of you,' Mum said. 'You must be ready for lunch.'

'I'll just go and change,' said Gil, running upstairs to his room.

He stripped quickly to his underwear, ripping away the camera equipment and tossing it carelessly into his school bag. The carpet tape had stuck too tightly to his skin and it hurt when he pulled it off, but he didn't care. He was utterly sick of his spying adventure. He had achieved almost nothing.

The film was so dull he might as well wipe the memory

card now. There was no blood, no pain, no torture, and apart from the nude mice he hadn't seen a single thing that really upset him. There wasn't even any point checking whether the camera had worked properly. Jude was going to be bitterly disappointed. It was nobody's fault, but Gil felt as if he'd let him down big time.

CHAPTER 18

Gil's punishments were lifted overnight without a word.

On Sunday Gil found his Nintendo and MP3 player lying on his bed, together with five pounds' pocket money and a big bar of chocolate. Dad disappeared off to work on Monday morning before Gil had even got up, so it was clear that he was allowed to make his own way to school once again. It meant he could go straight to Jude's house with the buttonhole camera instead of having to be dropped off at school first, and Gil knew he should have been delighted, but he was too full of anxiety about the way Jude was going to react to the video.

When Jude opened his front door, his face immediately broke into a huge grin.

'Oh my God, you did it,' he laughed. 'You bloody did it.'

Gil followed him down the narrow entrance hall to his room. Jude whooped with delight every step of the way.

'Oh, man,' he said, gasping for breath as he shut the door behind them. 'I was so worried for you. I thought about you all damn weekend. It was the longest two days of my life.' He stopped, and looked at Gil's face.

'What's the problem?' he asked, suddenly serious. 'Didn't the camera work?'

'Yes, I think so, but . . .'

'What?'

'It's just – the film's not very interesting. I think you're going to be really disappointed.'

'Oh.' Jude's face relaxed. 'I doubt that very much. Let's have a look.'

Jude connected the buttonhole camera to the laptop on his desk and dragged up the armchair for Gil to sit in. Then he perched on his wobbly office chair, with a big pad of paper balanced on his knee, and handed Gil the recorder part of the camera.

'OK, go,' he said. 'You play it back for me.'

The video flickered on to the computer screen.

Gil saw a blurred flash of the car park, filmed as he'd turned away from the car, followed by a shot of Dad unlocking the back entrance to the labs. The door swung towards the camera and there was sudden darkness. The lens readjusted inside the building in time to show the green lights blinking on the panel on the wall, and Gil could see Dad unlocking the next door, and then opening the door beyond that with his special pendant. The film swayed and jolted as the camera moved down the corridor and up the stairs. Gil was amazed at how much movement there was.

How did his eyes ever cope with that amount of bouncing around? It made him dizzy.

Jude was chuckling. 'I don't believe it,' he said. 'If that's all they can come up with, we're laughing.'

Gil opened his mouth to ask what he meant, but then Jude chuckled again as the camera staggered into the toilets, visited a cubicle and filmed Gil fiddling with buttons in the mirror.

'Nervous, huh?' he said, grinning sideways at Gil.

The video bumped along to the laboratory room where Dad had shown Gil the mouse embryo. Gil was relieved to see that there were some better shots here and he made a real effort to stand still and aim the camera. He watched Dad run through his speeches again, listened to his voice coming quietly out of the computer, watched the way his eyes became wide and bright as he talked about life and DNA and bricks building themselves into houses. The voice on the video didn't sound quite right. It was too thin. Dad's real voice was like sweet-and-sour sauce, thick and punchy.

A dreamy feeling came over Gil as he looked at the film he had made. It should have been exactly the same as the stuff he'd seen with his own eyes on Saturday, and yet it wasn't. Somehow the viewpoint had shifted slightly, but he couldn't work out how.

'Bloody Frankenstein,' Jude muttered.

The camera started to follow Dad out of the embryo room, and Gil reached for the buttons on the recorder.

'This bit's really boring,' he said, beginning to fast-forward. 'It's just shots of stairs and corridors.'

'Whoa, whoa,' said Jude. 'Go back a bit. Go back to that room.'

Gil rewound, wondering what Jude was looking for. This time, instead of watching the video, he watched Jude. He was flicking between the computer screen and his pad of paper, scribbling fast. He'd already covered several pages.

'This is good, this is good,' said Jude as the video neared the entrance to the animal rooms. 'This is where the animals are kept, yeah? Pause it a second. That's perfect.'

'What are you writing?' asked Gil.

'Eh? I'm not writing anything. I'm sketching a plan.'

'What sort of plan?'

'A plan of the inside of the building, of course.'

'What for?'

Jude turned his head very slowly and looked at Gil. 'Well,' he said, 'why do you think I wanted this film?'

'Um – to find out what's going on in the labs. To put the video on a website, maybe, if it was any good. To put pressure on people like Dad so they'd have to close the labs down. I don't know, really.'

Gil rambled on, wondering whether he'd missed something vital, wondering why Jude wasn't nodding in agreement. And then, just before Jude began to speak again, Gil suddenly knew what he was going to say. The words dropped around him like a shower of stinging fireworks.

'We're going in there, Gil. We're going to liberate the animals. We're going to show those bloody scientists that they can't get away with this. It's absolutely brilliant, what you've done. We didn't know much about the back entrance to the labs and now you've shown us everything. The security is completely pants, just a few locks and a burglar alarm – pretty much all the internal doors are magnetic, and we can get through those easily. We weren't completely sure where the animals were kept, either, and now we know the route through the building, which'll save us so much time. You've done a great job.'

'But you haven't even seen the animals yet,' said Gil, feeling dazed.

'I don't need to,' said Jude, shrugging.

'How could you possibly get past the guards and the dogs?'

'That's probably the easiest part to deal with. There'll be more of us than there are of them, and you'd be amazed how a nice bit of steak can sort out even the scariest dog.'

'Steak? I thought you were a vegan?'

'Sometimes you have to make compromises, you know. For the greater good.'

'But . . . but . . . I still don't see how you're going to manage the locks and the burglar alarm.' *Slow down*, Gil wanted to say. *This is going too fast.*

'I thought maybe you'd help us with that bit,' said Jude quietly.

'Me?' Gil couldn't look at Jude. 'What do you mean?'

'Do you know where your dad keeps his work keys and things like that?'

Gil knew exactly where Dad kept his keys. They were in the box he'd found in the locked desk drawer in his study.

'Yeah, I think so, but . . .'

Gil had to stop and swallow hard. Now he was seriously frightened, even more frightened than the time he'd found Sally sprawled on the path and thought she was dead. Jude wanted him to steal Dad's keys. He wanted Gil to burgle Dad's study so that they could break into the labs. Why the hell hadn't Gil seen this coming? All along he'd assumed that the video was the final goal, but it had turned out to be just the first step in a much bigger plan, and now Gil could see the whole picture it scared him to death.

'It's a big ask, I know,' Jude said very gently. Gil tried to hide his face. He felt sure Jude could see exactly how he felt. 'Maybe it's too much. You've already put yourself on the line to get the video.'

'No, no. It's fine. Really.'

'I'll totally understand if you tell me you've got cold feet. We'll find another way to do it, don't worry.'

'I haven't got cold feet. I just didn't realise what you wanted me to do, that's all.'

Oh for God's sake, get a grip, Gil told himself furiously. He was supposed to be a hero. He desperately didn't want Jude to start thinking he was a little scaredy-cat kid.

'You know, if you tell me where the keys are we can come and get them ourselves,' said Jude.

'You mean – break in? Break into my house?'

'Uh-huh. It wouldn't be a problem, honestly. In fact, I'd make an educated guess and say your dad probably keeps everything in his study, doesn't he? Which is on the ground floor, isn't it, with a small window facing the front garden?'

180

'You know my *house*? You know where I *live*?' Gil's words came out in an embarrassing squawk and Jude gave a smile that lit up half his face while his eyes remained cold and serious.

'Yeah, we've had a few plans for your house. None of them have come off yet, though.'

Plans for your house. The words lifted Gil up and swept him along in a flood of pure terror. *Plans. For your house.* Very clearly, he heard a voice speaking in his head. It was Dad, the time they'd come back from town on the bus. *Let's hope the house doesn't get fire-bombed. He's dangerous.* And now Jude was telling Gil he'd been there, outside Dad's study, examining the layout, making plans. Maybe he'd been in Gil's back garden under the apple tree where the mice were buried. Maybe Gil had even looked out at Jude from his bedroom window without realising there was anyone there at all. It was like feeling hands grasp your shoulders when you thought you were all alone.

But Dad can't be right, Gil thought, struggling to control his panic. There was no way Jude could be that dangerous. He was a friend, wasn't he? Jude was testing him, that was all. It wasn't such a big deal. He just had to face up to the test and show Jude that he could pass it.

'OK, I'll get you the —' Gil tried to say the word 'keys', but it wouldn't come out. He tried again, and thought it was going to make him throw up.

Jude nodded understandingly. 'Sure?' he said.

'Yup.'

'We won't need to keep them,' said Jude. 'We'll just need

to borrow them for a while so we can copy them, if that makes you feel any better.'

'Yeah. It's fine.'

'You know, the animals would thank you for it,' said Jude. 'If they had a voice.' He nodded at the computer screen, where Dad was still frozen in time with his head through the curtain. 'Play.'

Gil played the rest of the video.

Jude watched in total silence and with a face as still as stone. It was impossible to read what he might be thinking. Gil gave up trying and instead looked again at the animals on the film – the rabbits in their cages, the mice in their boxes. He looked again at Dad. Dad the monster. Dad the torturer. Dad patiently coaxing the mouse out of its hiding place. Dad rubbing the mouse's head with a finger, the way he stroked Mum's hair sometimes.

Who *was* Dad? wondered Gil. What was he?

The camera back-tracked through the animal rooms, through the washroom, round the corners to Dad's office. It glanced up at the sign that said *Dr Matthew Walker*. And then it stopped. The computer screen went grey.

'That's it?' said Jude. He took a deep, shaky breath and rubbed his face with both hands as if he was washing himself. 'Oh, God, it makes me so bloody angry,' he whispered. 'I don't know how you coped with it.'

'It wasn't as bad as I thought it would be,' Gil said, surprised at how upset Jude seemed to be. Then he wished he'd kept his mouth shut, because Jude blazed with anger.

'Not bad? You call that *not bad*?'

'It was just rabbits and mice,' said Gil defensively. 'There weren't any monkeys or dogs or anything.'

'And how do you know mice feel any less pain than monkeys? Or less pain than *we* do, come to that?'

'Uh . . .' said Gil uneasily.

'Did you actually see any experiments? Apart from that pathetic rubbish with the swimming mouse? Did you see what they *do* to the rabbits? Oh my God, those poor bloody creatures cooped up in cages, never allowed their freedom, poked and prodded and riddled with diseases and then just snuffed out when people like your dad have had enough of them. It makes me sick. He didn't tell you how they kill most of the mice, did he? Well, I'll tell you what they do. They hold the mouse down, stick a pencil across here —' Jude chopped viciously at the back of his own head '— and then they pull the mouse's tail until its neck snaps. You think that's OK, do you? You think just because you didn't see any blood that there's no suffering going on?'

'I didn't . . . I don't . . .' Gil wriggled in his chair, trying to find something sensible to say. 'I mean, those bald mice didn't look so great. But Dad said they don't know they're ill.'

'Oh, yeah.' Jude's eyes were furious. It was like being told off by Dad. 'I get it. He gave you that rubbish about consciousness, didn't he? It's supposed to be only human beings who are aware of themselves. It's only people who feel emotions, who care about each other.' His voice was bitter. 'Well, how does he *know*? How does he know what it feels like to be a mouse? Those scientists are always crapping

183

on about how much of our DNA we share with other animals. So if our genes are nearly the same, how can they possibly say that mice don't experience any of the same *feelings* as we do?'

'I don't know,' said Gil. He was too bewildered to think any more. 'I don't know anything about this, Jude.'

'Oh, I'm sorry,' said Jude, softening a little. 'I'm sorry. You're not the enemy. I don't mean to lay into you. You know something?'

He stopped, and Gil waited for him to go on.

'If I was dying, and somebody told me that the life of just one of those animals would save me, I wouldn't take it. You know that? I couldn't live with the knowledge that my survival had been at the expense of another living creature. Not a single one of them, let alone the hundreds they've got in there. We've got to get them out, we really have.'

Gil looked up at Jude. In the cold gloom of the little room Jude's face hung above him, alive with emotion, his sun-coloured hair falling into his eyes. The face almost seemed to shine with its own light, and Gil found it hard to look away. He kept his eyes fixed on Jude's face until at last he had the sensation that he was falling upwards, as if he was being pulled into a black hole. Once you stepped over the boundary of a black hole, there was no way back. Dad had told him about it, long ago, in the days when Gil was interested in science. The black hole's enormous gravity sucked you in to its centre. The problem was that you couldn't tell where the boundary lay until you were travelling towards it at nearly the speed of light. And by then you were doomed.

It was like that with Jude, Gil thought. He'd come too close to Jude to be able to move away now. Jude had pulled him in, and Gil was falling towards him in a great slow curve.

They played the video twice more from the very beginning up to the point where Dad dived through the plastic curtain, while Jude checked his plan carefully. He didn't watch the footage of the animals again. Then he deleted the film. It was one less thing to implicate Gil, he said, if things went wrong.

'Think about everything and give me a call when you're ready,' Jude said as Gil got up to leave. 'Don't use your own phone. Borrow this.' He opened a drawer in his desk and pulled out an ancient mobile phone. 'It's got some credit on it. Try and let me know by the weekend. And if you decide to do anything at all, use these.' He pushed a pair of thin disposable gloves into Gil's school bag.

It was getting on for lunchtime but Gil couldn't face going back to school. He ate a sandwich on the bus and then went to the library, where the librarian gave him a funny look but didn't actually challenge him. Gil curled up in a heap of cushions in the picture-book area and waited for a computer to become free. He played pointless computer games and endless rounds of Solitaire until his time ran out and he was kicked off the terminal. Then he went back to the safety of the cushions and read *Wibbly Pig* and *Postman Pat* books until it was just after school finishing time and he could finally go home without anyone asking any awkward questions.

'Hello, darling,' said Mum at the front door. 'Good day at school?'

'Actually, I feel crap,' said Gil.

He slid into bed with relief while Mum fussed around him with thermometers and cool drinks and painkillers, and let the world outside his bedroom disappear for a while.

The next few days passed in a haze. Gil was aware of his body keeping everything going, like a plane on automatic pilot. His body got out of bed and dressed itself and ate breakfast and managed to produce a few words for Mum and Dad and walked itself to school and found its way to registration. His body waded through lesson after lesson and solved problems and answered questions and handed in homework. But Gil himself wasn't there. He sat quietly to one side and struggled with the weight of the thing that Jude wanted him to do.

What was the right thing to do? When you were little, right and wrong were easy. Share your toys. Don't snatch. Don't hit people, or bite them. Say 'please' and 'thank you' in the right places. But he wasn't little any more, and all at once Gil found himself in a place where nothing was so clear-cut. No one was going to tell him what to do – or rather, Jude and Dad were both telling him what to do, and they were both claiming to be right. How could they both be right? Obviously it was wrong to steal Dad's keys, but was it still wrong to steal Dad's keys if it helped to prevent the suffering of innocent animals? Maybe some crimes were allowed, if they prevented bigger crimes. Even Dad had been prepared to break the law because he thought that nuclear weapons were wrong. But were Dad's mice suffering? And if they were helping to find cures for diseases, did that make the suffering acceptable?

Gil felt as if he was tumbling through the space between the stars with nothing to stop him falling. He sat in his room for hours at a time, staring, unable to do anything. He woke up often in the middle of the night, imagining he could hear noises from Dad's study, and wondering at what point Jude would decide to take matters into his own hands.

'Gil, we'd like to go out for the day on Saturday,' Dad said over supper on Thursday.

'OK,' said Gil, not really listening. 'Where are we going?'

'Actually, I meant just your mother and me. I want to take her out for lunch. Would you mind very much?'

'Oh. No, I don't mind at all.'

'I guess you'll be going ice-skating with Louis on Saturday morning, won't you?'

'Yeah, of course,' Gil said automatically. 'I haven't been for ages.'

'Do you think you could go home with him afterwards, so you don't have to be here on your own? We'd be back late afternoon.'

'Yeah, I'm sure I could. I'll sort it out with Louis at school tomorrow.'

Maybe there was no need to make a decision, Gil told himself. He would just drift along until he bumped into something that would make the decision for him. But of course he wouldn't talk to Louis. Even if he'd wanted to it would be difficult. They hadn't spoken all week. Gil caught sight of Louis occasionally, eyeing him from the other side of the classroom or the canteen. Sometimes he was on his own, sometimes he was with Ben, but he always looked away again as soon as his glance touched Gil's.

Gil allowed Mum and Dad to drive him to the ice rink on Saturday morning. Before they left the house Gil opened his bedroom window a fraction, hoping it wouldn't be noticed. When they got to the rink Dad escorted him in, paid the entrance fee, gave Gil enough change to buy a drink and a snack and took him through the door that led to the ice.

'Have a great time,' he said. 'We'll be back at about four.'

Dad waved cheerily to someone on the ice below and gave the thumbs-up. Gil knew without looking that it must be Louis. As Dad disappeared back out to the car, Gil stood at the top of the stairs with his skates slung over his shoulder and scanned the ice. There was Louis, standing as still as an ice sculpture in the middle of the rink while dozens of other skaters whirled around him. Louis' eyes were huge, staring up as if Gil had just emerged from the land of the living dead. Gil stared back, judging the time it would take for Mum and Dad to drive out of sight of the ice rink. When he thought he'd waited long enough, he turned round and walked out of the door.

CHAPTER 19

Gil walked slowly home with the skates bumping at his back.

It was about two miles. No plans, Gil told himself. No plans. But a plan began to seep into his head without permission. His bedroom window would still be open, unless Dad had checked and shut it before they'd gone out. So he'd be able to scale the conservatory roof and climb in the window. It must be possible – after all, he'd practised it the other way round as part of Dad's fire drill. And once he was in the house ...

Gil's mind slid away from the thought, as if it was too slippery to keep hold of. It would be nice to have the house to himself for a change, that was all. Gil began to count footsteps, trying to empty his head. One, two, three, four ... how many till he got home?

It took nearly four thousand steps, but Gil still felt he was there far too quickly.

It was hard to tell if his bedroom window was open or not. Gil thought he could see the tiniest crack, but he couldn't be sure. He stood looking up at the window for ages, listening to the quiet noises of the gardens around him – leaves rustling in the bushes, birds cheeping, the occasional plop of a big fish diving in the pond next door. Well, if the window *was* open it was fate, Gil thought at last. He wasn't really making a choice. He was just following a thread.

He dumped his ice-skates on the lawn and pulled the garden table across to the fence so that he could scramble up on to the wall at the edge of the conservatory roof. Then he inched his way across the wooden beams between the glass until he could reach his bedroom window. He tugged at the crack with his fingernails. The window was stiff, or perhaps it really was shut, Gil thought, his heart sinking. Trust Dad. He was obsessed with security. But suddenly the window swung open and Gil hauled himself head first through it, falling awkwardly on to the floor of his bedroom.

For a moment he lay there, and then he sat up carefully. *Don't think about it, just do it.* He'd need the gloves. Jude had told him to wear gloves so he wouldn't leave any fingerprints. Gil reached over for his school bag and dug about till he found them. They were made of thin clear plastic, not like the rubber ones Dad had made him wear in the labs. The plastic was both crackly and slimy and as Gil pulled the gloves over his fingers he felt as if he was preparing for some disgusting medical procedure.

It's bound to be locked, Gil thought, creeping down the stairs. But the study door wasn't locked. The handle was cold through his thin gloves, and the door felt even heavier than the last time he'd pushed it open. Well, the drawer will be locked, anyway, Gil decided as he stepped towards Dad's desk. It was, and this time the key was nowhere to be seen. Gil hesitated. Was it fair to look for it? Did that still count as fate, or was he making a decision? Maybe if he just lifted a few things here and there he could give himself permission to give up. He'd go and phone Jude and tell him he hadn't managed to do it and then . . .

Gil picked up the holiday photo that always sat on Dad's desk. Immediately a small key slid out from somewhere at the back of the frame and tinkled on to the desk. Gil stared at it. He really hadn't searched very hard. So that must mean the key wanted to be found. And that meant the desk had to be opened.

The top drawer slid open. There was the box, the one that held Dad's keys and the magnetic door release pendant. Gil took the whole box. He left the key in the drawer for now, and stumbled to the kitchen to make the phone call on the battered phone that Jude had given him. He had a completely irrational fear that if he made the call from Dad's study Dad would somehow be able to hear it.

'Jude here,' said the voice on the other end of the phone, sharp and crisp as a cooking apple.

'It's Gil,' said Gil huskily. 'I've got what you want.'

There was a cry so loud it hurt his eardrum. 'Woo-hoo! You star, Gil! I knew you'd pull it off!'

Somehow the praise didn't make Gil feel any better this time.

Jude launched into the plan so quickly that Gil knew he'd had it all thought out way in advance. It would be better if Gil wasn't seen at Jude's house, and it was definitely too risky for Jude to come to Gil's. Instead they would meet at the local library. Gil would bring Dad's key box hidden in his bag and sit in the kids' section. He'd put the bag down nearby, but not too near. Then Jude would come in and sit down too, and after a while he would pick up Gil's bag and walk out with it. They wouldn't say anything at all to each other. Gil would go home and wait for Jude to phone to say his friend had copied the keys, and then they'd repeat the process to get the bag back to Gil.

'It'll only take an hour or so,' said Jude over the phone. 'As long as your dad doesn't come home early it'll work like a dream.' He laughed loudly, although Gil couldn't see anything in the plan that was at all amusing.

It took about two minutes to get his bag from his room and then Gil was ready. It was far too early to leave, but he couldn't bear to hang about the house. It made his stomach churn. As he was about to pull the front door closed behind him Gil hit a problem. How was he going to get back in? He really couldn't face scaling the conservatory roof again. The only option was to leave the front door unlocked. Gil set off up the road, hoping that the local burglars would all still be in bed.

It was only a short walk to the library but by the time Gil got there his knees were shaking. He felt as if there was a hole in his ribcage and someone was poking at his heart with a pointed stick. *It's a normal day, a totally normal day*, he told himself, but when he pushed open the library door he nearly ran away. It was packed. The children's section was full of tiny kids with their parents and there was nowhere for Gil to sit. One or two of the older kids at the computers looked uncomfortably like people from school. The parents had occupied every single cushion and chair and the toddlers were climbing over them as if they were in a playground. Gil found a small piece of floor in a corner. He dumped his bag and sat down, swivelling round so he couldn't see the bag. Then he pulled a book off the nearest shelf and tried very hard to pretend he was reading it.

Some time later Gil felt behind him and found his bag had gone. It gave him a prickly feeling in the back of his skull to think that Jude had been so close and he hadn't even seen him.

When he got home, Gil sat in the front room and waited for Jude to phone. Time slowed to a standstill. It was midday, but Gil didn't want to eat. He couldn't even watch television. He had time to go over every single thing that could possibly go wrong. Mum and Dad would come home early. Jude would find that Dad's keys were special keys that couldn't be copied and then he would disappear and never bring the keys back. Mum and Dad would crash on the way back from lunch and he would never see them again – oh, this was ridiculous. Now he was starting to think like Mum. *Get a grip*, he told himself.

By the time the phone finally rang in his pocket, Gil had heard the sound in his head so many times that he was convinced he was imagining things. It was almost a shock to find Jude on the end of the line.

'Hi, Gil,' he said. 'We're all done. You can have your keys back soon.'

'Oh. Good. I was worried you weren't going to be able to copy them.'

Jude laughed quietly. 'Even uncopiable keys can be copied,' he said. 'You need to know the right people, that's all. Now, there's just one thing I want to ask you about. I think you might have more idea than me.'

'What do you mean?'

'There's a note in the tin and I've got a hunch it might be some sort of code, maybe for the burglar alarm. The paper's got some dates and times on it, and then it just says *Sigma*. Does that mean anything to you?'

'It's Greek,' said Gil. '*Sigma* is the Greek letter *S*, but it doesn't look much like an *S*. It's a maths symbol. You see it on spreadsheets and stuff.'

'Yeah, well, I was always crap at maths,' said Jude. 'What does it look like?'

Sigma was Σ. How could he describe Σ? Gil drew it in the air with a finger, zigzagging backwards and forwards while he talked.

'It's hard to explain,' he said. 'Sort of like a pointy number 3, only backwards. Or a *z* with an extra line.'

As Gil spoke, he glanced at the house phone sitting on the table next to him and had a sudden idea. Numbers on keypads were always arranged in a square – 1-2-3, 4-5-6, 7-8-9, with the zero on its own underneath the 8. What if you were meant to press the numbers in the shape of the *Sigma* symbol?

'It might be something to do with the way the numbers are set out on the keypad,' said Gil, thinking aloud. He imagined the Greek letter drawn on top of the numbers on the phone, and started to trace the shape with his finger. 'If you have one number for each point of the *Sigma* symbol, that would make . . . um . . . 3-1-5-7-9. Or possibly 2-1-5-7-8. Or even 3-1-6-7-9 if you had an extra long middle bit.'

There was a pause, and Gil knew Jude must be scribbling.

'Excellent,' said Jude after a while. 'That's really helpful. We could try disabling the alarm but it's a lot simpler if we've got the code. See you back at the library, then?'

'Yes, OK. Uh – Jude?'

'What?'

'When are you planning to do this?'

'Soon. Look, let's get this stuff back to you, all right?'

'OK. And then what?'

Gil waited for Jude to say something else, but there was just a dull silence that told him Jude had ended the call. What was he expecting Jude to say, exactly? 'Come with us, Gil.' Something like that?

This time Gil saw Jude come into the library. He was wearing a smart black jacket over his jeans, and his hair was brushed and tied back. Gil's school bag was slung casually over his shoulder. It made him look camouflaged somehow, as if he was making a deliberate effort to blend in with his surroundings. Gil watched Jude's eyes as they swept over him and completely failed to make contact. He felt a little flash of pain at being ignored. Of course it had to be like that, Gil said to himself, it wasn't safe for Jude to acknowledge him. But the hurt stayed, like a burn.

Before Gil returned Dad's key box to the drawer in the desk he looked for the piece of paper that Jude had mentioned. *12 noon 20th March to 12 noon 3rd April*, it read. *Sigma*. The note was in Dad's handwriting, and 'Sigma' was underlined twice. The third of April was the next day, Sunday. So if *Sigma* was the code, it would be changed at twelve noon tomorrow. Surely that meant Jude's raid would have to happen tonight?

Gil searched his school bag, hoping and dreading to find a note from Jude. *Midnight*, it might say. *Join us. Be there.*

But there was no note this time.

He waited in the front room until it was nearly time for Mum and Dad to come home, half-watching the television while he ate snacks. He hadn't really done anything, he told himself. He hadn't stolen Dad's keys, just borrowed them for a short time. The video he'd taken in the labs didn't exist any more, except in the memory of two people. What Jude chose to do now – well, that was his business. Everything was back in its place as if nothing had happened. So nothing *had* happened, had it? Gil went back over his fictional account of the day's events, adding little details here and there to make it more likely that Mum and Dad would believe it. By the time he'd finished it was so convincing he almost believed it himself.

The house phone rang twice while he was waiting. Each

time Gil picked it up and said 'Hello?', and each time there was a little click before the line went dead. It spooked him slightly. But there was nothing to be spooked about. Everything was fine. And at half past three he went out of the front door and deliberately locked it behind him. It would be much more convincing if Mum and Dad found him hunched up on the doorstep when they got home.

CHAPTER 20

'Oh, you poor thing,' said Mum. She put a hand on Gil's shoulder. 'Whatever happened?'

'He was just horrible to me,' said Gil. 'He said I was rubbish at skating because I hadn't been for three weeks and then he kept laughing and trying to push me over. I know I should have stayed there but he was really doing my head in. I couldn't cope with it.'

'It's so unlike Louis,' said Mum, shaking her head. 'What's got into him? I didn't think he was the sort to behave like a bully.'

Gil put on his most miserable face and looked at the floor. It was going well, but he still had to get round Dad, who was looking disapproving.

'So you came home on your own?' said Dad. 'All the way from the ice rink?'

'Yes,' Gil said. 'I was careful, Dad, honestly.'

'And what exactly have you been doing since you got here, given that you couldn't get into the house?' said Dad.

'Not a lot. Well, I did go to the library for a bit. I thought you wouldn't mind that,' said Gil.

Dad looked really irritated. 'The whole point of making plans is so that we know where you are and we know that you're safe,' he said. 'Now we find you've been wandering the streets for hours. You should have sorted it out with Louis. I'm not impressed.'

Mum stepped in. 'Come on, Matt. Gil hasn't actually done anything wrong. He just used his common sense in a difficult situation.'

There was a little pause, and Gil thought the worst was over, but Dad wasn't finished.

'I'm going to phone Louis and ask him what on earth he thinks he was doing,' said Dad, switching his anger to another target. 'He must have realised that his actions were putting you in potential danger. He should have stopped you leaving the rink.'

'No, Dad!' Gil protested, in genuine panic. 'You can't do that! It's too embarrassing. Look, *I'll* phone him.'

He went straight to the phone with his heart banging and pretended to dial numbers. Then he had a one-sided conversation, loudly enough for Dad to overhear.

'Oh, hi, Louis, it's Gil. Yeah, yeah, I know. Yeah, I just came home. Yeah, cool, I'll come over. Cool. See you in a bit.' He put the phone down and went back to Mum and Dad.

'Louis is sorry and he wants me to go over,' Gil said. 'Is that OK?'

'Sure,' said Mum, looking at Dad.

Dad just about nodded.

Gil heard the phone ring again as he was walking away from the house and it bothered him, though he wasn't sure why. There was no way Louis would call him, and Jude wouldn't be stupid enough to call the house phone.

Gil wandered up the road without being sure where he was going. After a while he found himself at the library again, but the instant he went inside he realised it wasn't such a smart move. He was sick of the sight of the library. The ghost of Jude lurked around every corner and the longer Gil sat and pretended to read books, the harder it was to persuade himself that nothing at all had happened.

Jude had everything he needed now to break into the labs. And Gil knew he would only find out about the raid when Dad found out, and then he would have to fake surprise or concern or something else he didn't feel. He longed for it to be over quickly.

After an hour Gil judged that Dad would have had time to get over his irritation. He went home and rang the bell, but when Mum opened the door she looked so white and scared that Gil wished he could just turn and walk away again.

'Oh,' she said. 'Dad wants to see you in his study.'

She didn't move away from the door. Gil stood looking at her, gradually filling up with fear. Seeing Dad in his study was bad news. It was like being sent to the headteacher's office. What had happened while he'd been out?

'You'd better come in and get it over with,' said Mum at last, pulling the door open properly.

It was a long way down the corridor to the study. The door was shut. Gil knocked and then waited.

'Come in,' said Dad's voice.

Gil pushed, feeling the bottom edge of the door catch on the springy carpet, and stepped inside.

Dad was sitting in his office chair. He leant forward as Gil came in. 'Ah, Gil!' he said. 'Good, good. You're back. You've had a successful time, I hope.' His voice was thick with sarcasm.

'Yes, it was —' Gil began.

Then he stopped. There was someone else in the room. Someone hunched up in Dad's armchair in the corner. Gil turned his head to look.

It was Louis.

Louis looked up at Gil, not speaking. His lips were set in a straight line and his eyes were hard. They fixed themselves on Gil's face until Gil had to look away. His legs felt as if they were about to fold underneath him and he badly wanted to sit down, but there wasn't another chair.

'Perhaps you'd like to tell us where you've actually been,' said Dad.

'At the library,' said Gil, as casually as he could manage. He had the weird feeling that Louis had suddenly morphed into a third parent.

'Oh, the library. I see. And where was it you told us you were going? I've quite forgotten.'

When Gil said nothing Dad went on, his sarcasm gradually curdling into something even more unpleasant.

'You see, shortly after you left the house we had a phone

call from Louis. He wanted to know if you were at home. Which was a bit of a surprise, as we were under the impression that you were on your way to see him. Given what we believed had happened at the ice rink this morning, I'm afraid I was rather harsh on Louis initially, until of course he told us what had really happened, and offered to come over and tell us about your behaviour over the past few weeks. About the way you've been treating him. About all the times you've slipped out of school without explanation. About the fact that you weren't at school at all last Monday, and apparently told Mr Montague you'd been ill at home – this is true, isn't it?'

'So you believe Louis without even bothering to listen to what I've got to say,' said Gil. 'That makes me feel great.' He tried to sound as sarcastic as Dad but he couldn't really summon enough energy.

'Yes, I believe Louis, I'm afraid,' said Dad. 'And now I want you to tell me what you've actually been up to.'

'You snake, Louis,' Gil said. But he couldn't give the insult any bite, and Louis didn't so much as blink.

'Yeah, Gil, you hate me, don't you?' he said steadily. He stood up. 'Is it all right if I go now?' he said to Gil's dad.

'Yes, of course,' said Dad, smiling so warmly at Louis that Gil felt a sudden rush of raw anger. It made him want to smash Louis' face against the study door until it bled. 'Thank you, Louis. You've done a very brave thing.'

Louis almost brushed Gil's arm as he went past to the door. Then the door clicked, and Gil was alone with Dad.

CHAPTER 21

'Sit down,' said Dad, waving at the armchair.

Gil sat down. The cushions were warm where Louis had been sitting and the warmth soaked into Gil's muscles, making him weak and tired. He had no idea what to do now. It was like being carried along in a fast-flowing river, waiting to drown. He should fight and shout and struggle, but he didn't know if he could be bothered any more.

'I'm waiting,' said Dad.

The tiny tick-tick-tick of Dad's watch punctured the silence.

'Gil, I don't know what you think you're trying to achieve here. I don't know how you imagine you're going to make things easier for yourself by not talking.'

What would happen if he just kept his mouth shut? What exactly could Dad do? Sanctions again, Gil thought. Permanent sanctions this time. So what? *You can't control me,*

Gil said to Dad in his head. *You have no power. It's too late to stop anything now.*

Dad picked up a piece of paper from his desk and thrust it out at arm's length. Gil saw that it was Jude's leaflet. 'Louis told me you'd tried to get him to hand these out with you at school. Is that true?'

Gil shrugged.

'He said you had hundreds of them. Where did you get them from?'

Gil shrugged again.

'I want to know what you've been up to. I insist that you tell me where you've been going when you've played truant from school.'

'It's none of your business what I've been doing,' said Gil finally.

'Oh, but it *is* my business. I'm your father. I have a right to know. You're thirteen years old, for God's sake. You're a boy. It's my job to protect you and stop you from doing stupid, reckless things that could put you in danger. Do you understand?'

'Yeah, I understand,' Gil said. 'I understand that you haven't got a clue.' He was almost beginning to enjoy himself. He was doing what Jude had done, calmly provoking Dad to the point of fury. Dad's breathing was quick and short now, as if he'd been running, while Gil felt more and more in control.

'Gil, I really thought we'd reached agreement on certain things. I took a huge risk taking you to the labs. I treated you like an adult. I showed you everything, I explained everything, you accepted it all. And then I find this – *this* . . .' Dad waved the leaflet violently right in Gil's face. 'I find you've gone behind my back. I find you've systematically lied to me. You lied just now, when you told us you were going to see Louis, and you lied yesterday when you pretended you had an arrangement to meet him at the ice rink. How many other times you've lied, I don't know. Perhaps you'd like to enlighten me, would you?'

'You know what your problem is,' said Gil. 'You can't bear to think that I still disagree with you about the labs. You just think you're right about everything.'

'On this subject, I *am* right.' Dad screwed up Jude's leaflet and hurled it at the wall. It bounced off and skittered away under his desk.

'Yeah, sure.' Gil had to fight an urge to laugh at the sight of Dad slowly destroying himself with rage.

'My God, Gil, you have no idea, have you? You are so woefully ignorant. Without the kind of techniques developed in animal experiments in places like my lab, you wouldn't even *exist*. You wouldn't be here at all. Or if you were . . .' He stopped suddenly and covered his eyes with a hand.

'Go on,' said Gil after a while.

He could feel that Dad's anger had vanished without warning, like water sinking into hot sand. He's just too pathetic to fight, thought Gil. He's given up. But his sense of triumph quickly evaporated. There was something wrong, something badly wrong, but he didn't know what it was.

'What do you mean, exactly, that I wouldn't exist? Dad?'

'I'm sorry, I'm talking nonsense,' Dad said, shaking his

head quickly, as if he was trying to shake away the words he'd spoken.

'I want to know what you meant. You said I wouldn't be here without places like your lab. Why did you say that?'

Dad rotated slightly in his chair so he was no longer looking Gil straight in the eye. 'It's nothing,' he said. 'Ignore me.'

It's nothing. Gil stared at Dad while Dad looked away, and in Gil's mind a little pile of memories began to fall one after the other, like dominoes knocking each other down. The time Mum lost it completely after Sunday lunch. *She's fine. It's nothing you need to worry about.* The times he'd asked them about Granny. *Don't worry. It's not your problem.* The time he'd told Mum and Dad how selfish they were for only having one child, and Dad had stopped Mum in mid-sentence. *Let's leave it like that.* The earthquake that had happened in Gil's head when he found out just what Dad did for a living. *I was going to tell you. When you were old enough.* His head was crammed with the things they didn't tell him, or half-told him, or brushed aside as unimportant when he asked a direct question. And now – *it's nothing*, Dad said.

But it's not nothing, it's not nothing, it's not nothing, thought Gil desperately. It can't be nothing. So what the hell is it? The noise in his head built to a roar that was like a train thundering through a station. He took a deep breath, and started.

'OK, Dad. So you accuse me of lying. You say I'm going behind your back. But there's all this stuff you and Mum are hiding from me, as if I'm too stupid to understand it. You never told me what your job was, you've never told me what's wrong with Granny, you try to pretend Mum's fine when she isn't. How many other things are there that you haven't told me? I don't see why I should tell you the truth when you never tell me anything. I don't know what you were going to say just then but it wasn't nothing, was it? I'm so *sick* of it.'

Gil was aware of his voice getting louder and louder until he was practically spitting the words at Dad, and then his throat became so tight it was impossible to go on. But Dad didn't react. He was quiet, looking out of the little window into the front garden. At last he turned to face Gil again.

'Yes, you're right,' he said. 'There are things we haven't told you. Perhaps it's time.'

'I want to know everything,' said Gil.

'I hope so,' said Dad.

He sounded tired, and his face was full of a sadness that frightened Gil.

Stop, Gil wanted to say. *Don't tell me*. But it was too late.

'I need to tell you something about yourself, Gil. I need to tell you the story of how you came to be. You see, your mother and I never thought we would have children. We never intended to. And then there came a day when we realised we wanted it more than anything else in the world. But there was a problem.'

'Are you trying to tell me I'm adopted?' Gil interrupted.

'No, you're not adopted. You're our child, our biological child. But you weren't made in the normal way. Actually, you were created in a lab.'

'You mean I was an IVF baby?'

'Yes, that's right. You were made in the same way that I make my mice.'

'But that's just because you couldn't have kids, isn't it? That's why people have IVF treatment. You create a baby in a test tube instead of it happening inside the body, that's all.'

'Not exactly, no. Not in your case. We had you made very carefully. We had you screened when you were a minute bundle of only eight cells. We got them to do something called pre-implantation genetic diagnosis, which means that they took one cell away and analysed the genes to make sure you were – OK.'

'What do you mean, *OK*?'

Dad looked down at his hands. 'It's possible that Rachel – I mean, your mother . . .'

'Dad, I know who Rachel is.'

'It's possible she carries a genetic disease, a serious disease that means she might die much younger than she should.'

'Is it cancer?' Gil heard his own voice as if it was coming from far away.

Dad gave a small, sad smile. 'No, it's not cancer. I think sometimes she wishes it *was* cancer. With many kinds of cancer now you have a chance, if you catch it in time. With the disease that runs in your mother's family there is no chance. If you are born with the genetic defect that causes the disease, you become ill, you spend the next fifteen years or so slowly losing control over your body and your mind, and then you die. That's all there is to it.'

'Isn't there a cure?'

'Not yet. There are treatments that help to some extent. But there is no cure.'

'That's what's wrong with Granny, isn't it?' Gil said.

'Yes. It's called Huntington's Disease.'

'So that's why you've never let me visit her,' said Gil. 'Because I would have asked too many awkward questions.'

'We wanted to shield you from it all,' said Dad. He didn't quite meet Gil's eyes. 'We had some very difficult decisions to make. Your grandmother started to become ill just at the time we began to think about having children. When she was diagnosed, and we realised that Mum could be carrying the disease too, we gave up on the idea of children. We couldn't take the risk of passing it on to another generation. We went off and did other things instead. Exotic holidays, lots of plane trips . . .'

'Screwing the planet up for me, then.' Gil tried to be angry, but it didn't work. He felt both weightless and tremendously heavy.

'Yes. In a way. Except nobody really knew about global warming then. But after several years of enjoying ourselves, we found we still desperately wanted children. And IVF made it possible for us to have a child that we *knew* would never suffer from the disease that has gradually destroyed your grandmother.'

Gil had a sudden memory of the gigantic photo of an embryo that hung on the wall of Dad's office. *I just happen to know it's a human being.* Gil remembered the way Dad had said it, and he knew at once why the picture was there.

'That picture in your office,' said Gil. 'It's me, isn't it?'

'Yes, it's you, when you were a cluster of cells just two days old,' said Dad. 'It's been there since you were born, as a continual reminder to me of what a miracle you are.'

Gil heard what Dad said, but it was like listening to a snatch of dialogue on the television, completely unrelated to anything in Gil's life. The photo of the embryo floated in his mind like an image from a dream and he struggled to make a connection with it. It was the weirdest thing he'd ever had to try and understand, like discovering he was an alien life-form. *That's me,* he told himself. *Those blobs are me. They built me.* Even now he was a collection of microscopic blobs, but there were a hundred trillion of them, all working away quietly to make him Gil. It made no sense.

Dad reached down to the bottom drawer of his desk and pulled out the photo album.

'It was hard on Mum,' he said. 'It was all she thought about for a couple of years. She kept photos of every embryo at the point they were tested for Huntington's Disease.'

He let the album fall open and Gil looked again at the smudgy blobs that he'd assumed were something to do with Dad's research. *Thomas. Imogen. Anna. David.* They were not mice or rabbits or guinea pigs. They were his brothers and sisters, all the brothers and sisters he'd never had, all the children Mum and Dad had never had.

'What happened to them?' Gil asked.

'They don't exist any more. We had four failed attempts at IVF before we had you – eight embryos that were put back inside Mum but miscarried shortly afterwards. Those are the ones she gave names to. I thought it was a bad idea, but she insisted. They were so real to her. You had a twin sister who died in the womb when she was twelve weeks old and nearly killed you too. And the others – when you were born, we let them go. We felt you were enough.'

'You let them die, you mean.'

'They weren't human beings yet, Gil. They were just cell clusters. They didn't feel any pain. They didn't know anything about it.'

'But they *would* have been human beings, wouldn't they? They would have turned out exactly like me.'

'Not exactly like you,' said Dad. 'You're unique. You're Gil.'

Gil closed his eyes and listened to Dad breathing quietly. Was it possible to cry if you had your eyes shut? But he wasn't going to cry, he didn't need to cry. He thought of the photos in Dad's secret album. *Why me?* he wondered. Why was he here and not Thomas or Imogen or any of the dozens of others who'd been kick-started into life and then never allowed to grow up? It was like the scene at the end of *Titanic*, the scene with hundreds of people floating frozen and dead in a dark sea. Gil was the one who was rescued, the only one who was pulled to safety, the random survivor. Everyone else was dead.

And now Mum – Dad was telling him that Mum was – she was . . .

'What's going to happen to Mum?' Gil managed to say.

'We don't know.'

'Is she ill or not? Has she got this – this Huntington's Disease or not?'

'Gil, we don't know. I promise you we don't know. We

made a decision not to find out. All we did was check to make sure that any child we had would be free from the disease.'

'But Mum could find out if she was ill?'

'Yes.'

'So why doesn't she?'

'Because she doesn't want to know.'

'Why not? I would!'

'Are you sure?' Dad's voice was warm and strong. 'You would risk being told that you had a disease that is completely inescapable, and that currently has no cure? Mum felt it would be like living on death row. She decided it was better just to wait and see what happened. But of course it becomes harder and harder the older she gets, and we didn't really anticipate that. She's about the same age now as her mother was when she started to show signs of illness. Whenever Mum thinks she's getting a symptom of the disease she panics. It's triggered by little things, like —'

'Like dropping a plate,' Gil said suddenly.

'Yes, exactly. The early symptoms of Huntington's are things like clumsiness and forgetfulness. Every time Mum drops something or forgets something she thinks she might be getting ill, even though it might well be nothing sinister at all.'

'But how would she find out? Is there a test?'

'Yes, it's quite simple. I could even do it in my lab, if I wanted to. You just take a sample of cells and separate out the DNA, then use a technique that makes lots of copies of the gene you want to test for, in this case gene IT-15. Huntington's Disease is caused when this gene is faulty and —'

'IT-15? That was on the labels for your mice in the lab, wasn't it?'

'Well remembered,' said Dad softly. 'Now maybe you can understand what I'm trying to do there.'

There was a moment where Gil saw the shock before he felt it, the way you always see the lightning flash before you hear the rumble of thunder. Then the room heaved under him as if bombs were exploding all around him. The mental world he had lived in for so long began to topple and collapse. His view of Dad, his view of Mum, his view of Jude, his view of himself – he watched it all changing, shifting, falling.

Dad was researching Huntington's Disease. He was trying to find a cure for the illness that might kill Mum, the illness that had destroyed Granny's brain so that she no longer recognised even her own daughter. That was what the mice were for. The mice were there to try and save Mum's life.

'Gil,' said Dad after a while. 'Talk to me. Are you all right?'

Gil didn't reply. He sat, stunned, and listened to the explosions as they continued in his head. One thought hung clear above the debris. How long did he have to stop Jude? How was he going to stop Jude?

'I've got to tell Jude,' Gil said. He thought he'd said it in his head, until he saw Dad's eyebrows knot together.

'Jude? Who's Jude?'

'No one,' said Gil.

'What do you mean, *no one*? Who is he? Is he that

213

appalling man who nearly got you arrested?'

'No,' said Gil. He couldn't really focus on what Dad was saying. The room seemed full of dust and smoke.

'You're hiding something from me, aren't you? What is it? What the hell have you got involved in? I insist that you tell me.'

'*Hiding* something,' said Gil slowly. '*Hiding* something. God, Dad, that's a joke, isn't it, coming from you? You've just told me – oh my God . . .' Gil clenched his teeth as a sudden shuddering rage surged upwards from his belly. 'Bloody hell. I can't – I can't . . . You've known this stuff my whole life – my *entire life*, for God's sake, and you've never told me any of it? And you call *me* a liar? You've lied to me about *everything*, Dad. I hate you. You're just a lying, selfish, smug —'

'Stop it,' snapped Dad. 'Stop that right now. You have *no idea* what it's been like for us. You have no idea how we've tried to protect you —'

'Oh yeah!' Gil leapt up from the chair, breathing hard. 'Well, you've done a really great job, Dad. Because right now I wish you were dead.'

'Grow up,' said Dad. He didn't move. 'Think about other people for once in your life.'

'Oh my God, I wish I could *kill* you. I *hate* you, Dad.'

'I've had enough of this,' said Dad, rising from his desk at last.

'I hate you. I hate you. *I hate you. I HATE YOU!*'

Gil hurled his full weight at Dad. Taken by surprise, Dad staggered back against the chair by his desk. The chair rolled gently away from him and he fell, banging his shoulder on the corner of the desk. Gil kicked the chair violently and it toppled forwards on to Dad's head. Then Gil ran from the study, his throat aching from screaming at Dad, his head howling with pain, tears of fury and terror and shock finally pouring down his face. Through the blur he saw Mum appear out of the kitchen door.

'Gil,' she said, catching his arm. 'Gil, what on earth's happened?'

He wrenched himself away and ran for the stairs.

She called after him. 'Gil!'

He ran, sobbing, and slammed the bedroom door hard behind him. He grabbed at the desk and dragged it across the door. His chest heaved with a life of its own, with gasps and sobs that he could not bring under control. Objects came into view briefly through the distortion of his tears and he picked them up at random and threw them viciously at the desk and the door. He could hear Mum outside, knocking, trying the door, calling urgently.

'Gil, what's the matter? Please let me in. What's happened? Gil?'

Gil sank to the floor at the foot of his bed. His face fell forwards on to his knees and he sat hunched up with his hands curled uselessly at his sides while the eruption inside his chest went on and on and the tears soaked the legs of his jeans.

'Please, Gil. Please let me help.'

But Mum's voice was impossibly far away. There was no one to help him now.

CHAPTER 22

As the storm in his head began to move away, Gil lifted his wet face, wiped his eyes with his hands and listened. There were noises coming from downstairs. After a moment he realised Mum and Dad were talking loudly. Really loudly. No, wait a minute – they were *arguing*. Gil got up with some difficulty and crept to the door. He moved the desk a few centimetres and opened the door a crack so he could hear.

'I don't believe you sometimes, Matt.' Gil couldn't remember ever hearing Mum sound so furious. 'I thought we had an agreement about this.'

'I've told you what happened. I didn't *mean* to tell him. It just came out.'

'You're starting to sound like a bloody teenager yourself.'

'I am not! Rachel, you forget this is just as difficult for me as it is for —'

'Oh, don't you dare. Don't you *dare*. This is *not* just as difficult for you.'

'Well, all right, I'm sorry, but —'

'You're the one who said we should wait till he was older. I wanted to tell him years ago.'

'For God's sake, Rachel, don't start dragging up accusations like that. It's not helpful.'

'But that's what you said! You did! Don't try and deny it now!'

'Yes, because I thought it would be too much for him. I thought it wasn't fair.'

'And how the hell do you think he feels now, with everything dumped on him at once? Tell me that. He's up there, barricaded in his room, crying his bloody eyes out. He won't even *talk* to me.'

'He'll be all right. He'll calm down. It's just teenage hysteria.'

'Matt, how can you *say* that? You're totally contradicting yourself. You know damn well he must have been feeling desperately unhappy even before he found out about all this if he's been bunking off school and lying to us about things.'

'He's not unhappy. He's trying to provoke me. God knows what he's mixed up in, or who this Jude character is —'

'That is just not relevant right now. Right now we have to stop him spiralling off into total despair.'

'No, we have to bring him into line and show him we're in charge.'

'Oh, great. Wonderful. It's really going to help if you're going to go on behaving like a control freak.'

'*What* did you just say?'

'You heard me, Matt. You want to control everything he does and everything he thinks. Well, congratulations. You've made him hate you. And at the moment I'm not sure I like you that much either.'

'Good God. I'm not staying here to be talked to like this.'

'Fine. Walk away from the mess. It'll still be here when you get back, though. Someone's going to have to deal with it.'

The front door slammed so hard that the whole house shook. Gil closed his bedroom door and pushed the desk back against it. Perhaps this was it, he thought unemotionally. Perhaps Dad had walked out and would never come back. He had never in all his life heard his parents have a row like that.

He stood for a long time examining the surface of his desk, not thinking of much at all. There was a big new dent, he noticed, from an object he'd hurled in anger, possibly one of the speakers for his MP3 player. He ran his fingers over the sharp edges of the dent, trying to smooth it and fill it, but it made no difference. The hole was raw and deep and irreversible.

Mum was coming up the stairs again. He heard her pause outside his room, but she didn't try the door.

'Gil, can I make you something to eat?' she said. It was such a normal question he couldn't think how to answer. Was he hungry or not?

'Gil?'

'No,' Gil said at last, hoarsely. 'No, I don't think I'm hungry.'

'Gil, I'm really, really sorry. You were never meant to find out like this.'

'No,' said Gil. The dent in the desk was really bothering him. He tried wedging his little finger in the triangular hole.

'Can I come in and talk to you?'

'Uh – not now. Later. I'm all right, Mum. I just want to be on my own.'

'Oh. OK.'

She padded away down the stairs again. Gil was grateful to her for swallowing such a blatant lie. There was no way she could believe he was all right. But he really didn't want to talk to Mum right now. He needed to think.

Think. Think.

He curled up on his bed and fell asleep as suddenly as if someone had hit him over the head with a cricket bat.

He dreamed of chaos. People ran shouting through dark corridors. Torches flashed, alarms howled, a door was kicked in. A curtain of plastic strips blazed in dripping flames and beyond was the stamping of terrified feet in cages. There was something behind the big silver door of the fridge – something waiting; he could not see what it was, but it was coming for him. It was going to snap his neck as if he were a mouse, and Mum was not there. He could hear her a long way away, banging furiously on the door, but she couldn't get in.

He woke up sweating and terrified and with one thought in his mind. *I've got to tell Jude . . .*

But what, exactly, was he going to tell Jude? Was he going to try and persuade him to abandon the raid on the labs?

Right this instant Gil wanted the raid to go ahead more

than ever. He wanted Jude to smash the labs into rubble. It would be revenge on Dad, revenge on his smugness and rightness, revenge for his secrets, for the lies he had told and the truth he had not told. He deserved that level of destruction.

But Dad's mice – when Gil thought about Dad's mice all he could see was Mum. He saw Mum sitting in the pan of a giant pair of old-fashioned scales, while mice fell one at a time like chocolate drops into the pan on the other side. Gil let himself think about Mum. He thought about her for a long time. If she was ill, if she was going to become like Granny and slowly slip away into a place where she could not remember who Dad was or who Gil was or even who she was herself, how many mice would he sacrifice to stop that happening? How many diseased mice would he make if he thought it might save Mum? A hundred? A thousand? A million? How many mice was Mum worth? Was it even possible to weigh lives against each other like that?

There were no answers. If the raid went ahead, Dad's research would be destroyed, and with it the hope of helping Mum if she was ill. If Gil tried to stop the raid he would be standing up for Dad when he hated Dad more than he had ever hated anyone in his life. Wasn't there anyone he could ask for help? Gil thought of Louis and all the childish messes they had survived together. Louis might have helped him. But he'd screwed things up too badly with Louis, and in any case it would never have been fair to drag Louis into this. The mess was too big and too frightening, and Gil had made it all by himself.

Gil lay in his room, thinking and not thinking, while the day turned into night and the room darkened. Mum came up the stairs from once or twice and asked him questions through the closed door, but he didn't really hear what she was asking, or what he said in reply. At some point he heard that Dad had come back, and Mum and Dad were talking softly together outside his room. He didn't move. It was like being an astronaut floating way above the world with only the sound of his own breathing for company. From time to time he thought about the battered old phone under the bed and wondered about calling Jude, but he couldn't think what he would say to him.

He would have to help himself this time. Gil didn't know if he had the strength. If he was going to act he would have to act tonight, because tomorrow might be too late. But he was terrified. He was terrified, it was dark, and everything he had ever believed about himself and his family lay in ruins.

CHAPTER 23

Sometime after midnight when he was sure Mum and Dad were asleep, Gil made himself act. It took less than ten minutes to pack his school bag with the equipment he needed. He left his desk barricading the bedroom door in case Mum or Dad tried to check on him in the night. Then he went to the window and pushed it open, slipping out of the gap on to the conservatory roof.

After the warmth of the day, Gil was completely unprepared for the chilly wind that swept out of the blackness of the night sky. As he crawled across the roof, the cold cut through his clothes and made him wish he'd put on a couple of extra layers. But he didn't go back. He reached the edge of the wall and dropped neatly into the back garden.

His old bike was still there under the lean-to at the side of the house. Gil pushed it through the front gate, instinctively looking up to see if there were any lights on, if anyone was watching. But the house was dark, and Gil quickly set off through the back streets with his hood up and his head bent.

It was silent and empty everywhere. Gil cycled swiftly through the pools of orange light that fell from the street lamps. His hands got colder and colder until they felt as if they were frozen to the handlebars. The thin plastic gloves he was wearing didn't help at all.

After a while Gil lost his sense of time. He was shaking with cold and pouring with sweat at the same time. Nothing looked familiar, even though Gil was sure he knew where he was going, and when he turned the last corner and saw he'd arrived it was like an electric shock.

Dad's building rose above the splashes of light from the few street lamps, looking more massive than ever. The stone that was so soft and yellow in daylight had turned grey and hard. The smoked glass entrance doors looked like black mirrors, and the steps were in shadow. There were no protesters on the pavement, but Gil knew there would still be security guards patrolling the building.

Gil slipped back around the corner and hid his bike in an alleyway. Then he ran to the bushes that edged the pavement opposite the labs. He crawled behind a bush and began to watch the building. Almost immediately a uniformed guard came out of the narrow road that Dad had driven him down, the one that led to the car park. The guard was being pulled along by a big Alsatian, and Gil could hear the man grumbling as he jerked the lead, trying to hold back the dog. He walked past the front of the labs, turned a corner and disappeared into an area that looked like a small garden. Gil thought he remembered looking down into it from Dad's office, and he scanned the side of the building to see if he could locate Dad's window, but the high walls disappeared into darkness. Moments later he heard voices and then a second guard with a much sleepier-looking dog stepped out of the garden and walked past the labs in the opposite direction, turning down the road to the car park.

For what seemed like hours nothing moved, and Gil began to slip back into the feeling that none of this was really happening. He was asleep, dreaming, and soon he would wake up in his own comfortable bed. He felt his eyelids begin to droop, and then suddenly the big Alsatian staggered round the corner of the building again. Gil jerked awake at once. It felt as if someone had punched him in the stomach. He had to make a run for it now, as soon as this guard turned the corner into the garden, and before the other guard appeared, patrolling the building in the opposite direction.

Gil began to straighten his legs. His knees creaked with the cold and the muscles in his thighs ached as if they were about to snap. As he watched the guard pace slowly across the front of the labs Gil felt something pull sharply at his back and for an instant he thought it was a hand. Just before he yelled out loud he realised it was only one of the straps of his backpack, tangled up in the twigs of the bush. He swore under his breath, wriggling the strap free, and when he looked up again the guard had vanished.

Gil leapt out of the bush and sprinted for his life across the road, past the grand glass entrance, round the corner and down the road towards the car park.

Everything hurt. His legs hurt, his lungs hurt, and the heavy box in his backpack bashed against his spine as he ran. Oh God, no one had seen him, had they? Gil dodged the barrier and ran on. The walls that rose on either side of him were blank and featureless and there was nowhere that would hide him, and the guards would soon be closing in. Gil skidded to a stop and frantically scanned the car park for a hiding place. There was a huge wheelie bin to his left, and Gil would have given anything to be able to climb inside it and collapse on to a pile of rubbish. But he didn't know if he had time, and in any case the guards might hear the lid slam. So instead he scuttled round the back of the bin and hugged the wall, praying the dogs didn't sniff him out.

The clump of boots on tarmac got louder and louder and Gil began to hear the wheezing of the guard's Alsatian. Then he could hear the guard muttering under his breath, and eventually a few words.

' . . . *stupid* bloody dog, stop *pulling* for Pete's sake, or I'll take you to the bloody river and drown you, you mutt. And get away from that rubbish bin! How many times do I have to tell you!'

There was a snuffling on the opposite side of the bin and then a sharp yelp from the dog.

'Serves you right. Now behave.'

'Go easy on him,' said a different voice. 'He's only young.'

'You wanna swap? He's a pain in the arse.'

'All right. But this one's half asleep, I warn you.'

Please, please just get on with it, Gil howled inside his head, hunched behind the bin. He wanted a pee so badly he thought his bladder might explode. Then the voices stopped and the footsteps started to fade. He peered over the top of the wheelie bin and saw a guard plodding away past the door to the back of the labs.

Gil ripped the bag off his back and pulled out the box that contained Dad's keys. Stealing it from the study for a second time had felt much easier, even though it meant having to wear those revolting plastic gloves again. Gil dropped the keys in his pocket, hung the magnetic door release pendant round his neck and shoved the box back into his bag. Then as the guard turned the corner of the building he stood up and ran towards the door.

This is where it all goes wrong, a voice said in Gil's head as he ran. Here he was, breaking into a building at half past one in the morning when he should have been fast asleep. The feeling of unreality was so overwhelming he wanted to laugh. There was the back door, almost within reach, but as Gil stretched out his hand the door was suddenly flooded with light and he stopped, bewildered. It was as if someone had just switched on the sun. It took him a few seconds to realise there was security lighting that came on as soon as you got too near the building. Why the hell hadn't he expected that? Well, at least it meant he could see the keyholes.

Gil pulled Dad's keys out of his pocket with shaking hands. There seemed to be about a million keys on the keyring and every time Gil grasped one it slid out of his fingers because of the slimy plastic gloves. At last both locks were opened and Gil pulled the handle as hard as he could. The door opened so easily it almost knocked him flying. Gil fell through the opening and the door swung shut behind him. Immediately he was thrown into darkness. And at once the panel on the wall started bleeping and little red warning lights flashed everywhere.

He'd triggered the burglar alarm.

He hadn't forgotten about the burglar alarm, of course, but last time he'd been here with Dad all the lights had been on. Now it was completely and utterly dark apart from the tiny flashes of red from the alarm panel. A towering wave of fear crashed over Gil and swept away the memory of what he was supposed to do next. He scrabbled frantically at the shut door and couldn't find any way to get it open again to let some light in. There was a torch in his bag, but how long would it take to find it? In about thirty seconds every siren in the place would be shrieking like crazy. *No-no-no!* screamed a voice in his head. *Get out get out get out get out get out!*

As Gil clawed uselessly at the shut door another voice spoke inside his head. *Sigma*, it said, very calmly and clearly. Of course, *Sigma*. The code for the burglar alarm was *Sigma*. He didn't need light to disable the alarm. He could do it with his eyes shut. Gil leapt over to the panel on the wall. It went on bleeping relentlessly, like a countdown to blast-off. The keypad glowed a mysterious white, and Gil could just make out the numbers, arranged in just the way he'd seen them on the phone when he'd told Jude what *Sigma* looked like. Quickly he punched in the pattern. Five digits, 3-1-5-7-9. If he was wrong . . .

The bleeping stopped.

Gil's legs gave way and he dropped to the ground in a heap, overtaken by panic. It gripped his stomach and twisted it until Gil was ready to throw up. His lungs gulped for air and he was aware of a tear trickling sideways out of the corner of his eye and dripping over his nose and into his ear while he rocked himself on the hard floor. Then just as suddenly the terror had gone, and Gil lay there in the dark while the shaking gradually subsided. He wondered why no one was coming to find him. He'd managed to stop the burglar alarm, but the guards must have seen the security light blazing away in the darkness outside. Or perhaps the light had gone off, and they had no idea that Gil was inside.

Before he'd left home, Gil had thought through two options and both of them now seemed crushingly stupid. It had all seemed straightforward in the safety of his bedroom. Plan A was to go to the labs, break in, find Dad's mice and steal them before Jude did. Plan B, if he bottled out of Plan A, was just to get the back door open, trigger the alarm and run, so that Jude's chances of raiding the labs would be ruined. Plan A was clearly madness, now he was actually here. He couldn't climb all the way up to the animal rooms and save Dad's mice. How would he get them out of the labs? He could hide them somewhere, maybe, but the thought of the journey up to the top of the building filled Gil with a feeling of hopelessness. It was too difficult.

But now he'd seriously messed up Plan B. He'd deactivated the alarms so they wouldn't go off. The back door would only stay open if he held it open, and there didn't seem to be a way of drawing attention to the break-in without getting himself into serious trouble. Gil didn't even know *how* to open the door from the inside – he hadn't paid any attention at all when he'd left the building with Dad. He rolled over on to his knees and got to his feet to examine the door, and at once he heard voices coming from the other side.

Panic blazed under Gil's ribs again. It was the guards, coming to find out what was going on. Angrily he squashed the fear down into his guts. He had to find somewhere to hide and that could only mean going deeper into the labs. Gil ran towards the door just up the corridor and fumbled again with Dad's keys until he found the one that worked. Outside he could hear the voices muttering, and there was a little thump on the back door behind him. Then Gil was through the door, and rushing to the next one. He touched the pad on the wall with the silver disc on Dad's pendant and the door slowly hummed open. Then he dived into the small space under the stairs beyond and waited.

Through the glass windows in the inner doors Gil could see a wedge of torchlight that grew wider as the back door opened. The beam shone straight down the corridor and made it impossible to see who was behind it. It moved past the first door and then, as the next door opened, the voices spilled out, sounding much too loud in the darkness. The torch beam swung wildly and Gil shrank as far back as he could and listened to what the voices were saying.

'Can you believe they didn't set the bloody alarm?'

'Those dogs were a total pushover.'

'I told you, didn't I? Piece of cake.'

'You don't think there's somebody in here, do you? Waiting for us?'

'They've got a bit of a shock coming if they are. There's some rope left over, isn't there, and gaffer tape?'

'Yeah, sorted.'

'So let's get on with it, eh? Just keep your eyes open.'

A familiar chuckle came out of the darkness and Gil held his breath to stop himself gasping out loud.

It wasn't the guards at all. It was Jude.

Jude took the stairs two at a time and was gone. Gil tried to count the people who followed him but quickly lost track. Six, was it, or seven? They merged into one long blur, like a giant maggot lolloping up the steps, and then Gil was alone in the silence.

He lay back under the stairs, utterly defeated. His plans had failed. All he could do now was raise the alarm and get Jude arrested, or walk away and leave him to liberate the mice that might be Mum's only hope.

Or perhaps, thought Gil, sitting up again, perhaps there was an alternative. Maybe he could stop Jude taking the mice. If Gil got there first he could move Dad's mice to a safe place. And if there wasn't time for that – well, Jude was still his friend, after all. Gil could argue with him, explain everything, beg him to take all the animals except the ones that Dad needed. It was a very long shot. But Jude would listen, wouldn't he, when he saw how desperate Gil was?

Gil began to creep up the steps after Jude and his gang.

He didn't dare to use the torch in his backpack. Instead he replayed the memory of the video he'd taken for Jude. You went up and up the stairs until they reached the landing where the toilets were. Then it was straight on, through the automatic doors and past the room where Dad made his mouse embryos. Gil found that every single automatic door he came to had been propped open, so there was no need to use the pendant. He carried on down the corridor, through more open doors, and left to another set of stairs. When you got to the top you went right . . . or was it left? Gil stopped uncertainly at the bottom of the staircase. It wasn't quite pitch dark. Faint streaks of light came from panels set into the ceiling, and ghostly fire exit signs pointed back the way he had come.

As Gil stood trying to make up his mind, feet pounded on the floor directly above and he managed to jump backwards out of the way as someone clattered down the stairs and charged past him. They were gone in a moment, breathing hard with effort, but Gil thought he'd seen a big box in their arms. There was a torch strapped to the person's head, and the beam of light bounced and wobbled ahead of them as they raced away from Gil down the corridor.

Without allowing himself time to think, Gil ran up the stairs and turned right, immediately diving into a side corridor as a second person hurtled past with a full box. This time he caught a glimpse of a rabbit's head with scared eyes gleaming red in the light from the headtorch. He kept going, along the corridor and up another flight of steps, watching out for the headtorches that gave him advance warning that someone was coming.

Then Gil heard footsteps behind him as well as in front of him, and guessed that the first person must be coming back for another cargo of animals. He slumped back into an alcove that was hardly a hiding place at all, but somehow nobody saw him. The two people shot past each other in the corridor, mumbling something under their breaths, and were gone in opposite directions.

By the time Gil reached the curtain of plastic strips that led to the animal rooms he was exhausted. He hid under a workbench in the washroom as yet another person burst into the room and puffed away with a box full of animals. It felt as if Jude's helpers had multiplied into thousands of shapes in the gloom. They were all dressed in black, they all wore balaclavas and gloves and torches on their foreheads, they all had the same big plastic storage boxes. Gil slipped through the air shower and the plastic curtain and into the room where the rabbits were kept, wary of bumping into someone. But there was no one there. All the hutch doors swung open. The sandpit was empty. The rabbits were gone, and he knew the mice would be next.

Gil stood hesitating at the entrance to the room where Dad kept his mice, listening and hearing nothing, and then he went in.

Empty mouse boxes lay in heaps everywhere. There was a smell of mouse pee and sawdust. Between the rows of cabinets where the mice lived knelt a figure who was pulling out drawer after drawer, scooping out the mice and dropping them into a big box next to him. The headtorch dipped and swayed as he moved. There was nothing to distinguish him from the other shadowy figures that Gil had seen flashing past him in the corridors, but Gil knew at once that this would be Jude.

Gil stepped behind the stacks of mice while he tried to think what to do. He heard someone come into the room, panting loudly, and there was a clatter that he guessed was their empty storage box dropping on the floor.

'Here you go,' said Jude's voice. 'Tell the others we're nearly done. Only two more after this, I reckon.'

There was a grunt and then the noise of the plastic curtain strips slapping together. Quietly Gil moved up behind the rows of drawers. On the other side of them Jude was steadily getting closer and closer to Dad's mice. It was too late to rescue the mice without confronting Jude. And when he sees it's me, thought Gil, what will he do?

He stood there for a moment, sick with a fear that was not like the fear he'd had of the guards and the Alsatians. He wasn't afraid that Jude would hurt him. He was afraid that Jude would laugh at him, ignore him, push him aside, tell him he was just a kid. He was afraid that Jude would have too many answers. The fear made his head swirl. Gil swallowed a few times, pushed back his hood and stepped out in front of Jude.

CHAPTER 24

Jude glanced up for a fraction of a second and then went on lifting mice out of drawers. The big box in front of him was heaving with mice – squeaking, nipping, clambering over each other, falling on their backs and getting up again.

'Not quite finished with this lot yet,' he said, and then he looked up at Gil properly. The beam of light from the headtorch shone right in Gil's eyes and he had to close them. He heard Jude swear softly, several times.

'Gil,' he said, 'what the hell are you doing here?'

'I need to talk to you,' Gil said very fast, without opening his eyes. The insides of his eyelids glowed blood-red in the torchlight.

'You what? Bloody hell, you pick your moment, don't you. Can't it wait till I'm a little less busy?'

'No,' said Gil. 'Can you move your torch a bit? I can't see.'

The light dropped away and Gil blinked his eyes open.

'Well, crack on with it, then, I haven't got all day,' said Jude.

Gil tried to judge whether Jude was being friendly, but it was impossible to tell from his voice alone, and the expression on his face was hidden under the same black balaclava that Gil had seen in the photo above his desk. Even Jude's eyes were invisible. As Gil struggled to put some words together one of Jude's gang whipped through the curtain into the room. He stopped dead when he saw Gil, but without even turning round Jude put up a hand.

'It's all right, it's all right,' he said calmly. 'Everything's under control here. Just give us some space for a minute, will you?'

The figure vanished again, like a black ghost.

'You followed us in, did you?' said Jude in the same calm voice. 'I guess you worked out we'd be here tonight?'

'I didn't follow you. I was here first,' Gil said.

Jude's head jerked in surprise. 'Don't be stupid,' he said sharply.

'I was the one who turned off the burglar alarm,' Gil said. 'It was off when you came in, remember? I heard you talking about it.'

'Oh my God. Never work with children or animals, isn't that what they say?' Jude laughed, and the torchlight moved from side to side across the box of squirming mice. 'You thought you'd be a hero, did you, and do your own raid? You could have screwed the whole bloody thing up for us, do you realise that?'

'Yes,' said Gil. 'That's what I wanted to do. I wanted to stop you.'

The mice squeaked and rustled in the silence.

'Oh, come on, Gil,' said Jude, in a voice that sounded dangerously quiet. 'Don't let me down, mate. We planned this together, you and me. Why do you want to ruin it now? You don't want these animals to suffer any more, do you?'

'You can have all of them,' Gil said. 'I really don't care. I just want you to leave the ones in these boxes, that's all.' He put his hand on the stacks that held Dad's mice.

'Oh,' said Jude. The torchlight flicked to the tiny clipboards on the front of the drawers. 'So these are your dad's little victims, are they? I thought you couldn't stand your dad. So why would you want to stop me taking his mice?'

'Because – because I've just found out my mum might have a really horrible disease and my dad's trying to find a cure. He's using the mice to find a cure. Please, Jude. Leave them.'

'Oh, I get it.' Jude laughed again. It was not a good sound. 'You've decided you're against torturing animals in experiments unless your mum's life happens to be at stake. *All animals are equal but some are more equal than others*, is that it?'

Gil almost stopped breathing. Jude had too many answers. There was no way to argue with him. Panic started to rise up Gil's legs. Jude was going to take all the mice, and there was nothing he would be able to do to stop him.

'No creature deserves to suffer and die to save the life of anyone, not even your mum,' said Jude. 'I'm sorry to say this, but your mum is no more special than anyone else.'

'She *is* special!'

'Really? How about my mum, then? Or your best friend's

mum? Or the bloke next door's mum? We've all got mums, you know. They're all special.'

'Jude, you're not listening to me!'

'In any case, these experiments don't work. Mice aren't people. Trying to cure a diseased mouse won't help your mum. It's a complete bloody waste of time. You might as well let me take them.'

'*Please!*'

'Sorry, Gil. It's got to be done. It's what we came for. This is the revolution, brother.'

Jude stood up and reached a hand towards one of Dad's drawers. Without a thought in his head Gil stepped forwards and pushed him hard. Jude stumbled back, almost tripping over the box of mice behind him, and Gil stepped into the space between him and Dad's mice.

'Just leave them,' Gil said, as firmly as he could manage.

'You're a good kid,' said Jude slowly, 'and you mean well, but you don't know what you're messing with. Now, just step back.'

'No.'

'Get out of my way,' Jude said, and Gil saw his lips move in the hole of the balaclava.

'*No.*'

Gil pressed himself back against the drawers of mice. An instant later his head hit the wall with a bang and he fell in a heap on the floor. It took several seconds to work out that Jude had picked him up and thrown him aside as if he was just a big stuffed toy.

'I'm sorry,' Jude said from somewhere above him. 'But I did warn you.'

As Gil's head began to throb, everything seemed to happen in slow motion. He lay slumped on the floor at the base of the wall and watched Jude's arm, lit by the torch beam, moving through the air towards the drawers of mice. On the wall above him Gil could see a square lump, lit up in the torchlight. He stared at the lump, puzzled, trying to work out what it was. At last he realised it was a fire alarm. And then, suddenly, he knew what he could do. He pushed himself to his feet and raised a fist, and just before he began to move he saw Jude tense up, preparing for attack.

'Don't, Gil,' Jude said, almost kindly. 'I really don't want to hurt you.'

Gil swung his fist backwards, and the edge of his hand smashed into the fire alarm.

The sound unleashed by the sirens made Gil feel as if his head was being smacked against the wall again and again. He saw Jude start to put his hands to his ears, and then grab the big box of mice and run from the room.

Gil nearly cried with relief. Dad's mice were safe. He leant back against the wall for a moment, his head jangling so badly from the noise and the bump Jude had given him that it took a moment to notice that his left hand hurt too, the one he'd used to break the glass on the fire alarm.

Gil fumbled in his bag to find the torch. When he switched it on he saw blood pouring from the side of his hand, halfway between the little finger and the wrist. He watched as his palm slowly began to fill with a pool of red under the plastic glove. Then Gil realised that the glove must have split somewhere, because blood was also dripping steadily on to the floor. There were already big splodges of blood on his jeans. The sight of the thick dark liquid shocked him into action. It was the middle of the night. The alarms were going off in a building he should never have been in. Jude had fled, and the police would be on their way. And Gil was marooned at the top of the labs, leaking blood and waiting to be caught red-handed.

He ran. In the washroom he grabbed a roll of kitchen paper and wound it round his damaged hand while he skidded through the corridors to the top of the stairs. Then he stopped, battered by the shriek of the sirens. If the police were coming, would he be able to make it to the back door before they trapped him? Oh God, he didn't want to be caught. Gil thought of the smell of the police car, days and days and days ago, and a morsel of sick started to rise up in his throat. But if he didn't go down the stairs there was nowhere to go. He didn't know any other way out.

Gil stood there helplessly while signals rocketed up and down the pathways inside his brain. He found himself wondering why the luminous fire escape signs on the wall were all pointing the wrong way. *You're wasting time, moron,* he told himself desperately. Why was it that you always noticed stupid, irrelevant things, especially when you needed to concentrate? The arrows didn't point down the stairs, they all pointed back the way he'd come, back to the animal rooms. It was crazy. Except of course . . .

Gil thought of Dad's office, and wheeled round suddenly. He had the key. That was it. He charged back through the corridors, the walls and floors and ceilings all vibrating with noise. It was left and left again as you came out of the washroom. Gil flashed his torch up at every door he passed, although he knew exactly which one was Dad's.

Dr Matthew Walker. Gil yanked the keys out of his pocket and shone the torch on them, but he couldn't think which keys he'd already used for the doors downstairs. The howl of the sirens assaulted him in wave after wave of sound and Gil had to try every key on the ring at least twice before he got the one that fitted. As he burst through the door into Dad's office he took a big sobbing gulp of air and headed straight for the window.

Then the smell of the room hit him. It was familiar somehow, like coming home after a long holiday. Gil sniffed, and as the smell filled his nose he knew suddenly it was Dad. A bit of aftershave, a bit of coffee, a clean shirt, warm skin, proper fountain pen ink, just a hint of mouse pee – Gil had a memory of sitting on Dad's lap when he must have been quite small. Dad was holding him while he cried. His foot was hurting. Gil had buried his face in Dad's chest and smelt his smell. *Don't worry, Gil. Your body will mend it. Your body is so clever.*

As Gil hesitated in front of the window he looked back at the picture above Dad's desk. That's me, thought Gil. He stared up at the cluster of cells, and could not begin to understand how he had travelled all the distance that lay between those specks of nothing and the person who stood in Dad's office with the scream of the sirens filling his head.

Go, he thought. Before you run out of time.

The window slid open fairly easily. There was plenty of

room to get through. Gil fiddled with the box under the window, trying to release the escape ladder. Inside the box, the ladder was packed in a neat roll. Gil pulled it out and hurled it through the window. The ladder didn't feel heavy enough, even though the entire thing was made of metal chains with metal rungs fixed across them. He heard the ladder rattle against the wall as it fell, and quickly he swung one leg and then the other out over the windowsill and found a foothold on a rung.

Then he stopped. One hand gripped the chain of the ladder but his injured left hand was too thickly wrapped in kitchen paper to be able to hold on to anything. Gil ripped at the paper with his teeth and it came away in blood-soaked lumps and fell to the ground far below. Immediately his hand began to bleed again but he made himself start to descend the ladder, feeling the blood drip warmly on his face every now and again. The ladder swung slightly and scraped the smooth stone wall.

Gil felt as if the descent would go on for ever. This was his existence now. There were no more choices to make. There was nothing but the stinging smell of the metal chains, and the drip of the blood from his hand, and the feel of his foot poking the empty air to find the next rung. The screams of the fire alarms were muffled, but other noises pushed their way into his head: dogs barking somewhere below, and police sirens in the distance. He took no notice. He just had to keep going down the ladder. That was all.

Without warning, Gil's foot touched something hard and flat and for a moment he couldn't work out what it was. It felt nothing like the metal rungs pressing into the soles of his feet. Then it dawned on him that it was the ground. He had reached the ground. Gil let go of the chains of the ladder and collapsed on to his side. The dogs sounded closer now. He should get up and run back to his bike before the dogs came. But he lay there for a minute longer, and the dogs didn't come, although they still barked. The guards didn't appear either. Gil wondered what Jude had done to them. He sat up carefully and found he was lying in the little garden that he had seen from Dad's window, the one he had watched the guards walk through on their patrol of the building.

Slowly, Gil picked himself up and began to make his way to the road. His legs were too shaky to run and so he stumbled as fast as he could away from the building, round the corner and back to the alleyway where he'd left the bike. The road that ran past the labs was empty and silent. There was no sign of Jude, no sign of the police, no sign of anyone. But the police sirens were getting louder.

Gil knew he would have to bandage his hand again somehow, otherwise he would leave a trail of blood that would lead the police straight to him, like Hansel and Gretel following the pebbles home through the wood. He couldn't think of anything to use as a bandage except the T-shirt he was wearing under his hoodie, so he stripped quickly to the waist and stood there shuddering with cold while he peeled off the gloves and dumped them and wrapped the T-shirt firmly round his hand. Then he pulled the hoodie back on, flipped up the hood and pushed his bike out of the alley.

At first Gil couldn't balance on the bike at all. His legs didn't feel part of him any more, and when he finally managed to stay on the saddle his legs didn't remember how to pedal. *Push. Now. Down. Up. That's it. Push.* About five minutes after leaving the alley he heard the police cars race up a street parallel to him, and he caught a flash of the blue lights of a fire engine at the end of a side road. He kept going, head down, the freezing air pouring through his hoodie and chilling him to the bone. *Push. Push. Push.*

When at last Gil fell off his bike in the driveway that led up to his front door, the house still looked reassuringly dark and silent. He parked his bike under the lean-to and scrambled in over the conservatory roof. Twice he nearly slid back off the roof. It was almost impossible with only one good hand, and the slightest touch to his left hand made it hurt like crazy. As Gil dropped through the bedroom window, a blanket of weariness fell over him and it was all he could do not to crawl into bed just as he was and give up. But he couldn't give up; he hadn't finished. He had to put all Dad's things back where they belonged before Dad discovered they were missing. He reached up to pull the rucksack off his back and yelped quietly with pain.

Carefully, Gil touched his hand. If he didn't sort that out first he was going to bleed everywhere again. The desk still blocked his bedroom door and he had to hook a foot around one of the legs to drag it away. It made far too much noise, and Gil made himself listen at his bedroom door for a while in case Mum or Dad had heard anything. Then he kicked off his trainers and tiptoed across the dark landing to the bathroom, where he locked the door behind him before he switched on the light.

Gil held his hand over the basin while he unwrapped the T-shirt. It was soaked with blood. He threw the T-shirt in the bath and began to run his hand under the cold tap. The stream of water immediately turned scarlet and the wound began to ache even more intensely. The gash was deep, so deep that it would not stop bleeding no matter how much water he ran over it. Maybe it needed stitching. Gil worried briefly about bleeding to death. He rummaged through the bathroom cabinet for wads of cotton wool and a roll of bandage and bound up the wound as tightly as possible. The T-shirt would just have to stay where it was, he thought. He could always claim he'd had a nose bleed.

Just before Gil switched off the light he glanced at himself in the mirror. He looked dreadful. There were bloodstains on his face but he decided to leave them there to back up his nose bleed story. There was also a spot of blood on the silver door-release pendant that still hung round his neck. He washed it as thoroughly as he could with one hand and dropped it into a towel.

Then he crept downstairs to Dad's study.

He'd dumped the gloves in the alley near the labs, so this time Gil used the towel to handle everything he put back in the drawer. It was awkward, and at one point he dropped Dad's keys with a gigantic crash that sent him scuttling away from the desk in a panic. No one came, and he had got as far as locking the desk drawer and was struggling to push the key back behind the photo frame without leaving fingerprints on anything when the phone suddenly started to ring in the front room.

In the quiet house it sounded as loud as the sirens Gil had set off in Dad's building, and it went on and on. When the answerphone clicked in there was a little pause before the ringing began again almost immediately. It wasn't going to stop until someone answered it. Gently Gil pushed the study door closed and stood with his back against it. *Please,* he pleaded. *I've had enough now. Let me stop.*

He heard the creak of a door above him, and then someone stepping very softly down the stairs. A few seconds later the ringing stopped in the front room and Gil heard Dad's voice, low and sleepy and muffled through the wall.

He took his chance to escape from the study, slipping upstairs and back into his room, where he put the backpack under the desk and climbed into bed just as he was. He left the door ajar so it looked exactly the way Dad would have seen it as he'd passed the room on his way down to answer the phone.

Gil pulled the duvet over himself. He lay on his back with his eyes wide open and tried to relax, but it was impossible. His whole body screamed with shock. Every pulse of blood in his injured hand felt like a fresh bruise and his mind jangled with voices and sirens and flashing lights. He felt Jude push him aside again and his skull rang with pain as it hit the wall. He felt mouse feet running over him. He was buried in mice. They would suffocate him. The feeling was so strong that Gil had to sit up and take a gulp of air. Then he heard Dad's feet on the stairs and quickly lay down again, turning away from the door and pulling the covers up to hide his clothes. The footsteps stopped by the bedroom door and Gil tried to fake sleep while he listened to Dad's breathing and imagined him looking in through the partly-open door.

'Gil?' Dad whispered at last.

Gil lay completely still until he heard Dad give a sigh and shuffle away.

The numbers on the alarm clock next to his bed shone red in the darkness. It was three o'clock in the morning.

What have I done? thought Gil.

He drifted in and out of sleep. Several times he jerked awake as if someone was holding his head under water and he was about to drown. When the clock said half past four Gil woke properly and knew that it was useless trying to get back to sleep. His jeans were as heavy as chain mail, and his feet were freezing. For a while he tried to warm his feet by gripping them one at a time behind his knees. He longed to be able to get up and wander into Mum and Dad's room, like he used to when he was little and had a nightmare. Dad would always sleepily roll out of bed without protest and go off to Gil's bed and Gil could climb into the warm hollow he'd left behind and fall asleep in safety. But he was much too old for that now.

Thoughts ran crazily through his head in a continuous flood. He had saved Dad's mice. He had got his own back on Dad. He had committed a serious crime. He had let Jude down and now Jude would despise him. He should have let the mice go free. He'd been brave. He'd been unbelievably stupid. He would get away with it and no one would ever find out. He would be hunted down and sent to prison. Dad would forgive him. Dad would hate him for ever.

He lay and gazed at the ceiling as the night crawled through hours of nothingness towards morning.

CHAPTER 25

After an impossibly long time, the birds started to sing. Gil lay in bed, his undamaged hand tucked under his pillow. At last he heard the small sounds that meant someone else in the house was getting up – the click of the bathroom door and the toilet flushing and the hot water tank in Gil's cupboard hissing as it filled up. He waited, listening, until he was sure that Mum and Dad had both got up and gone downstairs. Then he slid out of bed slowly. He struggled out of his stained jeans and stuffed them into the drawer under his bed. He found some pyjama bottoms and changed his hoodie for a clean T-shirt.

Then he touched the side of his hand. It was sore, but he couldn't see any blood leaking through the dressing. Slowly Gil began to unwrap the bandage until he could see the cotton wool underneath. There was a lot of blood but it didn't look fresh any more. All the cotton wool balls except one fell away. The last one was stuck in the cut, and he had to use a pair of scissors to snip away the fibres. When he had finished there was a hole over a centimetre long in the side of his hand, matted with hairs from the cotton wool. Gil slipped out to the bathroom and searched for a plaster that would cover the cut without looking too dramatic. He looked at the T-shirt in the bath. Oh yes, nose bleed. He would wander downstairs as if it was a normal Sunday morning, and then . . .

Gil gazed at his face in the mirror. The blood looked unconvincing, splattered in all the wrong places for a nose bleed. What was he going to do when he got downstairs and saw Mum and Dad? There had been a phone call for Dad in the middle of the night. It could only have been about the raid on the labs. Of course Gil would pretend to be surprised when Dad broke the news, but what if Dad saw through him? What if he started to probe for information? *You set this up, didn't you? Come on, Gil, I'm not stupid. Tell me what you've been up to.* Even yesterday Dad had been on the brink of working out who Jude was. This morning it would be blindingly obvious that Gil was involved somehow. How could Dad miss it?

He began to wash the dried blood off his face with one hand.

When Gil finally forced himself to go down to the kitchen he found Mum and Dad sitting quietly at the table drinking tea and coffee. It was only half past eight, but they were both dressed, and they looked up as Gil came in stretching and yawning strenuously as if he'd just woken up.

But he saw Dad's face and stopped at once. Dad looked as if he'd been in a fight. There were puffy circles under his eyes and his dark hair fell limply away from his forehead. For the first time Gil noticed it was streaked with grey.

'Hello, Gil,' Mum said. 'Did you sleep OK?'

Gil gave up his play-acting and slid on to an empty chair.

'Uh – not so well, actually,' he said.

'Did the phone disturb you?'

'No, I had a nose bleed. What happened with the phone?'

For a dreadful moment Gil thought Dad was going to cry. Mum put a hand on Dad's arm and spoke for him.

'It was the police,' she said. 'They phoned about three o'clock this morning. There's been a raid on the labs and the research animals have been stolen.'

Gil waited for Dad to say something, but he gazed deep into his coffee and said nothing at all.

'Oh,' Gil said at last. 'I'm sorry.'

'Yes,' said Dad, thinly. 'I bet you are.'

Gil flinched. It was like being stung by a wasp. Mum leant forwards, her face full of concern, and gave Dad's arm a little shake.

'Come on, Matt,' she said. 'I know you had a terrible row yesterday and we're all in shock, but —'

'No,' said Dad. He shook his head. 'Gil doesn't care. He doesn't give a stuff about my research. He probably thinks this is the best news he's had in ages. Don't you?' He flashed a bitter look at Gil.

Gil looked away.

'Don't you?' repeated Dad. 'In fact, I don't suppose this

raid has even come as much of a surprise to you, has it?'

Gil felt sick. Dad suspected him. This was exactly what he'd dreaded.

'I don't know what you're on about, Dad,' he said.

'Matt,' said Mum. 'What on earth are you suggesting?'

'Work it out, Rachel,' said Dad. Gil had never heard him sound so cruel. 'Use your intelligence.'

'Are you accusing Gil of being involved in this somehow?'

'That's exactly right, yes.'

'You can't be serious.'

'Yeah, Dad,' said Gil, trying to sound defiant. 'Where's your evidence?'

'Oh, there'll be evidence,' said Dad. 'The police will find evidence.' He stood up. 'I'd better go and get my head together. They'll be here soon to interview me.'

'Matt,' said Mum. 'Stop.' There was a tone in her voice that Gil hadn't heard for a long time. Dad stopped at once, looking taken aback. 'Be very, very careful,' said Mum. 'Do you understand me?'

Dad stood still, his face completely expressionless. After a few seconds he turned towards the door, but Mum made a tiny noise that stopped him again in his tracks.

'I need to know that you've heard me, Matt,' said Mum. She wasn't asking him, she was telling him, although Gil wasn't at all clear exactly *what* she was telling him. Then, abruptly, Dad nodded and left, and at the same time Mum got up and went to fill the kettle. The sudden silence in the kitchen was suffocating. Gil slumped forwards over the table and waited helplessly for Mum to ask him the inevitable questions. *What's going on, then? Is Dad right, that you're mixed up in this?* He toyed with different answers, ways of bluffing his way through it. As he went over it all in his mind he began to imagine it was not Mum asking the questions, but the police. He knew with absolute certainty that if he came under suspicion the police wouldn't let him off the way they had the last time. This wasn't littering in a public park. This was a serious crime with serious consequences. He'd never be able to get away with it. Gradually the secret began to weigh him down. The longer Mum asked no questions, the more desperate Gil became to confess. He felt as if he might explode with the pressure.

At last he heard the clink of a teacup on the table and the creak of a chair.

'What a mess,' Mum said from somewhere near him. 'I mean, I thought things were a mess yesterday, but this . . .'

Gil didn't dare to raise his head. He feared his face would tell her everything. He waited in agony for Mum to speak again.

'Do you hate me, Gil?' she said quietly.

Gil sat up in astonishment. It wasn't the question he'd been expecting. 'What?' he said.

Mum was pale and serious, but she was not crying. 'For hiding so many things from you,' she said.

'No, of course not, but . . .'

'You hate Dad,' said Mum.

Gil said nothing.

'We made all the decisions together,' said Mum. 'We tried to do the right thing. Now it's obvious we got some of it badly wrong. But we both have to take responsibility for that. It's not just Dad's fault.'

Was she asking him to forgive Dad? Gil didn't think he could do it. And anyway, Dad probably hated him now, after what he had done. Gil opened his mouth without any clear idea of what he was going to say, but to his relief Mum carried on talking.

'I'm not asking for any kind of confession,' said Mum. 'I appreciate I don't have such a great track record on being trusted right now. I just need to know that, whatever's been going on, it's going to stop.'

'Yes,' said Gil. 'I promise.' It was the easiest promise he had ever made.

Mum nodded. 'Please forgive me,' she said. 'I've made things very hard for you.'

'I just —' Gil swallowed. 'I just don't want you to be ill, Mum.'

'No,' said Mum. 'Well, I may not be. And if I am, at least now it's something we can face together, and that gives me hope.'

Gil felt the pressure in his chest begin to build again, the warning of the storm approaching. He did not want to be with Mum when it broke. 'I'm just going to —' he said, vaguely, pushing the chair back.

'Of course,' Mum said. 'See you later.'

Gil hurried back to the safety of his room and shut the door firmly behind him. As he battled to bring his breathing under control he wondered when the police would arrive and how much they already knew. A thought dawned on him, and he went and retrieved the old mobile phone from the back of the drawer under the bed. Then he sat and looked at it for a while before he got up the courage to call Jude's number.

It rang for a long time and then cut to voicemail. Gil rang off, prepared a brief message in his head and tried again. After two rings it was answered.

'Yes?'

The voice was so curt Gil couldn't be sure it was Jude, but he could not risk saying Jude's name aloud in the house.

'It's Gil,' he said.

'I know that.' Jude was clearly not going to make this any easier.

'I think Dad's worked it out,' Gil said.

He waited.

'Thanks for the tip-off,' said the crisp voice on the other end. 'Just get rid of the phone, eh?'

Then he was gone.

CHAPTER 26

A few seconds later, the doorbell trilled downstairs. Gil raked through the junk in his drawer until he found a pair of scissors, all the while listening to Mum as she opened the door, greeted someone and took them down the corridor to Dad's study. With the scissors Gil prised the plastic covers off the phone and took out the sim card and the battery. He snipped the sim card in quarters and then began methodically to destroy the keypad and the screen with the point of a blade. As pieces of the phone fell apart he collected them carefully and put them in a pile on his desk. It was weirdly calming.

If Dad tells the police . . .

He tried not to think about it. The work of dismantling the phone absorbed him for some time but when his mind swung round to the thought again, it had changed subtly.

When Dad tells the police . . .

255

It's all right, Gil told himself. *Jude will get away. He's not stupid. He's done this kind of thing before.* But that was not the only thing there was to worry about. Gil's hands started to shake so much he could no longer hold the scissors. He swept up the bits of the phone and wrapped them in a carrier bag which he stuffed in his backpack. Then he got unsteadily to his feet. It was the suspense that was unbearable. If he just went down and told the police everything perhaps it would be a relief.

But he was only halfway down the stairs before the study door opened and the voices spilled out into the corridor. Gil froze, his resolve draining away.

'Well, thank you very much, Dr Walker.' The voice made the hair stand up on the back of Gil's neck. There was something horribly familiar about it. 'We'll make sure we keep you informed.'

'Thank you,' said Dad's voice.

They were coming towards the bottom of the stairs and Gil tried to work out why he recognised the voice. Then he remembered. It was the policeman who had picked him up in the park when he'd first met Jude. Gil turned to run back upstairs, but it was too late.

'Well, well, if it isn't the ASBO boy,' said the policeman. 'I hope you've been behaving yourself.'

'Yes, sir,' Gil said faintly, leaning back against the wall.

'We scared some sense into you, then.'

'Uh . . .'

The policeman stood eyeing Gil up and down triumphantly. He seemed reluctant to move on. Any minute now, and he would put two and two together. He would say, *Hang on a mo. You were with that bloke in the park, weren't you? That troublemaker, Jude. We know all about Jude. So what have you been up to, then?* Behind the policeman Gil could see Dad frowning. The game was up. Maybe he should just put his wrists out for the handcuffs now.

'And just as well, from what your dad's told us,' said the policeman cheerfully. 'It's a good job we stopped you getting mixed up with that animal rights bloke, eh? Could have been nasty.'

'What?' Gil didn't understand. What had Dad said? Gil saw Dad's frown deepen. 'But it was . . .'

'Gil,' said Dad. 'Go and sit in the kitchen, please.'

'But . . .'

'Kitchen.' Dad tilted his head sideways. 'Go on.'

Gil slid down to the foot of the stairs and retreated towards the kitchen. Behind him he heard the policeman again.

'What's up with him? He looks as if he's seen a ghost.'

'Well, we've all had a bad night,' said Dad smoothly.

They moved slowly in the direction of the front door.

When he stumbled into the kitchen Gil could tell from Mum's expression that he must look terrible. She didn't say anything, but she came and put a hand on his shoulder as he fell into a chair. Then they waited together while the policeman chatted on the doorstep and Dad said 'Thank you. Yes, of course. Thank you,' over and over again, trying to end the conversation.

Then there was the click of the front door shutting and after a moment Dad appeared.

Gil was too scared to look at him. He was in turmoil. What had Dad told the police? He must have told them something. The policeman seemed to know about the connection with Jude. What was Dad up to? Was he just stringing things out to make it as unpleasant for Gil as possible?

'I need another coffee,' said Dad, sitting down heavily at the table.

'I think you need to tell us what's going on first,' said Mum, not moving.

'Well, I told them my suspicions,' said Dad calmly.

Gil felt the room begin to disintegrate. He wanted to be sick.

'And your suspicions are . . .?' asked Mum. Her fingers dug into Gil's shoulder.

'That this is likely to be the work of that animal rights activist who confronted me in town a couple of weeks ago. And I've told them that Gil —'

The pause was so long it sounded like a scream in Gil's head.

'That Gil may have passed on some crucial information without realising the damage it could cause.'

'You mean he did it unintentionally,' said Mum. For a moment Gil had no idea if this was a good thing or a bad thing. He had totally lost his bearings.

'Yes,' said Dad slowly. He reached out and began to fiddle with the handle of Mum's empty teacup. 'You know, it's very odd. There are a number of things that don't quite add up.'

'Such as?'

'Well, the policeman told me the raiders didn't manage to take all the animals. By some extraordinary quirk of fate, it looks as if all the mice from my project are still there. Just my animals, nobody else's.'

'But that's *amazing!*' said Mum. 'That means you won't have to start your research again from scratch!'

'Yes, it's amazing,' said Dad. 'Although not quite so amazing for my colleagues who've lost everything. Here's the next odd thing. The police are convinced that someone deliberately set off the fire alarms in the building. The burglar alarms had been deactivated – it's not clear when that was done. But the fire alarm in the room where I keep my mice had been smashed. It doesn't look like an accident. They found a lot of blood on the floor, and blood on the glass of the alarm too, as if someone had cut themselves rather badly when they broke it . . .'

Gil's hands were hidden under the table. He instinctively went to touch the place where he'd gashed himself, and winced with pain again.

Dad breathed deeply and glanced around the room, not quite managing to look directly at Gil. 'Look, Rachel,' he said, 'could I possibly have another coffee?'

In the interval while Mum made coffee, Gil stared at the table and furiously tried to fathom exactly what Dad knew and what game he was playing. Dad knew his mice were safe. But if he thought Gil had anything to do with it he wouldn't be talking about it now, would he? Had Dad really told the police that Gil was only involved accidentally? How much more than that did he know or suspect? How much longer could Gil sit here and pretend to know nothing about what had happened at the labs?

'Right,' said Mum at last, placing the coffee in front of Dad. 'Go on.' She pulled a chair up to sit next to Gil.

'The police are baffled as to why anyone would have set off the fire alarm,' said Dad. 'It suggests there was someone there who wanted to stop the raid. That's the only explanation that makes any sense. And then – whoever it was – they seem to have made their escape from my office by climbing down twenty metres of fire escape ladder. In the dark. Alone, perhaps. With the sirens going off around them, and the police on their way, and an injury that caused a fair amount of bleeding.'

He's talking about me, thought Gil. He can't know it was me, can he? In his mind's eye he watched his painful descent of the ladder, rung by rung, as if it were a scene in a film. He began to feel giddy.

'How strange,' said Mum thoughtfully.

'Yes,' said Dad. 'It's a mystery.'

Gil felt the kitchen spinning quietly around him. Eventually he could bear it no longer.

'I've hurt my hand,' he said, much too loudly. 'Look.'

He pulled his right hand from under the table and turned it palm upwards so that the wound was visible. A dark stain was beginning to show through the big square plaster. Dad reached across and took hold of Gil's wrist.

'That doesn't look so good,' he said. He started to peel back the plaster. As it came away it pulled sharply at the wound and Gil yelped in pain. Dad's eyes widened and

Mum gave a little gasp. The gash was oozing blood again and the edges of the hole gaped open. It looked huge.

'What did you do, Gil?' asked Dad.

'I cut it on some glass,' said Gil.

'When?'

'Last night.'

'Last night?'

'Yes, when I was —'

Gil stopped and swayed forwards as if he was teetering on the edge of a cliff. His hand hurt so much he thought he was going to faint.

'When I was —' he tried again.

'Oh, dear God, no,' said Mum suddenly.

'On some glass,' Gil repeated dizzily. 'On the glass of the . . . Dad, I need to tell you . . .' He reached for the rest of the sentence in his head but it swam away from him.

'No,' said Mum. '*No.*' She was not shouting, but the words were like gunshots. Gil looked up in surprise to see where they had come from.

'What do you mean, no?' said Dad. 'I want to hear what Gil's got to say.'

'No,' said Mum. 'You do not. I forbid you. I forbid you both.' She jumped up and grabbed some kitchen roll and held it gently against the wound in Gil's hand.

'Forbid me? I don't understand.'

'Listen to me,' said Mum. She spoke rapidly and with agitation. 'Over the last few weeks we have almost destroyed ourselves as a family. We have kept secrets from each other – all of us have. We are all responsible for this, and we are almost at the point of no return. If we stop now – if we turn back and deal with the awful things that happened yesterday – we have a chance. But this is a revelation too far. If we go on – if you insist, Matt, on hearing what Gil wants to tell you, and if you insist, Gil, on telling him, then I'm not sure there is any way out of this mess. At this precise moment I at least know very little about what happened last night. Can I beg you both that we keep it that way?'

Through his pain and guilt and confusion, slowly Gil began to understand. If he confessed, Mum and Dad would have to tell the police. Gil had no clear idea of what would happen then, but images from television police dramas filled his head – locked rooms with steel doors and no windows, a big policeman yelling right into his face, a courtroom with Mum and Dad miles above him in the gallery as he sat looking up from inside a cubicle of bullet-proof glass. And then prison – would they send him to prison? How serious was it, exactly, to take secret film of the labs and steal Dad's keys and crack the code for the burglar alarm to enable Jude to break in and liberate the animals? Did they send thirteen-year-olds to prison for that?

'But we need to know the truth,' Dad said.

'We know more than enough,' said Mum. 'And if you're going to start talking about justice being done and facing up to the consequences of your actions and accepting the punishment you deserve, then I think we've all experienced enough of that in the last couple of days to last us a lifetime.'

Nobody said anything for a long time. Then Gil made a decision.

'Picture glass,' he said, lifting his injured hand off the table. 'I smashed a picture last night with my fist when I was upset. That's how I cut it. Sorry,' he added.

He saw Mum and Dad look at each other. After a while Dad sighed deeply and ran a hand through his hair.

'You're going to need a couple of stitches in it,' he said.

'Good,' said Mum brightly. 'I'll run you up to casualty when you're dressed.'

'I think I just want to go back to bed for a bit,' said Gil.

'Me too,' said Dad. He looked exhausted.

'In a minute,' said Mum. 'There's something else I want to say first.'

In the short space before she spoke again Gil imagined all sorts of ridiculous soap-opera announcements. *I'm leaving. I'm pregnant. You're not my son, Gil. I'm in love with Jude.* What she actually said did not come completely out of the blue, although it was still a shock to hear it.

'I want to have the test for Huntington's Disease.'

'What? But Rachel —'

'Don't you think it's time?' said Mum. 'Don't you think it would be better for all of us now if we knew, instead of waiting in limbo for something that may or may not happen? At least then I can get on with my life. It's not done any of us any good to have me drifting about the house like a ghost.'

'I don't know,' said Dad. 'I really don't know. Are you sure you want to find out?'

Gil was suddenly aware of the pain in Dad's voice. There was no smugness, no certainty, just pain. For the first time

Gil thought what it might be like to be Dad, to have lived all these years in the knowledge that his wife might die from a disease that he had not yet managed to find a cure for.

'Yes, I'm sure,' said Mum.

Dad said nothing. He just put his head in his hands and gripped his fingers across the top of his skull.

'I thought perhaps you'd do the test for me, Matt,' said Mum. 'You did say you might.'

'I'm not sure I can face it.' Dad sounded in complete agony.

'Mum's the one who's got to face it the most,' said Gil. 'She's the one who might be ill.'

'Yes,' said Dad. 'You're right. I know.'

'It would really help me if we could all do this together,' said Mum.

'What are the chances of you having Huntington's Disease?' said Gil.

'They're exactly fifty-fifty,' said Mum very softly.

'Oh my God,' said Gil. A fifty-fifty chance meant Mum was balanced on a knife-edge. It was like having a choice of only two doors. If you opened one, you could walk through and live happily ever after. If you opened the other, you would die. No wonder Dad was scared.

'You have to keep hold of the fact that there's an even chance I'm OK,' said Mum. 'And if not – there's still Dad's research. But if neither of you want me to have the test, I will listen to you.'

Gil couldn't speak any more. At that moment he longed to have no sense of himself. It was too hard being human, being aware, having to choose. What should he say? Was it better to know, or not to know? Once you knew something for certain you could never choose to be ignorant again. Unless of course you had a disease like Huntington's, and then you had no choice. Your memory was eventually wiped clean whether you liked it or not.

'I think we need to know,' Gil said at last. 'Dad?'

'OK,' said Dad. He still didn't look up. 'OK.'

'Sleep on it for now,' said Mum. 'Go back to bed, the pair of you.'

Gil went back to bed, and buried himself deep under the duvet and both pillows so that the entire world was blocked out. He hoped he would be able to sleep without dreams.

CHAPTER 27

Gil was woken by someone coming into his room. He guessed it was time to go and get his hand stitched up.

'OK, Mum,' he mumbled. He rolled over and sat up, and then stared in amazement at Louis standing at the end of his bed.

'Wha . . .?'

'Your mum said it was OK,' said Louis quickly.

Gil watched while Louis hopped from foot to foot uncomfortably. He was too dazed with sleep to think of anything to say to him.

'Don't look at me like that!' Louis burst out suddenly. 'I'm sorry, all right? I came to say sorry. I feel so crap for grassing you up to your dad yesterday. But if you're just going to try and stare me out I'm not staying.'

'No, no, no,' said Gil. 'Wait.' He rubbed his face. What did he need to say to Louis? 'It's OK. You did the right thing.'

'Did I?' said Louis uncertainly.

'Yeah, you did. I mean, it needed to happen. It's a bit like . . .' Gil thought for a moment. His head was still fuzzy. 'It's like you found out I had gangrene in my leg and you knew you'd have to chop my leg off to save my life, and then you hacked my leg off with a penknife or something, and to begin with I was really angry with you but then I saw that you'd saved my life.'

'What? What are you on about?' Louis looked really agitated now. 'Are you ill? Oh my God, are you going to die?'

'No, you moron, we used to play that game, don't you remember? Shipwrecks. And I had gangrene and you had to hack my leg off.'

'Oh. Yeah. Actually it was *you* who always chopped *my* leg off,' said Louis.

'Was it?' Gil tried to remember properly.

'Yeah. But I still don't get why you're talking about gangrene.'

'Look, what I mean is that you dumped me in it big time with Dad. And I was so angry with you. But then . . . then I found out . . .' Gil tailed off. There was too much to tell Louis. Secrets writhed and wriggled inside his head like maggots in a dead animal.

'Your dad said you'd had a bit of a shock,' said Louis, frowning.

'Did he?'

'Yeah, when he phoned me up,' said Louis.

'When? What did he phone you for?'

'To ask me to come round. He said you needed a bit of –
um . . .'

'Yeah, well, Dad thinks you're wonderful, doesn't he?' said
Gil grimly. 'He likes you better than he likes me.'

'No he doesn't. Don't talk crap. Look, Gil – what's
happened? You don't look good.'

Gil began to tell Louis about Mum, about the way she
might be ill with the same disease that was slowly killing his
grandmother, about the way Mum and Dad had genetically
screened him as an embryo to make sure he didn't have
Huntington's Disease. He said nothing about Jude, about
the labs, about Dad's research. He picked his way around the
forbidden topics as if he was finding a path through a
minefield. All the time he tried not to look at Louis, but he
was aware of Louis' mouth hanging open in stunned silence
and his eyes bulging like giant marbles.

'Oh my God,' said Louis, when Gil stopped. 'Oh my
God. Is your mum going to be OK?'

'I don't know yet,' said Gil. 'I think she's going to have a
test done soon.'

'Oh my *God*. Didn't you know *any* of this?'

'No, but I knew there was something going on. I knew
there was stuff they weren't telling me. I think maybe that's
the reason I've been behaving like a bit of a —'

'Prat?' said Louis. 'Arsehole? Moron? Loser?'

'Yeah, OK, OK. Don't rub it in.'

'Well, it explains a lot,' said Louis. 'Especially that stuff
about your genes. I always knew you were a mutant
monster.'

Gil nearly managed a smile. He was suddenly grateful to Louis just for being Louis.

'Listen,' he said. 'Do you want to come over again later and do something? I don't know – watch a DVD maybe?'

'I can't.' Louis looked serious. 'I've got someone else coming round.'

'Who?' Gil's heart sank. How badly had he messed things up with Louis? 'Ben?'

'No, not Ben. I've decided he's kind of a pain in the arse. It's just a guy from skating. You don't know him.'

'Oh. All right.'

'How about after school tomorrow? You're not still grounded, are you?'

'I haven't got a clue,' said Gil, thinking of a catalogue of reasons why Dad might ground him for the rest of his life. 'I'll let you know.'

Gil waited for punishments but none arrived. In fact the opposite happened. A few days after the raid on the labs Mum and Dad gave him a mobile phone, a really good one. With the phone came permission to go where he wanted when he wanted, on his own – within reason. The sudden freedom almost scared him and for a couple of days he did nothing at all with it. But as he came out of school on Friday Gil knew there was something he needed to do. He needed to go and visit Jude.

He knew Jude wouldn't be there any more, but that wasn't the point. He had to make the journey. As the bus carried him closer to the rundown Tesco on the Chesapeake

Road, Gil wondered if this was what it felt like to visit the grave of someone who'd died unexpectedly – to go and say goodbye, or say sorry, or any one of the hundreds of things you hadn't managed to say when the person was alive.

The house looked just the same. The weeds in the front garden were taller, the tiles on the path were still cracked. Gil knocked twice just to make sure. There was no reply, but as he stepped back out of the gate into the quiet street a voice called from behind him.

'Hello?'

It was Sally.

'Hello, Sally,' Gil said.

'He's not here, you know,' she said immediately. She didn't open the door more than a crack. 'He's gone.'

'Yeah, I kind of knew that. Thanks.'

'I miss him,' Sally said. She began to cry. 'He was good to me. Do you know where he is?'

'No, I don't. I'm sorry.'

'I'm hungry,' she said through her tears. 'Can you lend me some money?'

Gil hesitated. Jude would not have walked away. Jude would have got her something to eat.

'I'll buy you some food, if you like,' he said.

They walked slowly to the kebab shop round the corner, and Gil bought Sally a wrap. He watched her eat it fast, saying nothing. When it was finished she sighed happily.

'That was nice,' she said. 'Thank you. You're just like him, you know. You're a good person.'

'I don't think I am,' Gil said.

'Yes you are. Most people ignore me. He didn't, and you don't either. You treat me like I matter, not just like I'm some mad woman. He was your friend, wasn't he?'

'I'm not sure.'

He had felt the connection with Jude so strongly, and now Gil wondered if he had imagined the whole thing. Had Jude just used him? Had Jude cared about him at all, really, or did the rights of animals matter more to him than any human being ever could?

'Will you ever come and see me again, now he's gone?' said Sally.

'Maybe,' Gil said.

He didn't really want to, but it was a link of some sort and he was reluctant to let it go. He missed Jude terribly. He missed the way that he had made everything so clear and calm and simple. It had been like standing in a street on a scorchingly sunny day, with the buildings on one side of the street shimmering in the heat, and the ones on the other side in the deepest of black shadow. Down the middle of the street ran the line that divided dark from light. Jude had made him absolutely sure which side of the street he should be on. And then the sun had gone in and the clouds had come over, and the street was plunged into shades of grey. Nothing would ever be that clear and simple again.

The next day, Saturday, Gil went back to ice-skating with Louis. When he arrived at the top of the stairs that led down to the rink Gil stood transfixed for a moment, with his skates hanging heavily round his neck. He had a powerful flashback of the last time he'd been there, the day he'd stolen Dad's keys for Jude, and it made him feel as if he was falling. He clutched the rail for balance, and then Louis came bounding back up the steps.

'You all right?' he said.

'Yeah,' said Gil. 'It's just a bit – loud.' It was a pathetic thing to say, but Louis nodded sympathetically.

'Yeah, it's a bit much sometimes,' he said. 'Come on, you'll be OK when you're out there.'

Gil put his skates on and followed Louis on to the ice. He made himself remember why he'd always enjoyed it so much. You could skate in a crowd of other people and still be completely alone on the ice, lost in your own imagination. Gil flew round the rink, barely making contact with the ice, and tried to visualise the hundred trillion cells in his body working together like a giant colony of microscopic creatures. They sent and received millions of messages, they produced chemicals, they burnt fuel to enable him to do this thing that should really be impossible – gliding on a thin blade on a surface almost too slippery to stand up on. And yet each individual cell was fragile and disposable, incapable of surviving by itself. It was a miracle. He was a miracle.

He thought about his beginnings as the ice sped away under his skates. He thought about the way Mum and Dad had cared about him when he was no more than a minute blob of eight cells. Had he been Gil then, when they had tested that embryo for Huntington's Disease? And if not, when had he become Gil? Was it a gradual process, or was there a particular moment when he had crossed a line that divided 'Gil' from 'not Gil'? He began to understand why some people believed that you were human from the instant the sperm and the egg fused together.

It made him feel special to know how he had been created, but it also made him feel abandoned, like Moses thrown into the river in a basket, drifting away in the hope of a better life. And sometimes he just felt weird, no matter how often he told himself that he wasn't a mutant monster. His genes hadn't actually been altered at all. He had just been screened for a disease, and chosen because he didn't have it. But he still sometimes wondered if he was a sort of half-cousin to the grotesque fishy strawberry Jude had told him about.

The stitches came out of Gil's hand and the wound healed steadily, growing a scary-looking scab that eventually fell off piece by piece to leave a purple line where the cut had been. The day Gil took the plaster off the wound, Louis had noticed it immediately. He'd been really impressed.

'Oh, wow! That's gross! How did you do it?'

'I cut it on some glass.'

'Oh, God, it looks well nasty.'

Things had almost returned to normal between them. Just occasionally Gil noticed that Louis was cautious of him, as if Gil was a dog that had bitten him and might bite again if he got too close. He couldn't blame Louis for feeling like that. But then Louis made up for it by putting up with Gil when he drifted off into his own thoughts, times when he knew that Louis had found him staring blankly into nothing and Gil hadn't heard a word he'd said.

There were lots of these times. Gil often wondered what Jude had done with the animals he took from the labs. He worried especially about the nude mice who had lymphoma, and the other ones who were ill. Sometimes he had a vision of a big green field at dusk, and rabbits and mice scurrying happily away in the grass. 'Be free, little ones!' said Jude's voice. But Gil knew it was a fantasy. The lab animals were as tame as household pets. There was no way even the healthy ones could survive in the wild. They wouldn't last the night.

He thought about Mum, too. Most of his thoughts were hard to put into words. They came and went in Gil's head like satellite pictures of clouds on the weather forecast. Mum seemed just the same, but Gil watched her more closely now, looking for any tiny change that might be significant. It was exactly what Dad did, he realised after a while. It had always irritated him to see Dad watch Mum in that special, secret way, and now Gil was doing it himself.

Without making a conscious choice, Gil still avoided eating meat. He wasn't sure exactly why he continued to be a vegetarian, except that it felt as if some sort of trade-off was needed. He'd prevented Jude from liberating Dad's mice, so he had to make up for it by not eating animals any more. Gil thought this probably wasn't strictly logical, but it made him feel better.

Dad accepted his decision without a word of challenge. Overnight their arguments had stopped. Without exactly avoiding each other, he and Dad kept their distance. They talked about trivial things – homework, dinner, sport – not about the labs, or Mum, or Jude, or any of the other things that occupied Gil's thoughts. It wasn't as much of a relief as Gil expected. For months he'd been wanting Dad to get off his back, and now, weirdly, he missed the rows. He missed the energy they'd had.

One evening as Gil was doing homework in his room, Dad knocked on the door.

'Busy?' he said, when Gil looked up in surprise.

'No, not really. I've nearly finished.'

'Can I come in?'

'Sure,' said Gil.

Dad came in and perched on the end of the bed, but he didn't immediately say anything. Gil wondered what he wanted. The silence was a bit awkward, and Gil pushed pieces of paper around on his desk while he waited for Dad to start.

'How's your hand?' said Dad at last.

'My hand?' Gil looked down at the place where he'd cut it. 'It's fine, thanks.'

'Let me see.'

Gil put out his hand. Dad grasped his wrist loosely and examined the scar.

'Mum and I have been talking about doing her test,' he said, looking at Gil's hand. 'We thought we'd do it this weekend.'

'Oh,' said Gil. It was a strange feeling, having Dad's fingers in a protective ring around his wrist.

'We'd like you to be there,' said Dad. 'If – you know – if it's not too much.'

'No, no, I'll come,' said Gil.

'Actually, I'd really appreciate it if you'd help me with the test.' Dad looked up at Gil, gently tapping the scar on his hand with the tip of a finger.

'Yeah, I'll try,' said Gil. He didn't want to think about Mum's test, but he knew he had to face up to it at some point. 'I'm not sure I'll be much use, though.'

'Oh, you will,' said Dad. 'I have complete confidence in you, Gil.' He gave Gil's hand the briefest squeeze and dropped it, getting up from the bed.

So on Saturday Gil went back to the labs with Mum and Dad.

For the third time Gil entered the labs by the back door, this time with Dad ahead of him and Mum behind. As he climbed the winding stairs that led up to the room where Dad made his mice, Gil thought about what they were going to do when they got there. Dad would take a sample of cells from Mum's body – cheek cells, maybe, because they were big and flaky and easy to scrape out from inside your mouth, or maybe a few drops of blood. Then he'd show Gil how to separate out the DNA and make billions of copies of gene IT-15, the gene that caused Huntington's Disease. It was a very simple gene, Dad had said – just the same three chemicals repeated over and over again, a recipe that told the cell how to make a kind of protein. But when the gene had too many repeats, it made a protein that was too long, like a big sticky worm. Over years and years the protein gradually filled the brain cells with a tangle of goo. And then at last, like Granny, you started to lose control of your body and your mind.

It might be good news, thought Gil, or it might be bad news. As the three of them walked together in silence down the corridor to the brightly-lit white-and-silver room, Gil looked back at the person he had been the last time he had been here, and the time before that. He wasn't sure how he was going to cope if the news was bad, but he had a sense that the Gil who had been in this corridor a few weeks ago, filming the labs for Jude, would not have coped at all.

He knew so much more now. He knew what Mum and Dad had tried to protect him from, and he understood why. He knew what had made him so angry. He knew which things were his fault and which things weren't. He knew that Dad wasn't a monster or a torturer. He knew that the truth looked different depending which side of the street you were standing on, and that right and wrong came in shades of grey as well as black and white. He knew you could hurt yourself and other people so badly that it seemed like the end of everything, and still find that it was possible to survive and mend and move on.

It was part of who he was, Gil told himself, as they got to the door of the room and he saw Dad looking round at him, and Mum trying to smile. He would face it, because he knew who he was now. He was Gil.

With thanks to:

Martha, for everything.

Phil,
for believing in me every step of the way.

Betty and Charles, my mum and dad, for giving me the
ability to see both sides of almost every story.

Celia Catchpole, my agent,
for her unflagging persistence and enthusiasm.

Anne Clark at Piccadilly,
for making this a better book.

Dr Roli Roberts, for his careful checking of the science
(all remaining errors are mine).

Stephanie Hale at the Oxford Literary Consultancy,
for her encouragement and support.

Pearl Flanagan and Alison Coles,
for their helpful feedback.

All the family, friends and colleagues who have been
so enthusiastic about this book.

Desperate Measures

LAURA SUMMERS

Vicky and Rhianna are twins but they couldn't be more different. For their fourteenth birthday, Vicky wants a card from the hottest boy in school. Rhianna wants a Furby.

Instead, they get a nasty shock. Their foster parents can't cope and it looks as if Vicky and Rhianna and their younger brother Jamie will have to be split up.

How can they stay together?
Desperate times call for desperate measures . . .

SIMON PACKHAM

Sam Tennant has been brutally murdered in an online computer game. What's worse, it looks like his killers are out to get him in real life too.

As the threats become more sinister, Sam faces a desperate struggle to identify his persecutors before things really get deadly.

An absorbing, fast-paced thriller.

DAMIAN KELLEHER

Luke's world is turned upside down when his mum
collapses at the hospital where she works as a nurse.
Fourteen-year-old Luke and his football-obsessed
younger brother Jesse each cope in their different ways,
and, as time passes, they must confront some painful truths.

Honest, funny and deeply moving, this is a story about
facing the worst and surviving.

'An important book everyone should read.'
Eoin Colfer

'*Life, Interrupted* is a lovely, warm, funny book – though
searingly sad at times. I wish I'd written it.'
Jacqueline Wilson

THE SPELLBOUND HOTEL

TOM EGLINGTON

Strange things are going on
in the village of Stagtree Knoll.

Determined to find out what is going on,
Bethany sneaks into the mysterious Stoames mansion
and discovers something very strange indeed –
a hotel for ghosts, spirits and non-material beings.

But Bethany is not a welcome guest here and if she
hopes to escape and save her parents, she must face
the sinister power at the heart of the hotel,
and break the spell it has cast over everyone

☆

www.piccadillypress.co.uk

Go online to discover:

☆ more thrilling books you'll love

☆ competitions

☆ sneak peeks inside books

☆ author interviews

☆ fun downloads

☆ and much more!